CASTRO IS DEAD

Cuba's new dictator has launched a reign of terror.

And his death would ensure political control—for the Americans . . . or the Soviets.

War is inevitable . . .

COUNTERSTRIKE

The electrifying new thriller by Charles D. Taylor, bestselling author of *First Salvo, Choke Point,* and *Silent Hunter*

"COUNTERSTRIKE is a wonderful what-if . . . fast, expert, and goes straight for the nerve points. A truly compulsive read!"
—Anthony Olcott
Author of *Murder at the Red October*

*Other books by Charles D. Taylor
from Jove and Charter*

SILENT HUNTER
CHOKE POINT
FIRST SALVO
SHOW OF FORCE
THE SUNSET PATRIOTS

Charles D. Taylor

COUNTER STRIKE

JOVE BOOKS, NEW YORK

COUNTERSTRIKE

A Jove Book / published by arrangement with
the author

PRINTING HISTORY
Jove edition / April 1988

ISBN: 0-515-09478-1

Jove Books are published by The Berkley Publishing Group,
200 Madison Avenue, New York, New York 10016.
The name ''JOVE'' and the ''J'' logo
are trademarks belonging to Jove Publications, Inc.

10 9 8 7 6 5 4 3 2 1

ACKNOWLEDGMENTS

With each succeeding book, I become more grateful to the wonderful people who are willing to contribute their time and knowledge to help me.

I had the good fortune to spend three days in Coronado, California, learning how SEALs are molded. I must first thank Richard Galotta and Rear Admiral Cathal L. Flynn, U.S.N. for helping to get me there. The BUD/S (Basic Underwater Demolition/SEAL) School is located in the Phil H. Bucklew Special Warfare Center. Young volunteers who aspire to become SEALs report there for twenty-six weeks of the most demanding training in the American military. Twenty-five to thirty percent of them eventually survive to pin on their "Budweiser"—the trident, eagle, and flintlock pistol emblem worn by approximately fourteen hundred of the most impressive military men in the United States.

The following men were willing to explain to me what it takes to become a SEAL, and Captain Larry Bailey, commanding officer of the center, allowed these members of his staff to help me: CDR Robert Nelson, LCDR Jim Keith, LCDR Ray Cottom, Lt. Tucker Campion, Lt. Al Morris, Lt. John Koenig, Lt. Charles Chaldekas, Lt. (jg.) Steve Simmet, and Master Chief Richard Knepper. A very special thanks goes to Lt. Jake Jaquith, who just happened to be the duty officer the day I arrived and won me for three days. After determining what I needed, Jake introduced me to the proper people, took me to classes, escorted me to various training events, loaned me his personal videotapes on SEAL training, and is still answering questions. These men train the elite of the elite!

Across the street at the Amphibious Base, CDR Richard Flanagan and LCDR John Timmerman, commanding officer and executive officer of Special Boat Squadron One, answered questions and allowed me to tour their Sea Foxes and patrol boats.

Captain David L. Schaible, U.S.N. (ret.), was the first SEAL I met in Coronado. He picked me up early the first morning, bought me a cup of coffee, and said, "This is what you're going to do." He commanded SEAL Team One at the height of the Vietnam conflict, he was Commander of Special Warfare in the Pacific, and when I walked beside him in Coronado, the instructors pointed him out to the students and said, "Let me tell you who that guy is. . . ." Dave and Betty Schaible treated me like an old friend in their home. Dave's library is a minihistory of SEALs, complete with photos of him with the presidents he served under and the Medal of Honor winners who served under him. He said, "If you're going to do it, do it right." He provided technical assistance for this manuscript, and whatever one may dispute is either my error or literary license. I'll keep working at it, Dave.

There is not a great deal of literature on SEALs; they prefer it that way. Data comes from articles in magazines such as *Armed Forces Journal International, International*

Combat Arms, and the *Proceedings of the U.S. Naval Institute.* I read about the earliest days of Naval Special Warfare in a manuscript from the Oral History Department of the Naval Institute. It came from a series of interviews with Captain Phil H. Bucklew, U.S.N. (ret.), the man who conducted reconnaissance at Sicily and Salerno in a kayak, was on the beach at Normandy six months before the invasion of Europe, slipped through Japanese lines in 1945, and traveled more than four hundred miles through occupied China to scout the coast for a possible invasion, and eventually produced the "Bucklew Report" on Communist infiltration in Vietnam. He set the example for ". . . anything, anytime, anyplace, anyhow."

I'd also like to thank Dan Mundy, Dominick Abel, Mel Parker, and Natalee Rosenstein for their efforts in developing the manuscript, and our own captain, Bill McDonald, for his continuing kindness in improving my proper knowledge of the navy. And thanks, as always, to Georgie for understanding me.

There are certain of us who are fortunate with in-laws.
Cheers to Matt and Pearl Laitala.

". . . anything, anytime, anyplace, anyhow."

SEAL motto

"There are things that in order to be achieved must be hidden. . . . Proclaiming what they are would only raise difficulties that would make it harder to attain the desired end."

José Martí (1853–1895)
Cuban patriot

PROLOGUE

Fidel Castro had been speaking for less than an hour from the platform at his favorite Plaza of the Revolution. He had never failed to experience a sense of awe as he faced the crowded plaza with the monument to José Martí behind him. Would there someday be such a beautiful monument built to honor him? Would the people experience equal love and devotion whenever Fidel Castro's name was mentioned? Not a day passed when he did not ponder those questions.

As he slipped a page of completed notes beneath the others, he experienced a chilling sensation of déjà vu. He had simply been shifting his gaze from face to face in the massive crowd when his eyes fell on the smiling countenance of Juan Duran. This man with the angular, almost patrician face was handsome in his colonel's uniform, standing tall and broad-shouldered among the citizens who elbowed their neighbors to be near him. Not a soul in Havana could remember the last time he might have been seen out of uniform, for it seemed like a second skin on him. He was the type of man the people clamored to be near at such a rally so that they could boast of their good fortune when they returned home. Duran was renowned for his adventures in Angola and Eritrea and Afghanistan, the lands where modern Cuban heroes were made.

Though Castro's glance held Duran's for only a second, the premier recognized the combination of arrogance, brutality, and anger that remained masked by a mysterious twinkle in his eyes that the people loved so much. And those eyes—they were intense and black and piercing, much like Ché's, though this man was clean-shaven. While Castro inclined his head slightly in recognition, without missing a word of his speech, the colonel gave no indication that he had been noted. His stare was cruel, as if Juan Duran were on the dais speaking to *his* people rather than Fidel Castro. And that is when the leader of the 26th of July Movement, the hero of the revolution for these past thirty years, sensed that déjà vu, for Duran's expression was no different than Fidel's had been when Batista recognized him one bright afternoon. In those days Ché and Raul had been at his side, and the three of them knew it was only a matter of time. Castro was sure there would have been a repetition of Ché's polemics if Duran had opened his mouth. And those eyes—those eyes were so cocksure that the bearded old man on the dais was destined to be a dead man!

The west wind blew a fluffy cloud across the sun, and for a moment the key words of Castro's speech seemed to blur on the white pages before him. Then the sun reappeared, so brilliantly that the reflection from the page forced him to squint. He shaded the paper with his hand, stopping in mid-sentence when the words seemed to swim before his eyes.

". . . and I emphasize for those to the north of us who hear only what they want to hear . . ." That was the moment when the cloud interrupted him and he was forced to repeat, ". . . who hear only what they want to hear . . ."

He moved back slightly from the dais to focus his eyes on the triple-spaced lines. It was only a few years ago, and then only on certain occasions, that Fidel Castro had taken to reading prepared speeches rather than exhorting his captive audiences for hours without once referring to a note.

The Central Committee members seated behind him shuffled their feet uneasily, shifting their weight in the uncomfortable folding chairs. It was the third time the premier had stumbled during this speech. Another man might have been forgiven for such weaknesses—but not Fidel. Cuban citizens had been accepting sacrifice as a part of their lives for many years because their leaders promised they would eventually become a perfect society. Now they were unable to accept the fact that he was old and susceptible to such impairments.

". . . that the Cuban people will not allow one dollar of capitalist money to soil our economy." He paused for his words to take effect. What he had just stated was contrary to the interview with the minister of economics appearing in that day's edition of *Granma*. The minister had just returned from an OAS meeting in Mexico City where the American secretary of commerce had proposed future talks on reopening trade discussions.

The minister's chin fell to his chest. He massaged his forehead in frustration, shaking his head from side to side when the man next to him whispered in his ear. Only days before, the Central Committee had agreed that a dialogue with the United States would not contravene party doctrine.

Castro shifted his weight irritably from one foot to the other, distracted momentarily by the rumbling sound as a fighter climbed toward the city from the airport. He took a deep breath preparatory to launching into his next topic. As his mouth opened he cocked his head to one side, listening. There was a distant clanking sound from the direction of the Columbia Barracks—tanks. There were no parades scheduled for that day!

Those behind him turned their heads at the roar of additional jet engines from the direction of José Martí airfield. As Castro launched into his next topic they watched four MiG-28s appear above the skyline, climbing into the wind. Then they turned east to circle Havana at an altitude that increasingly irritated the premier as he raised his voice.

"Our military strength has never been greater than it is today. We expect to have additional pilots training for another squadron of those"—he indicated the MiGs with a wave of his hand—"before the end of the year. Our navy will be adding a new submarine and a frigate shortly, and we have received assurance that ground will soon be broken for an advanced artillery school intended to draw students from the Third World." He pulled uncomfortably with his free hand at his graying beard while he shuffled the pages with the other.

The crowd sensed his discomfort. Their murmurs rolled across the great plaza as the jets continued to circle. The people had been released from work early to assure a large audience, but they were increasingly restless with this disjointed speech. Fidel had once been able to hypnotize his audiences. Until a few years ago they loved to cheer him at the least provocation. Today they found little to excite them. There had been the obligatory references to the Church to satisfy the Bishop of Havana, since Castro now was willing to reach a middle ground with liberation theology. They had been exhorted to set new records in the sugarcane harvest. And there had been a promise to lift rationing of certain consumer goods providing—there was always this escape clause—certain trade agreements were reached with other Third World nations. But it was all a rehash of what had been heard many times before.

The first indication of real trouble occurred at the far

end of the plaza along the Avenue de la Indepencia when the crowd began to pull back from that corner. Before the officials on the platform could fathom what was taking place, the same situation occurred from the direction of Avenue Carlos M. de Céspedes. Within seconds a sense of panic swept through the area. Then a tank came rumbling into view, its turret trained directly on the platform.

Fidel Castro turned first to his bodyguards, who were nowhere in sight, then to the front, where he gazed down on Juan Duran. The colonel's expression had become one of triumph, and his eyes reflected that mystical fire that had been so much a part of Ché.

It was not a revolution as the average person might imagine it. Certainly it bore no resemblance to the bloody street battles that the television networks coveted. It was much too well planned. The tanks that appeared in the streets of each Cuban city had no need to fire their guns. Each tank commander rode in full view, perched on the open turret. The soldiers patrolling each corner carried their rifles slung from their shoulders. Military vehicles cruised through the major streets of each city explaining that a potential revolution had been avoided. There were, of course, regulations to be followed until Fidel Castro could speak to the people. No one should appear on the streets in groups of more than three, and they should remain inside from sunset to sunrise; but this was only until revolutionary elements could be dealt with.

The planning was so exact, the execution so superb, that a gunshot was never heard. Yet, by the hundreds, Castro's trusted military and civilian cadre were whisked far away from the cities. Duran's initial solution to avoid any possible witnesses, emphasized by the threat of death to his district commanders, was for the establishment of staging areas. There, loyal Castro supporters were summarily executed and their bodies delivered to fishing boats in selected locations—and that was how an entire generation of loyal cadre vanished. Each boat disappeared over the horizon that evening. The sharks would ensure that not a single body would turn up. Dead men, especially those who would never turn up as evidence, could tell no tales of a perfect revolution.

The Cuban premier was not a prisoner. "We do not incarcerate our heroes," the defense minister had explained as he'd led Castro from the stage at the Plaza of the Revolution that fateful afternoon. The premier was, however, confined to his apartment for his own protection. "There are always those individuals in any change of government who lose control of themselves, fall victim to their emotions . . ." His voice was almost a whisper. "It would be a tragedy . . ." He let the final words drop as if he were unable to conceive of anything happening to the bearded man he faced.

Fidel Castro was a brave man who had never feared for his life. By the end of that day, as the last purple rays of the sun reflected off the walls in the apartment, he was almost convinced the fools meant to keep him alive. That, he knew from experience, was mistake number one if you intended to control a government—eliminate all opposition. Though it was his defense minister who carried the details to him as the day progressed, Castro was positive that Juan Duran was the leader of the coup. When the colonel appeared at his door that evening, there was no further need to speculate.

"May I have a few moments of your time?" Duran had saluted as he entered.

"Do I have any choice?" Castro could see the answer in Duran's eyes. The man was a clean-shaven Ché, his smile revealing nothing of what was transpiring in his mind.

"You are our leader, and you will remain so. There is no one capable of replacing you. I will admit that this aberration in the normal operation of government is my decision, but I want to clarify that I have no ambition to run the nation. I want only to influence it . . . to make some minor changes to our policy that many of us feared would be impossible any other way.'' His tone was humble, enough so that anyone other than Fidel Castro might have accepted such an explanation instantly.

''Does that mean that tomorrow I'll simply return to my office and resume where I left off?'' He knew that was an impossibility.

''Perhaps not. Of course, there are people who are opposed to what we are undertaking. They cannot remain . . . naturally.'' Duran paused as if deep in thought. ''And . . . one other thing. In most situations there are many who would call this a revolution. The terminology is incorrect . . . for that connotes a change in leadership, and you will remain our leader. However''—and again it seemed as if Ché were speaking—''it will be necessary to make this appear as if all of this was your idea and that my men were ordered by you to undertake such radical change . . . in your name.''

Castro smiled as he stroked his beard. ''No more than a family argument, eh?''

''Something like that.'' *Does Fidel really think he's making it hard on me?* Duran wondered. ''What is required is a statement to be issued under your signature detailing the realignment of your government. It will explain that there were certain subversive elements—trusted confidants—who were involved in a plot to overthrow you. You were able to uncover this rebellion and, with the help of the defense minister, coordinate a counter—''

''Ah . . . that's why Ramón remains alive. He's one of you. . . .''

Duran had no compunctions about lying, for he had learned in the desert tent at Assdadah that, like truth, it was a commodity manufactured to achieve an end. ''On the contrary, sir. He took part in this today because of his loyalty to you. When he learned of the undercurrents that threatened your government, he immediately agreed to take charge until you could be returned to power—''

"There. You've said it," Castro interrupted. "I am no longer in power."

"Under our laws, he succeeds you."

"There are three ahead of Ramón."

"Unfortunately, they were involved in the plot to depose you." Duran's voice was no longer animated, and that twinkle that was Ché's trademark when he won a personal battle had vanished. His next sentence was devoid of expression. "We can go along with this all night, but I have no desire to discuss philosophy at this stage. If I am assured that your enemies have been disposed of before morning, then—yes—you can return to your office. What I require before you do, however, is your signature on this statement to announce to the nation what I have just explained to you. In the meantime, you may resume your normal habits, although you will be under guard at all times. . . ."

"A prisoner . . ."

"For your protection." Duran's sense of humor appeared to have returned for an instant as he added, "You may even visit with Miss Arguello this evening if that is your pleasure—"

Castro bolted to his feet. "You will never use her name again." It was the first real sign of emotion he'd displayed.

"Whatever you prefer." The expression on Duran's face reflected his moment of success. He'd shattered the air of coolness maintained by Castro until that moment. Cora Arguello had been his mistress for less than six months. Her relationship with the premier was known to only a few of his most trusted aides, an inner circle that had now been breached.

Castro wheeled and stalked over to the window. "You

said you want me to sign something." There was curiosity in his voice.

"You may read it. It's quite simple." Duran joined him by the window and handed him a single sheet of paper. "We've nothing to hide. The objective is simple—to protect you. Is it so hard to believe that there were men close to you who would turn on you . . . or others who would die to ensure that your revolution survived?"

Castro cocked his head to one side and studied Duran curiously. "And you claim to be in the latter group?"

"We are—you and me—patriots. Cubans first . . . not greedy for money or all the trappings of power. Neither of us would go crawling to the Americans . . ." Duran growled.

"And you think there are some who would," Castro concluded.

"There were a number who would have done that."

"I see. And you have taken it upon yourself to dispatch them?"

"Me?" He turned to face Castro, tapping his own chest with an index finger. "Me? All by myself?" He turned away. "I should say not. People who assume such responsibilities alone are stupid. Call it a united decision by a patriotic group who support their premier but are first of all Cuban patriots."

"Are those who disagree with you enemies of Cuba?"

Duran turned and was about to respond when he thought better of it. "No, you can't trap me today." He smiled as he added, "All I can do is assure you once again that you have nothing to fear personally." He had learned such responses in the tent at Assdadah by the edge of the desert. One must always put the enemy at ease.

"Before I sign anything, I would like to find out exactly who is left in the government and who has replaced the others."

"That can be arranged. I would also request that you

make a brief appearance on the balcony so that the people will know that you remain alive and in charge of the government.''

"What will you do if I decline?" A curious grin spread across his face. One never cooperated with the enemy—unless there was a glimmer of hope, even one so slight as he now imagined.

Duran recognized that he was still being toyed with by a brave and arrogant man, but one who had few options. He smiled back in response. "You know, I have the feeling that I am being chided by my own father. No matter what I did as a youth, he was always challenging, even teasing me . . . and I had no idea how to respond, because he was my father. And you are the man who I have always looked up to all my life. There's no way I can simply say, 'Because I tell you to do it, Premier Castro.' '' He drew in a deep breath and sighed. "All I can ask is that you trust me, and we will survive this together.'' Another ploy from Assdadah learned at the feet of the strongest man Juan Duran had ever met.

"Let me read your paper . . . the one you want me to sign . . . and then we will talk about appearances,'' Castro concluded with finality. He had been a revolutionary too long to trust anyone.

That evening, when Juan Duran came to him again, it was Castro who began the conversation before the other had a chance. "I have not made up my mind about signing your paper. There is a great deal more I need to know before I can approve what you have done. But''—he wagged a finger at Duran—"I have decided to meet you halfway if that is possible.''

Duran nodded, waiting for what he knew was coming next.

"I would like to take advantage of your offer to see Miss Arguello. Does it still stand?''

Yes, Duran said to himself, *he sees it all very clearly, and he's ready to grab at straws.* "Of course. You are not a prisoner. You're simply under our protection until the streets are quiet again." Fidel was crafty, and he would be until his last breath. He would use her to try to escape. He was old now, certainly, but he was as cunning as he'd always been.

"You will allow me privacy once I'm there?"

"Most certainly. If I were in your position, you would do the same for me. I know that in my heart."

Cora Arguello was established in an apartment just two blocks from Castro's. The premier had never intended that anyone other than his closest aides would learn of his new mistress. As far as he'd been concerned, the people should feel that he was wedded to Cuba for his remaining years. So Cora remained literally a prisoner in the secret apartment to ensure that the nation remained ignorant of her existence. There was nothing she could ever desire, other than her freedom, that Fidel Castro could deny her in exchange for the affection and moments of peace that she offered him in return. Whenever he desired to be in her company, he was able to exit from a rear door and slip down well-protected alleyways to the apartment less than a hundred yards from his own.

Juan Duran escorted him to the rear door. Stepping into the warm evening, they were met by four of the premier's own armed guard, men selected for their undying loyalty. "I'm sorry you can't make even such a short trip unescorted, but there are still elements who could be dangerous to you." Duran turned to the guards. "You swore to protect the premier's life with your own. Nothing has changed since that day. Although I have been promised there isn't a soul nearby who could threaten his life, I can promise I will take my own revenge on each of you personally if any harm comes to him." Then he turned to Castro and saluted. "This is the only way I know of assuring you of where my loyalty lies. We will talk again in the morning."

"Yes . . . yes, I thank you for your concern, Colonel." Castro was mystified. If any but his own personal guard had been there, he would have been sure they were only a firing squad, yet here they were under orders to die if necessary to protect him. Was it possible that Duran really did want him as figurehead? So much had been racing through his mind that afternoon that he had been grabbing at straws. Wouldn't there be elements loyal to him who would make an effort? the people themselves? party hierarchy? Wouldn't those who were aware of Cora Arguello assume that her apartment would be the logical place for him to go where he could then attempt an escape? He looked over his shoulder as they moved away and saw that Duran had already gone back into the building.

The guard insisted that he move at a brisk pace, and there was little chance to think until they were in the back door and into the elevator to Cora Arguello's top-floor apartment.

As Fidel Castro stepped through her door with anticipation, reality greeted him. "Ramón . . ."

His defense minister smiled good-naturedly, saying nothing until the four guards were disarmed. "No shots now," he called out as they were led away. Then he turned to Castro. "Don't worry about them. They were loyal to you to the end. If they hadn't witnessed this, they might have been retrained, but I'm sure you understand. . . ." Then his expression changed to one of concern. "We've known each other a long time, so I won't try to fool a brave man. Miss Arguello was loyal to you also. Perhaps the two of you will be together again somewhere."

At the same time that he saw his defense minister nod his head, Fidel Castro felt a hand clamp over his chin and heard, rather than felt, his neck snap.

The former premier of Cuba, his mistress, and his four loyal guardsmen were disposed of just as so many others had been during the first twenty-four hours of Juan Duran's reign. They were stripped before their bodies were loaded on the fishing boats, their clothes were burned, and their corpses were methodically fed to sharks maddened by their blood, which had been carefully poured on the waters well out to sea.

On the following morning there had still been no shots fired, no bodies found, and absolutely no confusion. Havana was under tight control because dead men told no tales, nor was there a single corpse to question what had taken place.

CHAPTER ONE

When then-Major Juan Duran arrived at Tripoli International Airport, he'd neither been invited by the Libyans nor had he talked with one of them for two days. He had come directly from Moscow on an Aeroflot jet escorted by a KGB colonel. There was but a moment to savor the heat that was so much like home before they were whisked away in an air-conditioned car by two uniformed Russians. The first confirmation that he was actually in North Africa was the multilingual sign at the exit from the airport: "Welcome to the Socialist People's Libyan Arab Jamahiriya."

Though he could see the skyline of Tripoli in the distance to the north, the car turned away from the lush fields and headed into the desert for the camp at Tarhūnah. It was there that he would serve both as an observer and an instructor in the fine art of terrorism. He was there not only because he was one of the best, but because the Russians found that the Libyans were willing to take on Soviet dirty work for the simple price of professional training. With minimal encouragement, Moscow was able to convince Tripoli that actions against NATO or the

United States would eventually benefit the Arab world. Duran would show them how to increase the effect of their actions dramatically in just a few weeks.

"Do you speak our language, Major?" one of the officers asked Duran.

"If he does, he speaks very little," the KGB colonel responded. "I tried to talk with him on the flight down here, but he insisted on Spanish, and mine is very rusty."

Duran smiled inwardly. Languages had come to him naturally since he was a child, but he had long ago learned one of his most effective intelligence lessons: shut up and listen.

"Is this the same man who was so highly decorated in that African Legion of Castro's? I heard of that unit in the Battle of Lomba River . . . the one that almost secured the country. . . ."

"And you were also going to mention that a Cuban officer was expelled from the country because the UN was investigating torture claims. Yes, he's the one, and from what I've heard, everything is true." The colonel turned his head for a moment and added, "He never says much. He just stares and listens, and if I had to put my money on it, I'd bet that he understands a hell of a lot more than he lets on."

They lapsed into silence until the other officer finally asked, "Did they really let the Cuban complete Spetznaz training, too?"

"The top of the class. And he went to Afghanistan at his own request. He's the only Cuban whom the army ever allowed to fight there. I'll bet you heard the same type of rumors there, too. I don't know if they were ever substantiated. And I don't care," he concluded emphatically.

The other man, a KGB major, looked at the back of Duran's head with new respect. The Spetznaz units were designed to be used behind the lines, often operating in the enemy's rear for weeks at a time to disrupt communications and destroy civilian morale. Duran had arrived there as second-in-command of a unit, assuming leadership within two weeks when the leader was killed. From that moment forward, Duran's group became known for a savagery that neutralized the region almost overnight.

"Major Duran is sharing some of his talent here because the PLO and the Syrians have been experiencing second thoughts about alienating the Americans. Colonel Qaddafi's units love to antagonize the westerners, but they lack the essential sophistication that's needed today." The colonel lit a cigarette.

"I'm glad he's on our side," the major commented with a knowing grin.

"He is for the time being," the colonel answered acidly. "If you want my opinion, I don't think he cares for anyone particularly."

You're almost correct, Colonel, Duran said to himself. *But not totally—because you have never met Cara, who is beautiful and bright and intends to be the first lady of Cuba. Other than Cara, you understand me reasonably well.*

"Why is the major operating with us? I would think Castro would love to have someone like him close to home."

The KGB colonel looked out the window and squinted at the glare from the sand. "I wondered that myself. From what I've been able to gather, no one's anxious to have him return home quickly . . . not in Havana, where he apparently has a number of enemies . . . not in Moscow, where our leaders seem to think Major Duran has contributed mightily to some cause or another that I have yet to figure out."

They rode on in silence while Duran pondered his return to Havana. It would only be a few months . . . and Cara was patient.

The only individual who found it unnecessary to hover reverently near Colonel Qaddafi's helicopter was totally involved in directing the practice jump. Juan Duran would make sure it was perfect, or at least one Libyan officer would find himself transferred to a remote outpost on the Chad frontier. Duran concentrated on the aircraft swooping in below radar level, his breathing slowing as it rose just high enough for the men to jump. He was completely unaware of the tall, regal individual watching patiently a few paces behind him.

"Come on, Hammad," Duran growled into a transmitter, "you're going to be half a kilometer off your drop zone. You're not going after a bunch of goat herders this time. . . ." Duran's voice ended in a snarl as he switched channels on the radio. "Sharat," he ordered, "if they're off by as much as thirty seconds, you know how to make life miserable for them." He dropped the radio to his side, shading his eyes against the sun behind the approaching plane. "That stupid son of a bitch," he growled to himself as he marked the appearance of the first man against his watch.

"May I assume you've had this trouble before?" a soft voice inquired from behind.

Without looking over his shoulder, Duran answered, "I've told Captain Hammad twice before that he's on his way to nowhere, and nothing seems to make any difference to him or any of the others."

"What would happen if they were off by that much in an actual operation?"

"Dead men . . . twelve dead men if the unit on the ground was worth anything." Duran was watching through binoculars as they drifted toward the ground. "Maybe Hammad will break his neck this time and I can ask for someone else. . . ."

"What have you threatened this Hammad with if he makes one more mistake?"

"What else? Reassignment—that's all the control I have." He watched as Sharat's unit surrounded the parachutists. "None of them would have reached the ground alive."

"Why don't you hang him . . . as an example to the others?" The voice was soft, yet there was no doubting the seriousness of the speaker.

"Why don't I what . . . ?" Duran turned to confront the man standing behind him, a strikingly handsome Arab dressed in fatigues bearing a colonel's insignia. "I'd love to," he remarked even before realizing he had been spoken to in English. Looking more closely, he studied a face that seemed familiar, broad cheekbones, firm chin, blazing eyes. "It just might make the others pay attention."

"Good, Major Duran. You give the order and I'll see that it's carried out within the hour."

That was how Juan Duran and Muammar al-Qaddafi became acquainted. For Duran, it was also the beginning of a lifelong lesson—within one hour Captain Hammad was swinging from the end of a rope. Two hours later his replacement lead the detachment to the exact landing spot at the precise moment ordered, allowing Colonel Qaddafi to witness the effect of a well-trained Spetznaz-type unit working behind enemy lines. Before the sun had set that day, both men possessed a deep appreciation of the abilities of the other.

Duran's assignment was completed in less than six weeks. While this may have surprised the KGB colonel—no one, especially a foreigner, showed up a superior by finishing a job in less than the allocated time—it was anticipated by Qaddafi, who invited the Cuban to his tent for a farewell feast.

Though the Libyan leader remained away from Tripoli for all but ceremonial occasions, his tents were as magnificent as his city palace and were shifted in location according to the sensitivities of his intelligence staff. This time they were close to Assdadah, about a hundred kilometers southwest of the Gulf of Sidra. Qaddafi chose that site so that the people building the Wadi Zamzam Agricultural Project could share in their leader's enthusiasm for another successful socialist accomplishment.

"The people don't need to hear your speeches if they can see you actually involved in their work," Qaddafi boasted. "I used to give many speeches. I could talk for hours and they would cheer everything. And then one day I asked a worker some questions about what I said, and he didn't have the slightest idea—even though he claimed he'd attended each one faithfully. He was much happier that I was beside him and interested in his contribution. They are like children, my friend, and they get tired of being talked at. They like shows, public displays."

Duran was sitting on the floor opposite the Libyan leader, his legs crossed under him in the same manner. He sipped sweet tea from a bowl, then leaned forward and helped himself with his fingers from the platter in the center of the table. When he had finished chewing, he smiled and remarked, "I'm sure you are making a polite reference to Fidel Castro." He rinsed sticky syrup from his fingers in a carved bowl and added, "His best speeches are when he reminisces about the old days when there was a revolution and a new start. Now there are just problems." He shook his head sadly. "I don't think he's happy anymore."

"And he's old," Qaddafi concluded. "He's become a philosopher. I suspect that's the way we all become by the time the Americans and the Russians wear us down."

He's picking around the edges, Duran thought. *Testing. Getting ready to probe. He doesn't like Fidel, but he's got to be sure where I stand.* "I think he feels he has to depend more on the Russians today. The economy doesn't get any better. Rationing never seems to go away. Plus he just seems to be tired. It's been more than thirty years since it all started."

Qaddafi snapped his fingers for more tea. "Age wears men down. Most of them don't understand when it's time to pass their power on to another." He puffed out his chest and raised a fist, smiling at the same time at his imitation. "One must continue to rule with an iron fist, or the revolution dissipates around them. Fear delivers fantastic results.''

The thought passed through Duran's mind that perhaps the Libyan really was able to read minds. His eyes so often bored through his listener's, seeming to pry deep into his mind. It was said that Colonel Qaddafi could often start a conversation with almost the exact words you were about to say. And that was why Duran made a point of remaining as quiet as possible during the meal.

The Libyan looked off at a point on the far side of the tent, licking his lips as he selected his words. ''If you will swear yourself to secrecy, I will tell you everything you would ever need to know if you desired to rule your own country.'' Then those eyes slowly came back to Duran, so intense that only the bravest of the brave would hold his stare.

Duran never considered looking away. If what the man on the other side of the table was saying was sincere, this was indeed his golden moment. ''Why do you want to tell me this?''

''Because you are just like me,'' Qaddafi responded wistfully. ''Perhaps I should say you are just like me when I came to power here in 1969. You would bend the people to your will. In Cuba, your people have too much freedom today. That's why there's no progress.''

Too much freedom . . . too much freedom. The words echoed through Duran's head well into the night.

At the end of the evening Qaddafi said, ''I'm going to give you a gift that will explain much of what we have discussed tonight.'' He handed Duran a thin book. ''It is as close to a bible as you will ever have, and this translation is in your native language,'' he continued modestly. *The Green Book* was divided into three parts: Part One— The Solution of the Problem of the Democracy, ''The Authority of the People''; Part Two—The Solution of the Economic Problem, ''Socialism''; Part Three—The Social Basis of the Third Universal Theory.

"I've heard of *The Green Book*." Duran knew that this was doctrine as formulated by "the main representative of the people," as Qaddafi often called himself. One never underestimated a man who considered himself sanctified in the eyes of his followers. "I intend to read it at the earliest opportunity," he offered politely.

"If you follow what is written in those pages, you will find the people will follow you to their death. It's happened here." Again an almost mystical expression spread over his face. "Those unwilling to follow should meet their death as soon as you are aware of their feelings, even those once trusted. It's the only way. It allows the faithful more opportunity to follow the tenets of the new society. It's unfortunate that so many people have to sacrifice," he murmured softly, "but I'm sure you understand what is necessary for a revolutionary system."

Juan Duran spent a final, unanticipated week in Libya at the Assdadah camp, absorbing everything that Muammar Qaddafi was willing to explain to him. There was much that he hadn't considered, much that Cara would be able to handle for him. There was never an indication of why the Libyan sought to see Castro deposed, nor did Duran ever verbally commit himself to the concept. The Cuban simply listened to the enigmatic leader, who recognized himself when he probed Juan Duran's eyes, accepting advice proffered for an unknown reason.

Before returning to Cuba, he received word that he had been promoted to Lieutenant Colonel and would assume duties as a military advisor to Premier Fidel Castro.

CHAPTER TWO

A little less than a month had passed since Juan Duran's new government had taken up residence in the presidential palace near Castro's Museum of the Revolution, and the dusk-to-dawn curfew remained solidly in effect. The bodies of those few who dared to venture about the darkened streets were generally picked up by the morning patrols and dumped at the central morgue. Many went unclaimed, for to associate with a violator was often to admit complicity. And those who were found guilty of such association at the people's courts the following day were then dealt with each noon in the New Plaza of the Revolution. Duran was sure that it was only a matter of days until he could raise the curfew. There were hardly enough bodies to be concerned with anymore.

The streets and alleys around the University of Havana, especially the broad Avenue de San Lázaro, had remained unnaturally quiet in the aftermath of this revolution. However, on this particular evening, an armored personnel carrier (APC) rumbled down the Malecón and turned left onto San Lázaro. The vehicle lurched through a side gate at the university and moved down a sidewalk to an ancient moss-covered two-story building that appeared uninhabited. No light showed around the darkened windows. The muted grumble of the APC's engine was echoed by the ominous click of boot heels as a squad of troops emerged from the back and were directed to positions by their officer.

Then the floodlight on the APC snapped on. Like a gigantic flashbulb it illuminated the ancient stucco in a pale glare. Palms cast angled shadows matching those of the soldiers hovering in their lee. The stillness was shattered by a sharp voice magnified through a bullhorn. "You are surrounded by a unit of the New Revolutionary Army. You are required to exit the front door one person at a time, arms in the air. Anyone who disobeys an order will be shot without question. By the time I count to ten I expect the first person to appear at the front door. Failure to do so will establish the need for tear gas." After a short pause, the voice began, "One . . . two . . . three . . ."

The chatter of automatic weapons from behind the building shattered the night. An anguished wail erupted as the shooting stopped, punctuated in seconds by a single shot. The cry ended in a sharp howl of agony.

The officer waited patiently, bullhorn resting on his hip, until two soldiers came into the light, each dragging a limp body by the feet. Their clothing indicated both victims might have been young, but blood obscured their features. The woman's skirt was drawn obscenely over her upper body. Their corpses were dumped in front of the officer.

He raised the bullhorn to his lips again. "This man and woman, they tried to escape through a cellar window. Raphael shot the man through the head. The woman," he added, kicking at the female body, "made so much noise about him that they had to kill her, too.

"Two of your compatriots are dead because they tried to escape," he continued, stepping over the bodies. "I will begin my count again . . . but now you only have seven seconds left. Four . . . five . . . six . . . seven . . . eight"—he nodded his head at one of the men, who hefted a grenade launcher to his shoulder—". . . nine . . . ten . . ."

As he was about to give his order to fire, the front door swung back. Each weapon in the perimeter centered on the opening.

"Now! Out now," the officer barked. "I will hold fire for five seconds."

A man, a student by his looks, appeared in the doorway, arms raised, blinking against the glare of the floodlight.

"Your arms . . . higher . . . straight up . . ."

His arms stretched directly above his head, palms out. The fear in his face intensified as his head pivoted from one side to the other. He could not see who was behind the light.

"Walk straight ahead ten paces . . . and stop. No movement."

When the young man had taken ten steps, a soldier appeared at his side to pat him down roughly for weapons. The prisoner jumped as two hands running up the insides of his thighs slammed into his crotch. A rifle butt slashed out of the darkness into his stomach.

"You moved," the officer snarled at the man who now groveled on his hands and knees, gasping for air. "How many more in there?"

There was no answer, only a muffled choking sound.

"Next!" the voice snapped through the bullhorn.

An elderly man with a gray beard appeared tentatively in the doorway, screening his eyes against the glare.

"Arms straight up . . . take ten paces toward me."

One arm arched into the air, the other still shading his face. "I can't see you . . . I don't know where . . ."

"Ten paces now or you will be shot."

The man shuffled one step forward, peering down as the elderly do to see if there was a step, his hands now halfway above his head.

"Come on, asshole. Now!"

The bearded man shuffled a little farther. "But we were only having a meeting of a class. I'm a professor . . . we're with the university." Again he dropped an arm to shade his eyes.

The officer nodded to one of the soldiers. Two shots rang out. The professor's body flew back into the trunk of a palm, tumbling into the dirt in a forlorn heap.

"You, in the building. I'm losing patience. I want each of you to come through that door with your hands fully in the air and walk ten paces straight ahead to be searched for weapons. This building will be set on fire in exactly one minute. You will not be hurt if you follow orders." He glanced at his watch before calling, "Next!"

A man and two women, obviously young students, appeared in the doorway, then stepped gingerly outside. The man made an attempt to protest when the soldiers pawed the women and searched them for weapons. He was silenced by a rifle butt in the mouth.

The officer turned to one of the women. "Is there anyone else inside?"

She stared back, tears running down her cheeks, her features terror-stricken, unable to speak.

An open hand caught her flush in the cheek, jerking her head back. "If there are still some of your friends inside, they are going to be cooking shortly. Do you want that to happen?"

If there was an answer as she blinked through her tears, her mouth opening as if she wanted to speak, the words simply failed to come.

"Burn it," he growled. "And if anyone tries to escape, shoot them. These students seem to need more than one example."

As the flames climbed into the night sky there was more firing from behind the building. Soon two more bodies were hauled into the light, another man, and a girl who appeared to still be in her teens. Their age made little difference to the soldiers, who had been told only that the

University of Havana was a haven for subversives and that anyone meeting after the curfew was an enemy of the New Revolution.

The four surviving students were imprisoned with scores of others. They were among professors, businessmen, priests, lawyers, and a multitude of former Castro bureaucrats who still were unable to fathom what had taken place in the past month. The old government was gone, yet few really understood what had replaced it.

The following day they were all paraded onto a raised platform that had been constructed especially for the daily trials at the New Plaza of the Revolution. The old plaza had been Castro's pride and joy. Centered on the monument built in honor of Cuba's greatest patriot, José Martí, it was surrounded by beautifully maintained parks. Castro loved it because it reminded him of the humble origins of José Martí and thus of his own revolution.

Juan Duran had understood its purpose exactly and used it to further his own ends, first changing it to the New Plaza so that there would never be a moment's doubt about the status of revolutions in Cuba. He constructed a huge platform and backed it with his own revolutionary banners to gradually blank out the image of Fidel and Martí. It also allowed the crowds, who increased each day in anticipation of Duran's morbid circus, to see just who had been selected the previous evening. The number of prisoners continued to expand, yet there hadn't been a day when a single individual had been found innocent of the standard charge—subversion.

A cheer erupted from the crowded plaza when their new leader appeared on a raised section of the platform. Juan Duran, now displaying general's stars, strode to a judge's bench erected especially for these trials. There were to be no fatigues displayed in his government—they were worn only by prisoners. Duran was resplendent in a personally designed uniform that emphasized gold-braided shoulder boards and a variety of medals. A correspondent from Reuters had correctly noted that General Duran effected a great similarity to the Libyan, Qaddafi, both visually and in the image he projected to his followers. There was certainly that same mystical quality, and in the last few weeks he felt that Duran's eyes seemed to have taken on that fanatical glaze of the true self-believer.

The subversion trials, begun a week after Fidel Castro's disappearance, had become a rococo pageant in the new Havana. It was a lesson learned during late-night conversations in the tents at the Assdadah desert base: Control of the people is paramount and is achieved by making them an early and integral unit for revenge. While Havana was necessarily the central point for achieving this goal, similar trials were occurring throughout the country each day. Duran's military had neatly taken control of every government building in every major town from Santiago de Cuba in the east to Pinar del Río in the west.

There had never been an assassination or a reportable murder when control in Havana was achieved. Castro and his closest associates simply disappeared. There were no reports of sighting a single missing individual—dead or alive—nor were there any new graves to report. Senior military and government officials who remained in public view had either been involved in the coup or they were the first to be tried at the New Plaza. Sentences were efficiently carried out within moments of the verdict. Military prisoners were always shot. Civilians were either shot or hanged, though the latter fate was usually reserved for those Duran felt should serve as an example to the populace. Only those considered viable candidates for reeducation were sent to the prisons.

On this day the prisoner selections appeared unexciting. Though not a soul in the throng dared leave the plaza, the hot sun and lack of excitement created a mood that was both impatient and ugly. There was an inarticulate murmur, a shuffling of feet, that became disconcerting to Duran.

His military Judge Advocate, cloaked in black robes as he handed down a series of death sentences, responded instinctively to a wave of Duran's hand and moved to his leader's side. He was sure that the slightest mistake on his part might also have him at the wrong end of a firing squad.

"Carrero, didn't you say there were four students from the university . . . four who had been arrested last night for attending a subversive meeting?"

"Yes, sir. They insisted they were attending a class, even though the university had been closed down. Each one claimed there was so little left to complete their degrees that they took a chance. They intend to admit their stupidity and throw themselves at your mercy."

"Two of them are women?"

"Yes," Carrero said, grinning, "and one of them is quite attractive."

"Call them up now." That cast to the eye that the Reuters man recognized was definitely pronounced. "The people demand something unusual today." Give the people their revenge, he had been taught in the desert tent, allow them the taste of blood.

Duran moved to the microphone normally used by Carrero. "Today," he addressed the throng, "you will become witness to a very special case. There are four students from the university—each of whom resisted authorities—who were captured last evening. Why, you may wonder, are a few students so important?" He paused as his eyes swept the audience, his index finger pointing to individuals as if they were singularly important to his decision. He used his eyes to mesmerize his listeners. "The answer can be found in a single word—*communism*. And I am talking about the Marxist-Leninist threat that would reduce each of you to a number . . ." His voice fell off to a whisper before intensifying. ". . . and that number is reserved for a slave to a system more evil than the gulags and torture chambers that rear their ugliness in every Marxist-Leninist communist government. And that evil system had been taught by the university in this city until my government chose to halt it—to suppress an evil that festered in the heart of our capital city,'' he exclaimed in a now booming voice.

Juan Duran was a natural orator possessing the magnetic personality to enthrall vast numbers with his voice alone. In just a few short sentences he had been able to quiet the murmuring crowd and generate an enthusiasm unanticipated just moments before. First, they had been tempted with a crime against their new society. Although most hadn't the vaguest idea what that society might be, a gauntlet had been thrown at their feet. Few had been aware of this new evil up to that moment. Yet it had been molded in seconds, designed by their new leader to take the shape of a heinous effort to subjugate each of them personally.

Duran's eyes were shiny with excitement. ''Yet even after we succeeded in closing the door to this Marxist-Leninist evil, there were some who felt they had the right to flaunt their hideous philosophy in our faces . . . to insist that we allow them to continue to preach the overthrow of the people at the very instant we are trying to return Cuba to each of you. Some of them have claimed that they have nothing to do with any political philosophies, yet at the same time they are coddling the perpetrators of this evil system.

''That . . . *that* is why the university was closed. And we intend to keep it closed until we can be assured that only that which is right for the people will be taught to the future generations who will raise our nation to new heights.'' His voice, level for a moment, had once again increased in intensity as he brought his audience to a new level of anticipation. ''And today,'' he shouted at the top of his voice, ''we are going to try some of those who would force that Marxist-Leninist institution to open in opposition to your beliefs.''

The cheers reverberating across the plaza began as approval for the words of their leader, then gradually expanded into a bloodthirsty chant for the prisoners. A new dimension had been added to what had begun as a boring event. They sensed that an exciting day could be in store for them. Duran had already planned for it, but to him it was more like the smell of blood at a bullfight. Qaddafi had explained it precisely: *Give the people a good show, make them a part of it, and they'll eat from your hand.*

It was as Juan Duran was finishing his last sentence, even before the crowd's cheers reverberated over their heads, that Carrero realized his judicial duties would not be required that afternoon. He also now understood exactly why that stake had been erected near the front of the platform.

Duran moved to Carrero's position on the dais, arms raised to quiet the crowd. "The crime against our government—against each of you because each one of you is the government—is so serious that I will personally accept the responsibility of sitting in judgment of these prisoners."

Cara Estrada had been listening calmly, her face expressionless. Now a tiny place in her heart, a hidden, secret spot reserved for her most private feelings, grew a little emptier. Once again she'd sensed a subtle change in Duran's expression even before he beckoned to Carrero, though she was unable to determine which direction he would take. He'd become so unpredictable! It was almost as if power had transformed him.

Yet in just those few short weeks Cara had become almost as powerful as Duran. She was tall, slender, with a model's figure, and her long black hair hung down to her shoulders. High cheekbones accentuated soft dark intelligent eyes. When she spoke, men fell in love with her smooth husky voice. But she didn't think she had been altered by her new status.

Now her elegant eyebrows raised perceptibly, though there was no outward sign of concern. If there were aspects of his makeup that Duran failed to reveal to his mistress in the years before his revolution, there were very few. Over the past five years she was the individual singularly responsible for planning his career. When he was out of the country—leading the Africa Legion, training with the Soviet Spetznaz, assisting Qaddafi—she was the one who carefully cemented the political base for the coup. Cara Estrada had planned Castro's demise so perfectly that not a trace of the former leader existed.

But this sudden ambition to assume the mantle of executioner was not part of the scheme. This idea either originated with Duran or, worse yet, someone else she should be immediately concerned with. Though she gave no outward sign, this new twist was carefully catalogued in the complicated filing system that she maintained in her well-organized mind. Ever since he'd returned from Africa, there had been certain quirks in his personality that had surprised her. At times he seemed to be someone else.

"I will take the two women first," Duran announced quietly to Carrero. The latter realized he had now assumed the role of prosecutor rather than judge.

A murmur rose from the plaza as the two women were brought before Duran. Their clothing was the bizarre and colorful dress popular with the students at the university just before the revolution. On the platform, before the mass of peasants and workers, their clothes quite suddenly branded them as traitors against a new system. Designed at an earlier time to show sympathy for the lower classes, their peasant blouses and rough skirts had become an insult, and the reaction of the audience punctuated their dilemma.

Duran read the charges in a sonorous tone that echoed from the loudspeaker system to every corner of the New Plaza of the Revolution. When he spoke, the rustle of a cockroach could have been heard; during his dramatic pauses, the hum of thousands of whispering lips filled the air.

As he addressed the two prisoners he speculated on

which one should be first. Should he start with the pretty one or the less attractive girl? Which would the people respond to with more enthusiasm? The taller one had a fuller figure; the shorter was more pretty.

Duran appeared stern as he read the charges to the accused, though his purpose was really to incite the audience in the plaza. Duran went so far as to elaborate for the women's benefit exactly why the charges had been brought against them and the extent of the damage to the current government.

Prisoners were allowed to respond to the charges, but they were not given the opportunity to utilize the public address system. Anything they might say on their own behalf was strictly between themselves and the judge. Essentially they had no defense, for it was understood they would not have been on the platform if they were innocent. Their appearance was simply to establish before the people the extent of their guilt.

Neither of the women cared to speak for themselves. They had seen how the system operated, and their only effort was to place themselves at the mercy of the court.

"I generally support the death penalty in crimes against the people," Duran began as a hush spread across the plaza. "But these women are young . . . just girls . . . only twenty years old . . . and I do not believe their crime has been directed personally against the people. They were being used by the university, an institution that would undermine us all." He paused to allow that statement to sink in. "I will not impose the death penalty on young women who can still be educated to serve the country. The people . . . each one of you . . . have compassion. You can show mercy when mercy is deserved"—Duran had turned to face his audience as he spoke to the prisoners— "but crime cannot go unpunished. Before we start to educate people in the new system, we must be certain they renounce their crimes." He turned back to the women, and in a voice that echoed across the plaza, he shouted, "I sentence each of you to fifteen lashes at the post."

If anyone had been studying Cara Estrada, the first sign of surprise, or perhaps discontent, would have been obvious. Not only did her eyebrows again rise perceptibly, her mouth was drawn back for an instant in a grimace before her features once again became neutral. What she was seeing this day was a solid indication that Juan Duran had perhaps become more involved in himself than the revolution. There had been hints in recent days, but this time she sensed a distinct turn inward.

The crowd in the plaza also recognized a new element in their leader. He was prepared to offer them satisfaction, a new symbol they understood. Putting a criminal to death, whether it was by hanging or the firing squad, quickly solved the guilty party's problems. The dead no longer cared and the people were left with an empty feeling. It was difficult for them to take pleasure in a dead body. Vengeance became a momentary solution, but both the criminal and the crime were forgotten with the disposition of the corpse. Now their leader was dangling a new temptation—the opportunity to take part in the criminal's suffering, to see and smell the blood. It was a solution that appealed to each of the senses, and they roared their approval.

Another lesson from the Assdadah tent confirmed!

Duran enjoyed the expressions of dismay on the women's faces as they understood the real purpose of his sentence. They had been selected to be his new symbols—sacrificial maidens—and they knew their suffering was to be the high point in Duran's sense of theater.

"You." He pointed at the less attractive one. She would be first. Duran realized a sense of anticipation that he had never experienced in the past. It was alien yet pleasant. He had selected her for a specific reason—her breasts were much larger than the other girl's. He knew she would excite the crowd, but he had not been ready for the thrill he now knew he also would feel. The pretty one might be even more exciting after they saw how he intended to execute the sentence. There was even a slight tremor in his hands as he indicated that she should be brought to the newly erected post near the front of the platform.

Once she stood facing the plaza, trembling uncontrollably, Duran ordered two soldiers on either side to hold her arms out to the sides. They grasped her roughly, the eagerness evident in their faces. Tears streamed down the girl's cheeks as she recognized the look of triumph deep in Duran's eyes.

He placed his hands on the front of her blouse, pausing momentarily to savor the moment, then ripped downward. The material tore away, leaving the girl facing the crowd in her brassiere. A murmur of excitement, wild and ugly, rolled across the platform. Duran ripped the remaining shred of cloth away and stepped back to reveal her to the plaza. Her head hung with shame, dark hair flowing over her breasts while the people cheered. With a soldier still grasping either arm, she was lead to the post where her wrists were bound on either side.

Cara Estrada realized at this moment in time that *her* revolution had changed forever. She was reminded of the slave auctions of the past as one black after another was led to the front of the block and sold to the highest bidder. Her teachers had explained that slavery was the lowest level of humanity, and one of the lessons she never forgot was that nations became civilized only when they allowed all men to be free. Now the pictures from those old books flashed before her eyes.

The woman at the post lifted her head to glance back over her shoulder. Her eyes fell on Cara Estrada, who experienced a sense of revulsion that had remained below the surface during these trials—until that moment. Cara recognized an ugly sound from the crowded plaza as the people, men and women alike, rose to the bait of humiliation and blood. And she felt it as Juan Duran's exultant eyes held her own momentarily, for there was a lust in his glance that had never appeared until this moment. She had no idea if she could again gain control; but she knew that this act had transcended every goal she had fought for. This was another Juan Duran—one she had never known or anticipated.

As the whip curled back for the first blow, she saw the tremor in her lover's body. Then it ceased as the lash exploded against the naked back and Duran shouted triumphantly, *"Uno!"* An ugly red welt appeared.

The black cord flicked back, then forward. *"Dos!"* There was an echo from the crowd.

"Tres!" This time his voice was drowned out by an enthusiastic chorus from the plaza.

"Cuatro!" The chant rolled across the platform.

"Cinco." The voices grew louder with each blow.

The sixth lash drew blood, and Cara was no longer surprised when Duran stepped around to the opposite side of the post to watch the large breasts as the next blow fell.

After the tenth, he halted the proceedings so that he might turn the victim to face the audience. As his hands lingered on the hips of the semiconscious girl, Cara understood with a sickening flash of insight that the intellectual strength of the revolution had succumbed to the lust of power.

A hush fell over the audience as the second girl was brought forward. Her fear magnified her appeal. An outthrust lower lip enhanced a wild beauty, but when she saw the expression of pure pleasure in Duran's eyes as he reached for her blouse, that lip began to tremble. As his rough hands touched her, she closed her eyes, biting down hard enough on her lower lip to draw blood. When he stepped back to display her, they were met with a roar of approval.

Cara Estrada was not on the platform when Juan Duran delighted the crowd by laying on the last five lashes himself. In less than a month idealism had succumbed to a desire to control the people by appealing to their baser instincts; it had also instilled a fear they had yet to understand.

In the weeks that followed, pockets of resistance in Havana would cease to exist. Duran's unique methods of dealing with the opposition would cement his power both within the revolutionary superstructure and among the populace. The latter was willing to sell its soul for a satisfaction that had been offered successfully in history only by the Romans, the Inquisition, and the Nazis.

In the strategy room of the presidential palace later that day, a slide projection of the southern tier of the United States occupied the center of the wall behind Duran as he spoke. "I can't emphasize enough how important it is that your attacks occur at exactly—*exactly*—the same time. Remember, there is an hour's difference between Miami and New Orleans. When Major Pagos commences his attack at five forty-five, the sun will be above the horizon in Miami. But it will be an hour earlier, four forty-five, in New Orleans, and Captain Maceo's squad will have the protection of a dawn sky. It is as important that the Americans understand how efficient we have become as it is for them to see the effectiveness of the attack. More than their anger, I want their respect!"

CHAPTER THREE

The Russian ambassador to Cuba, Arkady Bunin, had been recalled to Moscow for consultation. In order to minimize suspicions in Havana, the ambassadors from half a dozen other major Soviet client states were also asked to return to the Kremlin, although they were not aware of Bunin's purpose.

The actual cause for this gathering had been Bunin's activation of a special code for the first time by any Soviet ambassador. Assuming that the intelligence arm of any host government can infer the purpose for most classified message traffic between an embassy and home base, an emergency procedure had been established. When an emissary determined that a crisis situation was pending that could severely affect Soviet policy, a warning was employed that could be broken only by the Kremlin decoder.

Arkady Bunin had been as close to Fidel Castro as two people from such diverse cultures could be. They went deep-sea fishing together, hunted boar on the Isle of Youth, and spent so much time at the Estadio Latinoamericano watching baseball that the Russian eventually took up watching American games on TV. On the day that Juan Duran appeared on Cuban television as the new leader, Bunin was as shocked as any other foreign statesman in Havana. But as far as the Kremlin hierarchy was concerned, his status remained secure because he was the only diplomat, Soviet or otherwise, who also knew Duran. They had been introduced a few years before by Castro, and it was Bunin who recommended that Duran receive training in the Soviet Union after his phenomenal success with the Africa Legion.

When the world is taken by surprise, as it was by Duran's accession, a nation must consider itself lucky if a relationship has already been established. Moscow had no choice but to accept Havana's new leadership, just as they allowed that Bunin's inability to anticipate Duran's coup was overshadowed by his earlier relations with the man.

"He is going to make Qaddafi look like an innocent in another few months." Bunin had no intention of softening his analysis. He was sipping a glass of strong black tea as he addressed the other individuals around the table. He'd insisted that the general secretary include the foreign minister, the secretary for Caribbean/Latin-American Affairs, and the head of the GRU (the Main Intelligence Directorate) of the Soviet General Staff. The latter, General Dotov, rarely appeared at such briefings unless the use of covert military forces was anticipated. "I was able to learn through one of his aides that he spent a number of weeks in the desert with the Libyan . . . and you can imagine what they talked about!" he added emphatically.

"I read in your report that he's denounced Marxist-Leninists publicly. But how much of that is show, and how much is just noise to appease those mobs of his?" asked the foreign minister.

Bunin withdrew a packet from his briefcase. He removed a number of photographs and laid them carefully in the center of the table. None of the men were shocked. Each of them had seen pictures of human slaughter from every corner of the world, and the corpses dangling from ropes, slumped against firing posts, sprawled in grotesque positions, or piled in shallow graves failed to impress them. But the photograph of Juan Duran whipping a half-naked woman caught and held each eye.

"Not all of the dead people were accused of being communists, but more than half of them were. And I'm willing to bet that seventy-five percent of the current prisoners are being held because they are party members." Bunin tapped the photo of the woman with a finger. "How often do you see a head of state personally stripping a prisoner and carrying out the punishment?"

He was met with silence.

The general secretary shook his head in wonder. The people saw him only on rare occasions and those were generally when he stared grimly from the reviewing stand in front of Lenin's tomb. Yet he possessed a human touch that few could imagine. "What will it take to convince people like Duran that wholesale slaughter isn't the only solution? If he keeps on, it will be no different than the Khmer Rouge. There will be no one left to manage the government. Every person intelligent enough to blow his own nose will be dead and—" He broke off, turning away from the table in disgust. There would be nothing left for the Soviet Union by the time this madman finished bleeding his country. The Russians had made a major and continuing investment in Cuba for over twenty-five years, and he was damned if this lunatic was going to run it down the drain. He stopped by a window looking down into a courtyard and folded his arms. "Why couldn't someone with some common sense take over?" he growled over his shoulder.

"On the contrary," Bunin responded, "you should be aware that this Duran is no clown. A madman? Maybe," he went on, answering his own question, "but a brilliant one. Whether you consider his military aptitude or his leadership, he is an absolute natural. He has the same law degree from the University of Havana as Castro, and he cultivated his political base in exactly the same manner from his first week on the campus.'' The ambassador sighed, stroking his chin thoughtfully. ''Maybe a little crazy . . . yes. But I guarantee that he is crafty, cunning—whatever term you care to choose—and he has a mind like a steel trap. With all that going for him, I think the best description of Duran is *volatile*.''

''I was aware of that,'' the general secretary snapped.

The room became so silent that the gurgling and squeaking of Bunin's stomach was clearly audible to each one of them. It continued until General Dotov broke the silence. ''Remind me never to accept an invitation to your apartment for dinner,'' he sniggered.

Bunin saw nothing humorous in either his stomach or the general's remark and, staring straight ahead, muttered, ''I can assure each of you that what you hear is a stomach in pain and that is the result of incredible tension over the past few weeks. It is not a laughing matter,'' he added wearily. Bunin was truly exhausted. Though he knew Juan Duran well enough to have dined with him one evening in Havana before his return to Moscow, he'd understood from the start that the new Cuban leader would not be taking advice from him.

The secretary for Caribbean affairs was willing to put into words exactly what the others were thinking. ''We are literally cutting our own throats each day we allow this Duran to live. First, he is costing us money. Second, he is making us look foolish every time he gives one of his anti-Marxist speeches while we continue to dole out another million rubles.'' He was touching the tips of the fingers of his left hand with his right index finger as he enumerated each item. ''Third, he has restricted our infantry brigade to base until further notice. Fourth, we now have to request permission for docking facilities for any military ship, and our reconnaissance flights have twice been forced to go on to Nicaragua because they did not request air space clearance in time—Duran's time I might add. How much more do I have to explain?" he sputtered.

"Perhaps you have a solution," the general secretary snarled. He would not turn away from the window. "Bunin has explained that he is protected twenty-four hours a day by guards who will happily commit suicide to please him. I suppose he even has eunuchs who hover over him while he screws that mistress of his?" he added, glancing back at the ambassador.

"I'd doubt that—but anything's possible in Havana. Nothing would surprise me these days."

"Well, Valery!" The secretary's eyes fell on the GRU head. "You've had little to offer. What would you suggest?" His expectant tone of voice indicated that he already anticipated the answer.

General Dotov shrugged, then winked at Bunin. "No single assassin is going to accomplish superhuman feats of strength and daring to get to this Duran. More than likely, the blame would come right back to us even if we were successful. You need the Spetznaz to create the setting, and you need a genius to work with them to make this Duran disappear exactly like he made Fidel vanish."

The secretary turned around from the window to face the table. The smug expression on his face confirmed that he had heard exactly what he wanted to hear. "And you have the man that can accomplish that," he concluded.

"I'd like to bring him here tomorrow morning."

"I'd like to meet this miracle man," the secretary countered facetiously.

General Dotov was amused by the reaction of the men around the table when he entered the room with his miracle man. "You expected a Spetznaz," he said, chuckling. "Someone in an army dress uniform with medals covering his chest. They are very good . . . but you asked for the best, didn't you?"

The stranger was of medium height and stocky, and he

wore black battle fatigues with such elegance that it seemed a crown belonged on his head. The uniform was custom fitted with sharp creases beginning at his shoulders and ending only where his pants were perfectly folded into the tops of the shiniest boots Bunin had ever seen. A distinctive black beret displaying an anchor and red star was canted jauntily over his right eye. A colonel's insignia appeared on either collar.

"Colonel Paul Voronov, Naval Infantry. This is the man you wished to meet, gentlemen." The general was thoroughly enjoying their surprise as he added, "Paul has also had the privilege of meeting your Juan Duran."

Each man in the room, including the general secretary, found himself scrutinized by the iciest blue eyes they had ever seen. Voronov's head never moved as he remained at attention. But his eyes held theirs for the briefest moment, and they knew he would remember every aspect of their faces forever. His own features were Scandinavian—short blond hair, a broad face with high cheekbones, and just the hint of Tatar around his barely slanted eyelids. His lips were thin and expressionless.

Bunin had to look down at the papers in front of him before he could look back at Voronov. When he did, he found the blue eyes riveted on his own. *The man radiates brutality,* he thought, *brutality and a love of violence . . . and he could care less about anyone at this table—he respects no man!*

"At ease, Colonel," the general said softly. "These gentlemen are pleased to meet you," he continued as he sat down in the same place he had occupied the previous day and extended his hand toward the free chair next to him. "Please make yourself comfortable." He passed some papers to each of the other men at the table. "Allow them to study your service record first and I think they may want to ask you some questions."

After a few minutes, the general secretary looked up at Voronov and tapped the papers with his fingers. "Very impressive,'' he murmured uncomfortably, ''very impressive.'' Then he looked away from those eyes and shuffled through the service record again.

The foreign minister looked instead at General Dotov. ''I . . . we are surprised . . . I must say. We all assumed that you would recommend your Spetznaz for this operation. Their training is more attuned to what we had in mind. . . .''

''I have every intention of making this a Spetznaz effort. However, I thought I made it clear that we needed a very special type of leader to coordinate the operation. Spetznaz officers are trained to lead Spetznaz teams. Each team acts as one man. That is why they have been superb wherever they have been sent. But my understanding is that there are two objectives here: one is to reclaim a client state and the other is to alter the leadership of that state.''

Bunin's eyes fell hesitantly on Voronov before they returned to the GRU head. He was absolutely correct. It would take a man like Paul Voronov to remove Juan Duran if Moscow was to avoid the censure that came from efforts such as Prague or Berlin or Kabul.

Voronov's service record read like the epitaphs in the Hall of Heroes. There was naval service in the Baltic and Red Banner Northern Fleets, destroyer command, experimentation with high-speed attack craft, development of amphibious tactics culminating in acceptance by the elite Black Berets of the Naval Infantry, superb decorations in Angola and Afghanistan, and letters of merit for covert operations around the world that of necessity remained undocumented.

''You know the Cuban . . . Duran . . .'' the general secretary ventured.

''Yes, sir.'' Voronov's mouth barely moved, but his words cut the air like a whip.

''I know that,'' the general secretary responded with more confidence. ''Why don't you tell us exactly how you came to know him.''

"General Duran—he was a major at the time—was a guest of the Soviet Union. He spent time at Simferapol training in terrorist activities and then was recommended to train with our Spetznaz forces. Since I, too, had been accepted as an outsider, I was assigned as a guide to work with him through the course. You understand, of course, that very few qualify for such training and that less than half complete it successfully."

Spetznaz were special operations forces functioning specifically under the GRU. They trained in teams of approximately a dozen men for sensitive missions abroad, generally behind enemy lines. In Afghanistan, they were known for their aggressiveness and ruthless tactics. Each team member was trained in reconnaissance and target location, infiltration tactics, sabotage with explosives/incendiaries and chemical/biological agents, clandestine communications, hand-to-hand killing and silent killing techniques, psychological operations, language skills, and survival behind enemy lines. Teams were also trained to operate from submarines or amphibs and to jump from planes. Unit pride allowed little room for outsiders.

"General Duran and myself are the only non-Spetznaz members to have ever completed the course successfully," Voronov added nonchalantly.

"Would Duran have been able to survive this course without you?" the foreign minister asked.

"It's a matter of culture. He understands our language and, to a lesser extent, our traditions. He wasn't prepared for the hatred of outsiders that's part of Spetznaz. I suspect that if I wasn't there, they might have killed him. But I can assure you that a number of Spetznaz would have died before Duran." Voronov blinked for the first time. "He's superb; he is Spetznaz."

"Would you object to taking Duran's life?" Bunin inquired.

"No more than he would mine."

"Has General Dotov explained the purpose of this meeting to you?" asked the general secretary.

"He has."

"And do you have any questions?"

"No."

"None at all?"

"I understand the purpose of the mission." Voronov's face gave no indication of what he was thinking. His voice remained a polite monotone.

"Well, then, do you think there is a probability of success for this mission?" the general secretary asked.

"I expect all missions I decide to undertake will be successful."

"Have you had any failures?"

"One."

"Do you care to tell us?" The general secretary found this one-way conversation increasingly irritating.

"Failure to complete the mission of holding the canal during the revolution in Panama."

"To what do you lay that failure?" The general secretary expected complete answers to his questions, and he wasn't about to allow a mere colonel to buffalo him.

"I underestimated my opposite number." Then, to quell the pique that he could perceive in the general secretary, he added pleasantly, "It was this close." Displaying a tiny space between his thumb and forefinger, Voronov continued, "I was using Cuban troops at the time. They were no match for American SEALs, nor can they expect to compete with Spetznaz. I do understand exactly what is required of me," he concluded emphatically.

"And you want to go to Cuba?"

"It's as good as any other place." Then with the tiniest hint of anticipation, more a smirk than anything else, his lips turned up at the corners and he explained, "It's a challenge."

Another day was spent with the experts familiarizing Voronov with the country and the names he should recognize. It was Arkady Bunin, the ambassador who understood Duran and Cuba better than any other man, who explained how he had compiled a list of possible replacements for Duran.

"There are a number of capable people representing every conceivable interest you could imagine. Even though it is considered a socialist country, you can find a dozen political views from a dozen people on the street. I will not suggest anyone who could be considered a puppet of ours. If you consider who we can work with after that, the list is considerably shorter. And if you look for talent and a name respected in most quarters, there are hardly any. But I suggest you meet with Jorge Anaya as soon as you can. He is a justice of the Supreme Court, yet his moral values are based only on what benefits him. He might suit you."

CHAPTER FOUR

There were five bridges, or causeways, connecting Miami Beach to the mother city on the mainland, six counting old A1A at Bal Harbor to the north. Major Pagos considered mining only the lower five at first, but changed his mind after Duran emphasized how necessary it was to demand the Americans' respect. To allow one mainland connector to remain was a sign of weakness. As a result, he authorized an additional team of sappers and assigned them a double-span mission on the old highway. Since the major was certain there wouldn't be time to pick up either them or the adjacent team at Biscayne Park, their personnel were selected from a unit just completing survival training. Pagos was sure they would have to escape inland and establish contact with him.

Transporting his troops into a country accustomed to terrorism would normally have been a demanding mission. But Major Pagos had studied the tactics of the drug smugglers and their process of transporting their product. He soon appreciated the fact that getting any sort of contraband into the United States was a simple matter of entering where authorities were either not available or spread too thin. It was also perfect for inserting teams of five men at a time. Their gear would be delivered through other points. If any of them were caught, they would be considered illegal aliens rather than insurgents.

The first stage of the attack was so perfectly timed that Duran would later express disappointment that it was witnessed mostly by park-bench drunks and early-morning joggers. At precisely 5:45 A.M. Miami-time, the charges placed by Major Pagos's special forces detonated. The blasts from the northern end rolled down Biscayne Bay in delayed echoes to punctuate the vision unfolding before the eyes of the few watchers.

An orange sun was already climbing above the hotels to the east when dust and minute sections of the connecting highways arched skyward in unison. To a professional, it was a work of art. Even an amateur could create a mess with a couple of tons of the stuff, but swimmers were severely limited in how much they could carry. High explosive was heavy, and it was important to understand how to design a bridge in order to blow it up with a limited supply of explosive. The largest, I-195 required special placement and, as a result, was more impressive than the rest. Thick clouds of dust surged into the air, rising more than a hundred feet and blotting out the sun as the sharp blasts reverberated off the bay's surface, rebounding in one tremendous thunderclap. Vehicles directly over the explosives were hurled piecemeal into the water, while some fortunates were able to jam on their brakes in time to avoid certain death. When the smoke and dust cleared, each span had lost between thirty and forty yards of highway. Miami Beach was totally cut off from the mainland.

As a span of the old Tamiami Trail erupted in a thick cloud and sank to the bottom of Biscayne Bay, the second phase of Major Pagos's operation was taking place under his personal supervision. The massive underground storage tanks at Miami International Airport burst through the runways as tongues of flame clawed a thousand feet skyward. Airliners parked at the gates for early-morning flights ruptured like ripe grapefruits as the fire engulfed them. Thousands of square feet of glass were hurled into the terminal buildings by the intense heat, creating a firestorm that licked horizontally at early-morning travelers. Pagos smiled grimly from his position to the west near Palmetto Expressway. His watch read 5:47 A.M., and already the city of Miami had sustained damage that would require years and untold millions to return to a normal level of economic survival.

If his executive officer, who had coordinated the mining of the causeways, remained as efficient as ever, two small high-speed boats would already be careening through Biscayne Bay, plucking his sappers from the water for the fifty-mile trip across to Bimini. Before the Americans ever figured what had occurred, or who had done it, they would be back in Havana. The teams that had taken the two northern connectors would soon melt into the large Cuban community to make contact with Pagos.

Within days every single man would be back in Havana— without a single loss!

The sortie at New Orleans replaced one initially planned for Pensacola. Duran had eventually acceded to wise advice, acknowledging that it would be unlikely even a small force could escape from a military base unscathed; nor was it impossible to imagine that the United States might counter an attack on one of their bases with one on Cuban soil. The source of terrorist action directed against cities would take more time to identify, and forceful reaction would be initially limited. That time would allow Duran to introduce the second stage of his scheme.

The New Orleans operation actually commenced earlier than that in Miami because of the sophisticated preparations required. Since the crescent of the ''crescent city'' was formed by a wide bend in the Mississippi River that created the city's half-moon shape, the river became the objective. Economic impact was Duran's goal—after all, hadn't the Americans attempted to strangle his own little country's economy?—and the river was the key to New Orleans's pocketbook.

Captain Maceo was overjoyed at the opportunity to employ some initiative in achieving Duran's goal, which was to block the Mississippi. Three days beforehand he had checked into a downtown hotel. Obtaining schedules for all the shipping in the river and memorizing the navigational charts was accomplished the first day. The second day involved identifying a serviceable number of loaded fuel barges that would be accessible on the following night. On the final day his team arrived one at a time, assembling in a safe house in a rundown section of Gretna where part of their weapons allocation had been stored. The balance of their supplies would be obtained from the various drops established earlier the previous week.

The Mississippi operates on a twenty-four-hour basis, especially on its lower stretches. The river never sleeps, nor is there ever a moment when tugs aren't chugging back and forth on their endless missions. There was no reason to question two of these tugs as they moved four fuel barges down the western side of the river, slowing as they approached the bridge connecting Gretna to New Orleans. As they neared their destination crewmen separated two of the barges, while the two remaining were moved to the opposite side of the river. The time was now just a little after four in the morning. Captain Maceo uttered the expected words over the radio to his men, and the final part of the operation began.

The first barge was made fast to one of the immense cement pilings of the bridge on the Gretna side. The second was moved across the river to a piling on the New Orleans side. A small boat then picked up the crewmen from the barges and whisked them across the river to the docks on the far side of the bridge.

Captain Maceo's orders to his remaining men loitering about the docks became the death knell for the few crewmen remaining aboard selected freighters, and they also began the second phase. There was no necessity for gunplay. The Cubans quietly dispatched the deck watches, then moved below to take care of those asleep. While three men on each ship scurried down to the engine rooms to set the charges, the former barge crews cut the mooring lines, then assisted in securing a tug along the outboard side. Once away from the dock, a second tug moved the next ship away, following the other toward the center of the river. Then a third was moved out behind the other two in the same manner. The ships eased into the stream, pushing against the current toward the bridge. It was now four-forty, and the sky showed gentle traces of light to the east.

Maceo remained in constant contact with his team leaders, pleased with their efficiency in such strange surroundings. It really was going to work just as they'd anticipated back in Havana!

At exactly four forty-five, no more than five seconds apart, the barges pressing against the bridge pilings exploded in sheets of flame that climbed instantly above the high steel towers. The soft morning clouds, so common above New Orleans that time of year, reflected the yellow-orange light across the river where the two remaining barges had been released to bump down the dockside. These also detonated within a few seconds of the others, cascading fuel across the docks into the warehouses and business establishments facing the river.

The three ships began to separate, one being pulled toward either shore of the river before the tug crews cut them loose. It was a little shy of four forty-seven when the ship on the Gretna side exploded, breaking in two with the force of the blast. The second and third followed in the same manner within ten seconds of each other, the middle ship rolling on its side as water poured into the gaping hole in its hull. The last ship stayed afloat just long enough to crash into a Greek freighter frantically trying to avoid the holocaust. Within minutes the three holed ships were at the bottom. The Greek was blazing its full length as it reeled out of control.

The last item Captain Maceo noted for his report was that the bridge superstructure seemed to be melting while the New Orleans docks near Jackson Square appeared ablaze for at least half a mile. Then the scene of destruction was left behind as the high-speed boats that had picked up each team sped around the bend. Maceo's men were deposited at Chalmette. Their rescue craft were sunk. Pick-up trucks transported them across to Lake Borgne, where they boarded fishing boats for the trip back to Cuba.

Juan Duran became a fan of the *Today* show that morning. He had been told previously that one could learn a great deal about American culture, and there were always Washington politicians willing to air their complaints. And when there was a crisis, the producers of the show were willing to give up their normal format to bring it to their audience.

The aerial shots of the causeways to Miami Beach were satisfying—mostly because Major Pagos had executed his job properly—but the scenes from Miami International Airport and New Orleans were more effective. When the news began at seven that morning, the local Miami station provided superb live coverage until NBC could take over. Fires remained out of control until well into the morning.

In New Orleans the flames appealed even more to Duran. He expressed pleasure any number of times at the twisted steel of the bridge and the decimated dockside area. But the knowledge that nothing would be moving on the Mississippi for an as yet unknown time was his triumph.

It was much too early for the Americans to do anything but speculate. The trauma of these two separate catastrophes would remain long after the fires were controlled. Even though there was little for the authorities to trace at this stage, Duran knew that eventually the CIA or FBI would pick up the scent. But it would be hard to prove. Well before any charges could be formulated by the Americans, he would counter with something else to occupy their time. Juan Duran had no intention of allowing them breathing room, not after they tried to squeeze his own poor country economically.

Cara Estrada's talent for public relations had been appreciated over the past few years, when she could magnify every irregularity that could possibly have been blamed on Fidel Castro. Even when Fidel attended one of his beloved baseball games, she had been able to make his appearance the kiss of death for the losing team. Sugarcane fields seemed to wilt soon after he spoke to the workers. A gift of older tanks from the Soviet Union for a newly formed armored battalion became an insult to the Cuban people. Cara had mastered the ability to manipulate the negative until it became an art form.

But her ultimate feat was to turn the egocentric Juan Duran into a great communicator. She claimed that ninety-nine percent of leadership was the ability to tell people not only what they wanted but why they were supposed to appreciate what they got. Any leader who could accomplish that could write his own ticket for as long as he cared to rule. There was also the added necessity of creating unity, in this case convincing the people of Cuba that their position as a David of the world could eventually bring down the Goliath to the north, the United States.

It had not been a simple task to initially teach a man with Duran's ego how to appeal to his people verbally, but over the years Cara transformed him into a natural orator. This talent faded when he achieved power. He was so captivated by managing the kangaroo courts in the New Plaza that arrogance interfered with his speaking ability. For a short time Cara's renewed task was imposing, for she once again was required to transform him into a peasant for those days he was to speak to the people.

She began by encouraging him to expand his wardrobe. While Duran leaned toward the custom-designed uniforms that Qaddafi favored, Cara emphasized light-colored trousers and loose-fitting, open-necked shirts. Then she insisted that the huge old desk that impressed him so much never appear on television. She also took away the rostrum because she said he looked like a hawk when he leaned on it with his elbows.

In these early days she made sure that he gave formal talks on national television at least once a week, and that every possible public appearance received major attention. His speeches were broadcast from a studio in the palace designed to look like a middle-class living room, complete with sofa, easy chairs, lamps, and a coffee table covered with the current periodicals. There was even a large old dog—hated by Duran—that Cara coached to sit at his feet. Juan Duran became the composite neighbor-next-door for the average Cuban, neither a military man nor the robber baron that had become a symbol of hatred for most Latin Americans. He was one of them, a leader who could come home from a hard day punishing miscreants at the public trials in the New Plaza to an evening of leisure in the type of home many of them aspired to.

That was the way he had appeared the night he made his speech against the Americans—two days after the incidents in Miami and New Orleans. Cara had orchestrated the speech into a major event by explaining to the international media that there would be revelations concerning the recent disasters in the United States. Almost every major media service was present. It took little time for Juan Duran to make his point.

"In the past few days the United States has finally suffered what they have been exporting throughout the world for so many years—terrorism! Apparently carefully planned and thoroughly executed, the cities of Miami and

New Orleans have experienced what the peoples of the Third World and some European nations have suffered under for years. Through their efforts to control the governments of young nations seeking independence, they have finally become the victims of their own repression of poor people. No act of terror or aggression ever seemed to impress the Americans as long as nothing came home to their shores. They remained aloof to the savagery that affected so many of us on a day-to-day basis. Now . . . now they understand that the rest of the world suffers as a result of their imperialism and arrogance . . ."

Juan Duran had carefully prepared for this moment, placing himself in Cara's hands even before Major Pagos and Captain Maceo left on their missions. Together they studied tapes and movies of other orators. Cara selected the highlights, which were repeated again and again. Then she had run videotapes of Duran rehearsing this very speech from a variety of angles to convince him of exactly what she was grasping for. Now, as he spoke, his foot would occasionally tap the sedated dog who would then very slowly raise his head for a scratch, exactly as if it were all a nightly occurrence. The speech unfurled in giant letters on a prompter so that Duran appeared to be speaking directly to the nation without a prepared talk. Behind the camera Cara waved hand signals to help him emphasize each point.

". . . and the rest of the world joins in prayer for the families of those who have died." Duran's head nodded forward for a moment of silence, as if intoning a silent prayer. *"But what has taken place in these American cities is a direct result of Washington's interference in the small nations of our globe. Many of us would call this sweet revenge—if our hearts did not go out to the innocent victims."*

Duran went on to list a series of terrorist strikes that had caused injury and death to innocent people in a number of countries, mostly Third World, before he concluded each example with exactly how the root cause could be traced back to American foreign policy and interference in the daily life of another country. His speech was carefully designed to appeal to popular anti-Americanism. The arguments were logical to an extent, bending the truth when it came to the actual atrocity. To Cara's distress he would occasionally depart from her words to elaborate on his personal hatred of the United States. *That's all he has to do,* she thought, *just add a couple of sentences that will provide a clue . . . and the Americans will jump down his throat.* Why was he doing that? She'd noticed these little quirks in the past couple of weeks—hints of arrogance— and they disturbed her.

"If I have impressed upon you the seriousness of American imperialism and the twist of fate that brought terrorist retaliation to her shores, let me appeal to your sense of fairness at this point. My government is a young one, barely free of the womb, born of the necessity to free all Cubans from the shackles of the powerful nations that were monopolizing our chance for freedom. Yet, at this very moment, we are in danger . . . from our powerful neighbor to the north. Yes—the United States. I have already learned that Washington has chosen to lay the blame for her misfortune at our feet . . . that Cuba will soon fall victim to American revenge for acts I knew nothing about until I, too, witnessed the results on my own television set."

At this stage of his speech Duran had been perfectly choreographed by Cara. He inserted dramatic pauses as she directed from behind the prompter, her hands moving like those of a conductor to create the inflections in his voice. Now she beckoned him to lean forward, as if each person watching were being addressed personally. For the only time that she could remember, his arms rested naturally on his knees as he implored each individual to understand his predicament.

"Every nation, large or small, must utilize an intelli-

gence network for its own protection. I am sorry to admit that such an operation is important even to a country as small and poor as my own—but it is vital in today's world.

"I have been informed that the United States intends to retaliate against Cuba for the tragedies in Miami and New Orleans. There is no proof available that I am aware of as to exactly who might be to blame, but I can assure you that Washington possesses nothing to justify any actions against my country beyond the economic sanctions she has forced upon us . . . beyond the invasion forces—including the Bay of Pigs—she has mounted against us . . . beyond the funding of illegitimate forces and arms to overthrow our people's government . . . beyond the desire to annex a nation that cries out to the world to remain sovereign."

The dog, prodded enough times by the same foot, was finally induced to sit up and accept a tidbit from his master. If Duran appeared on the television screens as Cara intended, the world was watching a sensitive, concerned individual. No man could have been more sincere.

"When Third World nations are faced with imperialism —no different than the threat now looming large against my own country—it becomes necessary to establish a defense of some kind. Now, it is obvious that there is no way Cuba can possibly defend herself against the United States. What is our alternative? What can we do that will make this giant stop for a moment and reconsider her intentions?

"I can assure you that a great deal of thought was involved before a solution of any kind was devised. The decision reached was a mutual one involving leaders of nations friendly to the Cuban people. The answer is to present the Americans with an alternative more frightening than that which they are planning for our country."

He spread his hands in guilty supplication, as if he would regret what he was about to say more than anything else in the world.

"The nations of the Third World, unable to face the might of the United States, either economically or militar-

ily, have joined together to determine how we might neutralize this threat to our independence. The result is a promise to the American people, one that I can assure you we are united in seeing through to the end. To make what I have just said as clear as possible, I implore the American people to send a message to their government before it is too late to curb this insanity. The combined Third World nations are committed to unleashing a wave of terror in retaliation against any aggressive acts by the United States against any of our countries. But,"—and here he waggled a finger toward the camera—*"this retaliation will take place on American soil . . . not overseas . . . not in countries who have left us alone. . . ."* Duran's face showed regret as he shook his head solemnly.

"And you will hear me and many others repeat over again in the coming days that we did not want to come to this point. We have been forced to the edge and this appears our only method of retaliation." He shook his head from side to side once again as if disagreeing with himself.

"Only weeks ago we determined that we would never threaten until one of us was driven to the edge, and that is now the case. You have my promise. Should the United States direct any form of aggression against the Cuban people, I assure everyone listening to me that we will retaliate with a fervor you cannot imagine—each time the Americans choose to attack our nation in any form—and all the gods that any of you have ever worshipped know what that means to the world. Our capability is small in comparison to their own, but our will is mighty. It was not our choice to be in this position, but from this day let it be known that a union of Third World nations will no longer cower beneath the whip of American imperialism . . ." His voice drifted off to a whisper. That was supposed to be the end. And then to Cara's shock he growled, *"Cuba has been chosen to face them. I have been chosen to lead."* He

shook a contemptuous fist at the television camera, his face contorted in rage.

Cara Estrada was truly frightened as Duran's face faded from the screen. Those final words were those of a madman. *He sounds just like Qaddafi,* she thought.

That evening a section of the causeway connecting the Florida Keys exploded and collapsed into the ocean. The warning was self-evident, a blatant punctuation to Duran's speech.

CHAPTER FIVE

Bernie Ryng had been through the folder three times—
the first after it had been handed to him over a cup of
morning coffee. The next time was at a borrowed desk
where he had analyzed each detail he considered important
enough, then jotted down a few of his famous unreadable
notes. He took a final glance just before he joined Hoff at
lunch.

He had never met Hoff before that day, though the
man's reputation was known in a very small, very select
group. It was always the same with those types—they
would never be called public servants holding jobs like
his—because they tended to operate a little beyond the
proprieties followed by career diplomats or intelligence
specialists. It was possible Hoff might have been with the
CIA when he was a youngster, just to get a feel for what
the game was like, but he was too smart to stay in an
organization that became a whipping boy.

Ryng's superiors had called early, before dawn, to explain that a guy named Hoff would be in touch—and, not
only was he for real, but be nice to him. When they met

that morning, Hoff explained that he worked for the national security advisor, which signified that he hung his hat in the White House on occasion. What all that meant to Bernie Ryng was that whatever was coming at lunch carried more weight than the classified orders he was accustomed to receiving.

Bernie Ryng appeared to be of medium height and build. Yet when one studied him more closely, it became apparent that his neck was much thicker than the average man's. And when he removed his uniform blouse or a jacket during warm weather, his bare arms displayed long thick muscles, and his chest strained the buttons on his shirt. He radiated sheer power. In uniform, the gold emblem over his service ribbons offered a simple explanation for his physical strength—the trident, the eagle, and the flintlock pistol denoting the *SE*a *Air* *L*and capabilities of a navy SEAL. His blue eyes and broad cheekbones were distinguishing features, as were his thin blond hair and light complexion—he was one of those rare people who appeared ageless.

In contrast, Hoff was tall, balding, and nondescript in his rimless glasses. He drank mineral water with a wedge of lemon. The message to Ryng, who was drinking a beer with his lunch, was that the man across the table was a no-nonsense type. Bernie wished there were more of the same in Washington. Maybe there were those days when Hoff liked to run half a dozen miles instead of eat lunch, too.

"Have you read the folder I gave you this morning to your satisfaction?" Hoff asked.

Ryng nodded. "Sure. Want it back?"

Hoff reached across the table to take it. "Did you take any notes?"

"A couple, just some things I wanted to get straight in my mind."

"Are they now?"

"Are they what?" Ryng asked.

"Whatever you had to get straight in your mind—are those things straight now?" Hoff wasn't being rude, just abrupt with his curiosity.

"I guess so. It's all pretty cut-and-dried, I guess."

"Then if you don't mind, I'd like the notes, too, please." Again he extended his hand across the table. "If you're finished with them," he added politely.

"Sure . . . if it's that important to you. They're pretty hard for anyone else to read. I always sort of jot things down in a kind of code I understand, just in case someone were to see. . . ."

"I do appreciate that, believe me," Hoff replied with a half smile, his hand still in front of Ryng. "But there is no such thing as too cautious, and I assure you there is no one more careful than me, Mr. Ryng."

Ryng smoothed out the notes and glanced at the scrawl for a moment before offering the wrinkled sheets to Hoff. He nodded his approval. "I like you already."

"Considering the people you run with, I'll take that as a compliment. May I call you Bernie? I'm told you prefer—"

"Don't be surprised if I look over my shoulder if you call me Mr. Ryng again."

"I answer to Alf . . . since it looks like we'll be working together."

"Am I assuming too much? I mean, are there orders that will be cut for me to cover whatever we're supposed to be doing?" Bernie Ryng was military—no way around that—and he was comfortable when things were handled that way. Whenever the CIA had been involved, he'd always been transferred to their jurisdiction. But he'd heard of people like Hoff, and generally their operations left no trails.

"You're assuming too much." Hoff smiled without showing his teeth. "But if you want to call some of your people, please feel free."

"Then this isn't going to be a military operation. . . ."

"On the contrary. It's entirely military—outside of people like me, of course. It's just that no one in the Pentagon is going to be involved, not directly, especially if they're asked.''

The folder Ryng had read covered the years before Juan Duran's assumption of power in Cuba, the short period of his rule, and some analyses of Cuba's political, economic, and cultural future, along with psychological profiles of Duran and those close to him. The projections concerning Cuba's regional influence in the coming years were especially unattractive for the United States. As lunch progressed Hoff explained, without ever mentioning the White House, that his superiors had obviously come to the conclusion that there was little to be gained by sitting back and waiting for Duran to shoot himself in the foot.

"Just how crazy do these shrinks think Duran is?" Ryng asked. "It seems to me he's shrewd as hell most of the time."

"*Crazy* is inexact terminology in his case. It denotes individuals who are wild and unpredictable in their daily lives. We think Duran is about as predicatable as any leader today after watching him for two months in power. He appears to have a master plan, and he appears to be following that plan to a tee. In a way, I'd say he is more of a Cuban patriot than even José Martí . . . and that's going some." Hoff poured himself some more mineral water. "We both know a psychologist could probably have a field day with people like us, so you can understand why we hesitate to categorize Duran. There are any number of psychoses we could choose from—he exhibits a wide range. But remember that there have been some very effective leaders who would have kept a baker's dozen of shrinks busy for years—Stalin, Hitler, even Abe Lincoln, who a lot of his contemporaries thought was a bit soft."

"But Duran's not all there," Ryng finally interrupted.

"In a broad sense, yes. That's what makes him so dangerous."

"And there are enough people who feel he presents a continuing problem for the U.S.?"

"That's why we're enjoying this pleasant lunch." Hoff dabbed his lips. "As a matter of fact, since we're about done here, we should get down to the basics. I hate to drag conversations too far past coffee. You can imagine why you've been recommended to me."

"Go on."

"You don't seem to have many questions. I thought I'd be dodging all sorts of things." Hoff grinned.

"So far, there haven't been all kinds of answers for me to dream up questions. But . . . covert, right?"

"Extremely."

"Something I'm supposed to do myself?"

"At first . . . yes. Later, absolutely not. We have much larger things in mind. You can be more specific with me once we have everything in perspective, but I expect you'll want at least one of your SEAL platoons. You people do operate in large groups, don't you?"

"SEALs operate by themselves, in pairs, detachments, platoons, teams, whatever's necessary to finish the job. It all depends on the operation. We organize for the task . . . no wasted motion . . . no unnecessary people. We give you everything you could ever hope for for your dollar, and then some."

"And I think you may have a need for other Spec-Ops types if you like—an Army A-team, perhaps?"

Ryng shrugged. Why did people suggest things like that before they knew what shape the mission would take? A-teams were terrific, in the right place, but they didn't swim. It was better not to attempt an explanation then. Better to change the subject. "Wherever I've been in the past, I've been able to see exactly how we're affected directly. Do you have actual proof that Duran was involved in Miami and New Orleans?"

"Satellite. They knew better than to get away by plane, but they sure as hell haven't the least idea they can be tracked by something they can't see. Each operation was a hell of a job, very professional. No one can really prevent terrorist attacks if there's no warning. But you can follow them afterward. We had an eye sitting right over Cuba—almost always active there—and we were able to reorient the cameras. It was all Havana-directed, believe me.''

"And there are prospects for more . . .''

"Already have been. Small stuff until they see how we're going to react. But it's the need to keep prodding—you saw that in the profile, just like Qaddafi—and Duran keeps at it. So far, it's been directed against money. They grab an armored car, something like that, but they burn the cash rather than keep it. Just a method of keeping the pressure on. And there's one other.'' Hoff brought it up as an afterthought, and Ryng could see that it was designed to be the kicker. "Coast Guard cutter the other day was called out for a rescue. Fishing boat was taking on water, the radio said. No need for a helo to drop pumps. Just needed a tow back to Key West . . .''

"They were bushwhacked, right?''

"First-class petty officer was commanding, four kids crewing for him—all dead. The patrol boat was burned to the waterline. The helos that were sent out to chase around after anything suspicious found fishing boats, nothing but fishing boats, although there were some strange ones. Three ended up back in Matanzas, and the photos we got show there wasn't a fish aboard. They returned to port drawing probably the same as when they left—and they tied up at the naval piers.''

Ryng tapped his forehead. "There's so much good gray matter up here that I bet I don't need those notes I gave you. But my memory tells me that Duran seemed to be avoiding military targets. Why change his stripes at this stage?''

"Don't ask the shrinks.'' Alf Hoff smiled for the first time since they began lunch. "That was the last thing I was told by one of them. Once they've established this profile of Duran, the guy said to me, Duran's going to do the opposite. That, he said, is what's frightening. It's when he changes colors that you've got to get nervous. And if he's willing to start bugging the Coast Guard, anyone has a shot at being next.''

"You want him gone forever—that's called assassination. And it's not in my job description." Ryng's voice had an odd serious tone to it. "I don't know who put you on to me, but they missed something along the way. I do military operations. They have a beginning, a middle, and an end. You just have an end in mind."

Hoff became just as serious. "You're anticipating me. I don't appreciate that. If this was a straight muscle job, the CIA could handle it. I was told you were a good listener."

"To a point, Alf, to a point. You're circling. Tell me why you're not insulting my intelligence."

"Because I was told that the SEALs—you—were so good you could start a revolution in another guy's country." Hoff's eyes wavered between seriousness and humor as he studied Ryng. "And that means doing it with a Soviet Spetznaz unit looking over one shoulder and a hell of a good secret police operation peering over the other. You've got to make it look like a rebellion, and you've got to make sure that every single person associated with Duran is gonzo so that a new government has a chance to get its feet set. I guess I really don't care how you go about it. I understand you even like to operate independently. . . ." His voice drifted off in an attempt to effect a halfhearted smile at his own humor.

"I guess it comes back to: Why do you want to do it this way—and with me?" Not once in his career as a SEAL had he ever questioned *if* a job could be done. It had always been a question of how many SEALs were needed, how long it would take, or why a mission had to be completed in less time than he wanted.

"The CIA's record isn't something we want to chance, and anything coming out of the Pentagon gets so overorganized that sooner or later the word gets around. I think you—even a few well-chosen friends, if you like—can slip into

Cuba without anyone but me being any the wiser. After you've analyzed the mission, you can have as many men as you need . . . whatever it takes. What do you think?''

''I think you're one of the wildest people I've ever met, Alf. And I like your ideas. Behind those funny-looking glasses you're a hell of a fun guy, aren't you?'' It was all he could think of to say. In retrospect, it wasn't so funny after all. ''I don't mean to be wise. It's my way of thinking.''

''I wouldn't imagine that would take a lot of time. I was told this is right up your alley.''

''It is.''

SEAL teams are the Navy's special warfare force, a derivative of the original UDT (Frogmen). Since survival is fundamental to successful special operations, only the best are accepted for the twenty-six-week BUD/S (Basic Underwater Demolition/SEAL) course undertaken by both officers and enlisted together, and only twenty-five to thirty percent of those usually graduated. After that—jump school. Those few survivors of the toughest military course in the world are capable of operating in tropical or arctic conditions underwater and on land, or they could arrive anywhere in the world by parachute. Once assigned to an actual SEAL team, they begin their advanced training.

While their tactics are covert and silence is golden, there is no weapon they are unfamiliar with if silence must be broken. They are medically self-sufficient and able to survive off the land in any environment. Since they are rarely seen and never heard, and prefer to avoid publicity, they are lethal beyond imagination.

While it was possible that other U.S. units might have been capable, none of the others would ever have had Bernie Ryng as a leader. That made Alf Hoff extremely comfortable when he returned to the White House that afternoon. He told his boss to report that everything would soon be under control.

CHAPTER SIX

Unless they are shooting when they arrive, Spetznaz units materialize quietly, secretively. Their unique advantage is the fact that their presence is unknown. If they operate properly, no one need know they were ever present—for the only people to come in contact with them will generally end up dead.

Paul Voronov and his Spetznaz unit arrived in Cuba aboard a Russian freighter that docked without incident in the port of Cienfuegos. The city is about one hundred forty miles southeast of Havana and lies on one of the best-protected harbors on Cuba's Caribbean coast. Since it is the country's center for industrial development, and exports more sugar than any other port in the world, it is the constant host to the Soviet ships that help to support the island's economy.

Cienfuegos was the perfect port of entry for Voronov, since the Cuban government still insisted on clearing all Russians through customs. While there was little that could be done if a Soviet citizen appeared an unacceptable visitor, it was a way of saving face. On the other hand, when Russian ships arrived to bolster trade, Cuban customs was willing to do what customs officials did throughout the world—they came aboard briefly to shake the captain's hand, certify medical clearance, and accept their bribe from the purser after a few glasses of good Russian vodka. The crews were free to come and go as they pleased, since most ships remained in Cienfuegos only long enough to offload and refill their hulls.

Voronov's men were no less innocuous than those from any other ship. The Russians favored shorts and V-necked T-shirts in the warm climate. Perhaps an observant customs agent might even have noted that a certain element in this ship's crew were in exceptional physical condition, well-muscled, narrow-waisted, and definitely less tanned. Yet their beards and well-worn clothes blended in with the others, and like any other crew, they spent as much of their time as possible lounging against the railing and staring at the longshoremen on the dock.

As the day progressed they meandered ashore, sometimes singly, a few in pairs. By the time the sun had set that evening, Paul Voronov's entire unit was ashore. A Soviet engineer battalion was permanently billeted in barracks on the outskirts of the city, and one by one the members of the Spetznaz unit made their way to the installation. As with any port in the world, certain crates hoisted by certain forklifts found their own way to the Soviet installation.

Since any major increase in personnel at the base would eventually be noted by Cuban intelligence, they remained less than forty-eight hours. On the morning of the third day the engineers moved out to conduct exercises north of the city. When they returned that evening, Paul Voronov's team had melted into the countryside to establish a base camp near the village of Congojas. They were also very close to the main east/west highway that led to Havana, a little more than two hours away.

On the following day, outfitted in civilian clothes and carrying the identification of a Soviet civilian, Paul Voronov drove to Santa Fe, on the coast west of Havana. This small town was home to the largest Russian intelligence gathering station outside the Soviet Union. There, more than two thousand technicians, civilian specialists, and military personnel monitored U.S. military operations throughout the Caribbean and Central America. They were commanded by General Major Komarov, who reported directly to General Dotov, the head of the GRU in Moscow who had selected Voronov. General Komarov was said to know only slightly less about the workings of the Cuban military and government than Cara Estrada, and his closest associates claimed that was only because he did not care to sleep each night with Juan Duran.

"You're not afraid of being recognized by Duran?" Komarov teased. "After all, you trained the man in your own trade."

"There is only one time that Duran will have the opportunity to see me again and that will be too late as far as he is concerned."

"For your sake, I hope so. You know, one of my people picked up a rumor from a contact inside the palace that Duran was pleased we were angry with him. It was even said that he anticipated a Special Operations unit might be sent to Cuba to teach him a lesson—and he laughed at that." Komarov's eyes were fixed on a point beyond Voronov's shoulder. "I don't know if that was just rumor or hard intelligence . . . but it is something to keep in mind."

"If what you say is correct," Voronov said, his voice level and devoid of emotion, "then it would appear you have a weakness internally. I doubt that such information would find its way from Moscow, but it could have leaked from here."

Komarov's expression remained the same, although the tone of his voice reflected his irritation. "That charge would appear to be unfounded, Colonel, and I'm willing at this point to keep it between us."

"My men are trained to live off the land, and we'll do just fine if we're allowed to do so. If we have to dodge Cuban troops or, even worse, their damn militia, then my mission takes twice as long." He leaned forward slightly. "If we have to kill Cubans to protect ourselves, then that means the job also becomes twice as difficult. I can promise you we're also very good at tracing these leaks back to the source, and I'll make sure that any man in your organization selling any sort of information to the Cubans dies very slowly. Is that unacceptable?" he concluded, again sitting back in his chair.

Komarov shrugged. He appreciated Dotov's detailed message explaining why this Voronov was so highly regarded, and now he also understood even more the reason for the inclusion of a subtle warning from the GRU head. "My only desire would be to share in your efforts to render punishment. Is that fair enough?" he countered, answering the question with another question.

"Understood." Voronov allowed a long enough pause to indicate he was now changing the subject. Then he continued politely, as if they were two old cronies who understood each other. "My intentions are to discredit Duran before he is deposed. It must appear to the Cuban people, especially to the mass of peasants, that their leader will stop at nothing to solidify his power, including a reign of fear. Right now, only the unpopular element—students, teachers, the liberal set—is suffering from his excesses, and he's turning those public displays into an art form. I intend to turn his military into the most vicious secret police organization you can imagine. To begin with, I need four dozen of their uniforms, if you would please arrange that for me."

"Done."

"What kind of weapons are they carrying these days?"

"For some reason these Latins love the automatic weapons—mostly AK-47s, though the officers often carry

Makarovs in a holster. The younger ones think they look tougher that way.''

''We have the Makarovs, but our standard issue is 74s. I'll need the same number of the 47s, ammunition, and some manuals. Some of my men are so young they've never worked with a 47. I want them to be able to field-strip them just like any of the others. What else?''

''Very little. They wear our boots, use our ammunition, our tanks, our artillery and missiles. Only the militia lacks our new equipment, and much of what they use came from us years ago.'' Komarov looked the other man up and down. ''What you don't want, Voronov, is blue-eyed, blond Cubans. . . .''

''Once my men are properly outfitted, I doubt you would be able to determine whether or not they're Cubans. Even in a group your intelligence specialists would be completely fooled . . . no blue eyes . . . no slant eyes. All but a handful served alongside Cuban troops in Angola at one time or another. Most of them speak Spanish as well as I do. By the time I get back to camp, all my men will look more Cuban than Duran.'' Paul Voronov's hands were locked easily behind his back and he eyed Komarov as if he'd made an off-color remark. ''You know very little about the Spetznaz, General,'' he added with a grin.

''If I've underestimated you, I apologize. My specialty is intelligence, not indigenous warfare. I am a worrier over details.''

''Spetznaz survive by attention to detail,'' Voronov replied curtly. Then, again pausing just long enough to indicate the previous discussion was concluded, he continued, ''I need Cuban supplies, whatever it is that they take into the bush when they're on operations. When I break a camp, I expect anyone who stumbles across it will know that Cuban troops have been there. I want a supply of their soap, razor blades, toilet paper, everything they might carry, including the magazines with the pictures of naked girls, the dirtier the better, so the peasants will fear for their women as much as their own necks.''

General Komarov, arms folded, glared at Voronov with distaste.

''These requests won't go on forever—just long enough for my men to get a feel for their new identity. Once they're comfortable, I want them to go into the stores and buy everything themselves . . . but I can promise you they will steal a great deal.''

Juan Duran had been in a playful mood for the entire day, to the distress of those around him. The evening proved to be no different, for he entertained Major Pagos and Captain Maceo, his operational leaders in Miami and New Orleans. Qaddafi had taught Duran an important lesson before they had separated at the Assdadah camp: treat your heroes exactly as you would want to be treated yourself, and entertain them well with whatever they desire. In the case of Pagos and Maceo, both of whom were bachelors, there were many beautiful women circulating around tables loaded with more food and drink than either of them had ever imagined.

The root cause of the problems that followed, Cara Estrada was sure, was the champagne. It had been rarely consumed in Havana since the days of Batista, and Castro allowed it only when foreign heads of state visited. To Duran, it was a just reward to those who triumphed. And as far as he was concerned, his triumph over the doctrinaire Fidel Castro justified every drop of this capitalist excess. Pagos and Maceo deserved it for their victories. The result had been a reception that began quietly with all the participants in uniform for the speeches and formal awards to the two men being honored. From that point on, the popular image that Duran hoped to project to Cuban citizens would have been shattered—if any had been lucky enough to be invited.

The women who had been hired for the reception not

only appreciated the fine food and drink, they understood exactly why they were being well rewarded for their attendance. They also knew that if they were to be well tipped, it would help if everyone drank as much as possible.

These women were beautiful, the men handsome in their uniforms, and the entire party out of hand within hours. Cara was thankful that the ladies were smart enough to lead the men out singly, for she had been convinced that sooner or later one couple at least would end up completely naked on the dance floor.

Once again she recognized that reoccurring quirk in Duran's nature, and she was surprised that this time she experienced disappointment rather than shock at his weaknesses. It was becoming too easy for Duran to succumb to excesses. Since they were so close to the surface, Cara thought a few words might suffice. Most men in his position would normally reorient their behavior toward a strict course of moderation, or so she hoped. His reactions were frightfully similar to the day on the platform at the New Plaza, when he insisted on taking over punishment of the female prisoners. There was that look in his eyes again, almost the exact expression that possessed his features as he lay the whip on the large-breasted girl.

His eyes magnified the change when a gorgeous girl with black hair cascading over her bare shoulders began a seductive dance with Captain Maceo. Cara saw that same faraway, cloudy cast beneath Duran's lids. There was no doubt that he was becoming drunk, nor did he seem concerned. A glisten of sweat stood out across his forehead. She saw his lips twitch in anticipation of something he could only imagine, something repressed—as she was sure it was in most men.

With an intuitive shudder she recognized the primacy of his desire—whether it was power over another, sexual domination, or perhaps a flirting with ideas that normal people attempt to conceal below the surface. The moment she realized what it was, she hoped it would remain hidden to the others. Much of Duran's own reaction was caused by the way the girl looked at Maceo as she danced with him. The manner in which her body moved, sometimes touching, other times moving away to be watched by appreciative eyes, matched the suggestiveness of her lips and eyes. Maceo's reaction seemed to captivate Duran almost as much. It was as if they were both peeking in the girl's bedroom window. Cara could see his mind toying with a depravity she could only imagine, and she wished desperately she could have those early days back again.

The Juan Duran that Cara Estrada first met at the University of Havana was idealistic, so young and excited with the world of ideas that he had little time for sex . . . or that was the way it seemed to a young girl in love with the man she was positive was the greatest man at the university. Looking back on those days, while Duran's eager eyes reveled in the seduction of Captain Maceo, she yearned for that time when she had taught him what it was to love—not the kind he was now so entranced with, but that first sensitive, sensual love that made two people believe that they were the only lovers in the world.

The intensity! She would never forget those moments.

Those were also the days when he would miss an entire day of classes because he had discovered another philosopher. Cara would go to his room at noontime and find him sitting on the little balcony outside his window, totally oblivious of the fact that he was still in his underwear. More than likely he hadn't eaten a thing, and often he had been engrossed in his reading since she last saw him.

Juan Duran, she became convinced, had no need for the structured life of a college student. He was able to involve himself in an idea, whether it was a religion, a social theory, a political system, even an individual's life work, and gather in almost every possible fact gleaned from every possible opinion. His concept of what Cuba should become was a derivative of his study of the history and political evolution of the most powerful nations of the twentieth century. Juan Duran was neither capitalist nor communist. Cara had fallen in love with a purist who had no doubt that he knew more than any other man. That superiority complex, a sense of intellectual stubbornness, had been there from the beginning. And she was sure that as a student he probably was better read than any other Cuban.

Why . . . he seemed more powerful in those days than . . . *than now!*

If he had one glaring weakness, it was his devotion to the ideas of the totalitarians—men who brought power to their countries by the sheer weight of their determination and their unswerving beliefs. When he finished his analysis of their failures, he was convinced that their weakness came from a dependency on other nations. He claimed that once he obtained power—that was when Cara understood how pure his idealism really was—he would ensure that the big countries who preyed on the little ones like Cuba would have no place in his new society.

What a man! What a man to have for your very own.

Cara taught Duran love, and then she taught him about sex. He was an eager student, and he had tried very hard in those days to remain sensitive to her feelings.

Where had that part of Juan Duran gone?

In those days he drank little, a few beers with his friends, some wine from time to time. She never saw him drunk with anything other than the absolute determination to fashion Cuba in his own image.

Where had that part of Juan Duran gone?

His desire for power had been a pure one. It was based on the concept that there would be no more poor, that there would be enough food for everyone, that government could answer every question, solve every social problem, remove the necessity for crime—it was an endless litany that Cara was willing to listen to for hours because she believed in Juan Duran, believed he was the one man who could accomplish it all.

Where had that part of Juan Duran gone?

Where was the Juan Duran who had made a pilgrimage to the Sierra Maestre to trace Fidel Castro's early days as a rebel? Cara was ecstatic when he invited her to join his retreat. They had visited the Moncada Barracks, arriving there on a July 26th to observe the anniversary of the movement. From there he'd gone into the city to the Santiago Civil Hospital, where the survivors of that fateful attack on the barracks were tried. Later that evening he recited with amazing accuracy Fidel's famous "History Will Absolve Me" speech to an unbelieving Cara. For almost two hours he spoke as he imagined Fidel did that day in 1953, enunciating Castro's famous five points with equal vehemence. Two days later he and Cara were on the Isle of Pines, where Castro had been imprisoned for twenty months developing his revolutionary reeducation program.

Again and again, Juan had repeated that famous sentence culled from one of Castro's letters written during his Mexican exile—"From trips such as this one does not return, or else one returns with tyranny beheaded at one's feet." Cara still shivered with delight when Juan explained how he would some day return to Cuba in that exact manner . . . for there was never a shred of doubt in his mind.

Cara still loved this wild, strange man called Juan Duran— but she had fallen in love with an idol, and now she knew that idols were made to be shattered. That was all so obvious as she stared about the dance floor where the revelry for two heroes had become a debauchery, where idealism had been trampled by reality.

Then Maceo and the woman were gone, and Cara was dancing with the man she was sure she would always love. She was thankful that once again she had his complete attention. Then she became even more thankful the others were so drunk that they paid little attention to their leader at that point. Duran held her tightly, drunkenly, and whispered dirty words in her ear until she was positive everyone in the room could hear him. His body moved against hers with increasing demands until she pulled him from the room, once again thankful, only this time it was because those few remaining never noticed their departure.

As they climbed the stairs to their apartment Duran's voice rose as the words he had been whispering gushed out in a filthy torrent echoing off the high ceilings and down the endless corridors. He alternated between pawing Cara and tearing at his own clothes as she dragged and pushed him to the door. Once inside he forced his hand into the front of her gown, tearing the material away with a loud, guttural laugh.

"Wait . . . please . . . wait . . ." she pleaded as she ran to pull the drapery cords of the high windows with one hand while she held up her dress with the other. "There," she said, turning with a smile, "there's no need for your people to invade your privacy."

"Why not?" His voice was a whisper as he dropped his shirt to the floor. "They should be aware of the hidden powers of their leader . . . their emperor!" he ended with a shout, sitting back on the bed to yank off his shoes when his pants would not pull over them.

"Shh . . . I know what will calm you." She let the remains of her gown drop around her feet. This was not the way she had planned to end the evening, but she understood now that this man had moments when someone—Cara Estrada was better than any other—had to protect him from himself. "I know what Juan Duran needs," she added seductively. She walked toward him one step at a time, wearing only bikini panties and spike heels. "Let Cara take care of you. . . ."

"But first," he said with a giggle, "the people must see their emperor . . . for their emperor has no clothes." He kicked his shoes into the air and rolled back on the bed to remove his pants and underwear. Then, stark naked, he bounced to his feet and rushed to one of the great windows, yanking at the drapery cord. "I'll show them that I have no fear of anything . . . at any time . . ." He stumbled backward as Cara slid an arm around his waist and pulled him back. "*Madre* . . . I just want to . . ."

"I know what I want from the emperor," she murmured, closing the drapes. "And no man would want me to share that with the peasants." With her hand firmly buried in his crotch, she drew him slowly back toward the bed. "If you think Maceo was going to have fun tonight, Juan Duran will experience things his friends never dreamed of." She pushed him down on the bed and climbed up to stand over his chest. "Now we'll forget the peasants." In the days at the university such antics had been a game that they laughed about later. Now Cara saw it as the only way she could control him. There seemed only one thing that could attract a man drunk with both alcohol and himself.

His eyes focused on her for the first time. Then he smiled in anticipation. "Oh?" His eyebrows raised.

"Take off this shoe," she said wickedly, placing one foot on his chest and pressing down hard with the point of her heel.

His eyes traveled up and down her body. "All right," he answered meekly, removing the shoe and dropping it on the floor.

She placed the other shoe on his chest, increasing the pressure. "This one, too." When he had done the same thing, Cara bent slightly from the waist and stuck her tongue out. "Shall I remove my panties by myself . . . or is that your job?"

As his hands reached up she knew that she had the "emperor" back under her control. He would soon be sleeping soundly. There would no longer be any danger of him charging naked to the window to show the people that another Juan Duran lay hidden just below the surface.

While the Cuban dictator snored drunkenly beside Cara Estrada, a fishing boat slipped down the channel from the Key West docks. Stars sparkled like diamonds, their reflections blinking in the water, as the darkened boat quietly eased into the Straits of Florida before any eye might identify it.

As the day progressed it moved into normal fishing grounds with nets over the stern. If there had been the slightest thing unusual about it, an experienced fisherman might have noticed that the draft remained the same even after hauling nets. But there were no prying eyes to notice the catch falling back through a sluice into the ocean.

Later that afternoon a single ping picked up by the listening gear indicated that a submarine had taken station three hundred feet beneath. Their course gradually took them south-southwest until they paralleled Cuban boundary waters.

Once darkness fell the sporadic Cuban patrol boats returned to base. Night belonged to the invisible eye of coastal radar, which no fishermen cared to challenge for the sake of a few tons of fish. But the electronic radiation detected by their countermeasures gear allowed the fishermen to ease closer to the island in the radar dead zones. The submarine's movements imitated the boat's, remaining just deep enough to avoid fouling the nets. The overriding noise produced by engines and fishing gear successfully masked that of the submarine. If there were any hydrophones resting on the ocean bottom, there was no chance of the Cubans detecting the submarine.

The fishing boat turned west at a preplanned time to a course paralleling the coastline ten miles abeam. With the glow of the hotel lights of the Veradero disappearing astern, the submarine slowly rose to ten feet below periscope depth.

Bernie Ryng listened to the familiar sounds as two other SEALs helped him rig the swimmer propulsion unit (SPU). The check list was second nature—it had been for more years than he cared to remember—but it had also saved his life and so many others over the years. Everything on a mission of this type should be perfect. Yet . . . the SEAL

on his left wasn't happy with one of the straps and reset it
. . . the one on his right tinkered with the pressure gauge
on his tanks, tapping it again and again until he was
positive he couldn't influence it.

"I'm going to double-check your gear again."

"Hey, I went through that myself twenty minutes
ago . . ." Ryng began.

"You did—but I didn't, sir." SEALs retained one overriding lesson as long as they lived: always work on the
buddy system. Don't ever accept your own perfection
because that's when you make the first and only fatal
mistake. Each one looked after the other. That was why so
many SEALs remained alive through a career of covert
operations.

Ryng knew instinctively there was no chance to argue.

"Two minutes, Mr. Ryng." The hollow voice echoed
over the speaker in the tiny space.

"Do either of you care to check the label on my skiv-
vies? I guarantee they're Soviet-made." Ryng appreciated
the care they took. He would have insisted on the same for
every one of his men.

"No toothbrush or toothpaste," the SEAL said, reseal-
ing the neutrally buoyant container that was attached to the
SPU. "Weak personal hygiene."

"Nope. False teeth," Ryng responded.

"It looks OK to me, Mr. Ryng. Nothing to identify you
if you wash up on the beach."

"I've never washed up on any beach before and you can
bet your ass I'm not about to start now."

"If you did, Mr. Ryng, every SEAL would consider
himself in deep trouble."

"One minute," said the voice from the speaker overhead.

"That's it, gents. Time for me to lock out." Ryng gave
each of them a gentle grin and stepped through the hatch.

Within moments the lock was full of water. The outer
door opened, and Bernie Ryng emerged into a world of
total blackness, kicking easily to clear the submarine. He

couldn't see it behind him, but he could sense it, immense and lethal in its natural element. But Ryng was in his element also. There was a feeling of security to know that once again he was doing what he did best. Every movement until he was ashore would somehow feel right. He'd been at it for more than twenty years—he was a human shark.

A sharp sound behind him confirmed that the door on the submarine had been secured. Satisfied that he was entirely clear, he engaged the SPU and moved away, increasing speed to open his distance.

Everything had been rehashed in the submarine before arriving on station, but the navigator, like the SEALs who had prepared him for the lockout, had taken it upon himself to ensure Ryng had memorized his movements precisely. After two minutes of maintaining a straight line, he slowed to check his watch and wrist compass, then turned to the course that would take him to the beach. There was hardly a sound in the all-enveloping blackness that surrounded him. It was like flying . . . soaring through the warm inky waters off the Cuban coast.

Ryng's first indication that he was nearing the coast was the slight drag caused by wave action on the shore. He'd checked his wrist compass periodically for reassurance on his heading, but it had been perfect . . . or almost perfect. He'd only been a few degrees off at one time. His watch indicated that he should be near the drop-off zone.

Precision was vital now. His landing point was between two rock outcroppings, and he had no interest in fighting the currents around those rocks to correct his position. Except for a highway, that area was uninhabited according to intelligence photos. It was a secure place to haul his equipment ashore and there would be more than enough time to stow it.

Your timing had better be accurate . . . see how perfect you are now, you old son of a bitch, he said to himself as he began to ease toward the surface. The undertow was becoming more pronounced and the distant rumble of wave on rock was increasing in volume.

When he surfaced, the stars were stark in the black sky. No moon. His eyes were accustomed to the dark, but it required an extra moment to get his bearings. Staring hard toward the land, he concentrated on the whiteness of the crashing waves until he was absolutely sure. Not bad . . . not bad at all. He was less than a hundred yards off the beach! Couldn't have gotten any closer, or he would have had to swim out a way to scuttle the SPU. Now it was just a matter of a sidestroke to wrestle his gear ashore.

A few hours after midnight Bernie Ryng crawled onto the beach near Santa Cruz del Norte, about fifty miles east of Havana. The main road between Havana and Matanzas ran close to the shore. It took less than an hour for him to move his gear across the highway and disappear inland. Then, like a nesting animal, he circled his area to establish security. It was ideal. He camouflaged the location and slept for four hours.

The following morning Ryng moved inland to a railway stop and rode the train into Havana. It was time to find out as much as possible about the Russian Spetznaz unit, which was of more concern at this point than the mission.

CHAPTER SEVEN

For a full ten minutes Sergeant Fedor Kurochkin, dressed in the uniform of a captain in the Cuban army, remained crouched in the brush at the side of a dirt road leading into the village of Potrerillo. He'd remained in the same position the entire time, moving only his head to peer in either direction down a road that rarely witnessed motorized vehicles. The piles of horseshit were certain proof that four legs were the primary transportation. Kurochkin was so quiet that the birds in the trees never interrupted their constant chatter, nor were they aware that fifty yards to the rear his three men waited out of sight for the signal to join their leader.

This was the second day of a patrol that had been more successful than Paul Voronov had hoped. Cuban troops from the barracks in Cienfuegos often conducted exercises in that area, and their scheduling had been most appropriate to his plans. He'd sent three teams into the same area with one goal: to create enough havoc to establish a negative image of the Cienfuegos Barracks among the local peasants. Undermining trust was a necessary factor in stirring up any population. Voronov enjoyed the psychological boost it created. He felt sorry for the locals when such an operation was necessary because he knew they never understood that they were being forced to suffer for their own good.

One horse, shuffling slowly down the dirt road in front of a two-wheel cart driven by a young boy, was the only object to interrupt the peace and quiet. The birds had arisen from the trees as it approached, wheeling and screeching in protest before settling back on their perches as it passed on. It was adequate warning and, like anything else, had not escaped Kurochkin's eye. He would be sure the birds did not announce their approach when they moved into the village.

They had come from San Fernando de Camarones, another village rarely visited by the military. There, they'd stolen one of the town's few operating vehicles, an ancient Buick with no rear window. It came from the front yard of the house that had to have the newest outbuilding in the village, so Kurochkin assumed it also must belong to the wealthiest person in the area. He made sure there was no doubt about who had taken it. Then they drove it into the village square and loaded the back end with beer removed from the single store in town. When the owner protested, he had been beaten. Then Kurochkin bent over the poor man groveling in the dust and pressed his pistol to the man's head. In no uncertain terms he explained what the army did to people who interfered—he also explained that the next time it was quite possible that the man's wife and daughters would be taken along simply to keep his troops happy. In vivid terms Kurochkin explained how much the young girls would be appreciated.

There was a single gas pump, dented and scraped, leaning toward the door of what Kurochkin assumed must be the local garage. After driving the Buick across to it, one of them filled the tank. There was no sign of life until the hose was replaced, and then an old black woman in a shapeless dress wandered out from the open door of the garage with a beer can in her hand.

"You can pay me," she mumbled from a toothless mouth. Her free hand was extended toward Kurochkin.

"Not today, *madre*," he answered. "We have better things to do with our money. Go back and drink your beer."

"No. Pay me." She was standing before him now, breath stinking, her hand extended just under his chin. "Pay me . . ." she repeated, her voice increasing to a wail.

Kurochkin's hand lashed out, knocking the beer from her hand. "You should learn more respect for the military, *madre*. There's a new policy now in this province—free petrol for the military."

"That's not even your car," the old lady whined, stepping back a pace. "It belongs to Fernand—"

"Shut up, *madre*." Kurochkin's arm moved forward, pushing the woman backward so quickly that she fell to the ground. "Be glad that we are kinder to old ones like you. I should kick in your ribs for your insolence. Why don't you crawl back into your shack and thank God that the army wants only your petrol."

The three men behind him had been making crude remarks. When she fell backwards, one of them called out, "Why don't you screw her right there, Pedro," and all of them laughed raucously.

The woman began to cry silently, covering her face with both hands.

"The next time the army comes to this village," Kurochkin snarled, "I want to hear that the peasants have been more cooperative. You tell everybody that just as soon as we leave . . . understand?"

She nodded without saying a word.

Kurochkin wheeled about with a perfect touch of arrogance and returned to the car. "Let's move on to Potrerillo. Maybe we can find some rum there," he concluded loudly.

Watching now from the bushes until the horse and cart disappeared around a bend in the dirt road, Kurochkin thought about the old woman and was sure that she wouldn't forget him. When he rose to his feet, satisfied it was safe to move on, the three others came up soundlessly to join him. A timing device had been left on the Buick from San Fernando de Camarones and in less than an hour it would explode in flames.

Paul Voronov knew that communications were almost nonexistent in that part of the province, certainly slow enough that the government would never catch up with them. But he also knew that the word would spread from one village to the next as the other Spetznaz detachments accomplished the same objective. Word of mouth moved faster than any electronic means, and the peasant population of Cuba would soon accept the fact that the army of the new government had become lawless overnight.

Just outside the town, Kurochkin's group uncovered the military truck that had been stolen from the Santa Clara Barracks the previous day. After removing supplies from under a tarpaulin in the back end, they switched into fatigues. On their left shoulder a red badge with a black scorpion identified a unit that had been highly decorated in Angola—the Scorpions. Grenades hung from the web belts at their waists, and they were now equipped with automatic weapons.

Each village in the Cienfuegos highlands seemed to have a central square. Often it was no more than a dirt plaza with a couple of trees where the old men lounged in the shade, yet it was the heart of the town. Near the square one could usually find a store, a gas station, a small church, and a town hall that often doubled as the local school. The few citizens of Potrerillo who were not in the cane fields would never forget the day the Scorpions roared into the square. Each of Kurochkin's men had taken a swallow of rum before pouring it over their uniforms. They were firing their rifles into the air as the truck careened to a halt in the center of town.

Kurochkin vaulted out of the driver's seat with a bellow

and trotted over to the store, carelessly smashing an empty rum bottle against the outside wall. He peered through the large single window, then wiped at it with his arm and squinted into the interior again. Apparently unable to see what he was looking for, he pounded in the plate glass with his rifle butt and leaned inside. Then he turned and waved to one of his men, who backed the truck up to the window.

Their noise alone had attracted attention—a small crowd that hung back just far enough to avoid recognition by these wild men. The Scorpions proceeded to loot the store, throwing whatever appealed to them into the back of the truck. The people outside could hear howls of protest that were soon interrupted by screams of pain. These were followed by the appearance of a soldier dragging the owner outside, where the terrified man was braced against the side of the truck.

After slapping the man hard with an open hand, the soldier placed the barrel of his rifle against the man's chest. "Should I shoot you now," he said with a grin, peering down the sights, "or should I save you for target practice?" As his finger curled around the trigger the owner's eyes closed and he began mumbling under his breath.

"Hey, Carlo," Kurochkin called through the broken window, "don't kill him right away. There's a locked door in the back that we can't break down. I think your friend has the key."

"Well, you piece of shit, where is it?" The rifle barrel ripped open the man's shirt as it slid down to his belly. The soldier leaned forward until the muzzle disappeared in a roll of fat. "You can hand it to me and save yourself a lot of trouble . . . or I can take it away." He pushed harder. "What do you say?"

"It's . . . it's in my pocket," the fat man whimpered.

"Which one?"

"The right one."

"Reach in very carefully and hand it to me. If you do anything I don't like, I'll splatter your belly all over the truck."

Very slowly the man's hand slipped into his pocket. He was shaking so much it was almost impossible to remove the key. "I do . . . I really do have it . . ." he offered.

"Captain," the man named Carlo called out, "you asked for a key, and this idiot decides to play with himself. Look at this."

"Please . . . I have the key. Here . . ." The key appeared briefly in his hand before falling to the ground. "I'm sorry . . ."

"Pick it up!"

As the man bent over, Carlo playfully cuffed him in the back of the neck. He fell to the ground heavily with a whimper. Carlo picked up the key and tossed it to the waiting Kurochkin. Then he kicked dirt in the man's face. "If you move—just once—you're a dead man."

There was rum in the locked room, and Kurochkin and his men made a great show of drinking out of the bottles. As soon as they had taken whatever they wanted, gasoline was thrown on the outside of the wooden building. A single match turned it into an inferno.

Kurochkin directed the truck over to the building that evidently served as the town hall and school. There his men took turns shooting out the windows until there was nothing left; then they turned their attention to the other buildings. By this time not a soul could be seen in Potrerillo except for the owner of the burning building, who had been forced to stay with them.

Though the town seemed deserted, Kurochkin knew that everything they did would travel to the neighboring villages by nightfall. "What shall we have to eat tonight, Carlo? How about some fresh chickens?"

"That sounds like a good idea, Captain." He turned to their prisoner and snapped, "Where can we find some chickens close by?"

A shaking hand pointed behind the little wooden church. "Father keeps some behind the church—but that's all he has . . ."

"I'll watch your man," Kurochkin said. "Go get us six fat chickens—just six, now! Since they belong to a priest, we'll take only what we need."

Carlo obtained a bag from the back of the truck and set off for the rear of the church with one of the others. The sound of squawking hens announced their success. But when the two men came back with their prize, they were followed by a rotund little priest with a shiny bald head. Totally distraught, he was wringing his hands, plucking at their sleeves, and imploring them to listen all at the same time. He appeared anything but a priest as he begged them to return his chickens.

Noticing that Kurochkin seemed to be in charge, he scurried over. "Please, sir, please have your men release my birds." It was a rapid-fire, high-pitched whine. "They're all I have. They're—"

"I'm doing you a favor, Father." The Russian's arms were folded across his chest in irritation, but an amused expression remained on his lips. "You have more birds. I know that. We're taking only what we need. You wouldn't call that a sin, would you?"

"You're stealing," the priest replied, sensing incorrectly from the look on the officer's face that he could be a bit braver. "That is a sin in itself. And look at what you've done." His arm swept around to include the burning store behind him. "The government will punish you for that. . . ."

"We are the government now, Father." The swaggering Kurochkin couldn't remember when he'd attempted to effect a more serious expression. "When Juan Duran took over, we became the government. Now, what do you think of that?"

The priest took a step backward, his eyes traveling from Kurochkin to each of the Scorpions, then falling to the ground. His lips began to move—but there was no sound. His head inclined forward slowly as a barely audible sound emerged from his mouth.

"What's that, Father?" Kurochkin leaned forward. "I can't hear you." There was no answer. Then he reached out, placed his hand under the priest's chin, and slowly lifted his head until their eyes met. "I said I couldn't hear you. I'm not used to anyone ignoring me."

"I was saying to myself that I should no longer be afraid of you . . . and I was praying. I thought you were bandits of some kind, but I understand now." There was a touch of bravery that surprised Kurochkin. "Tell me, is the army free to roam the countryside like this, raiding—"

"Foraging, Father. *Foraging* is a much better word. It's more like collecting taxes. Life has been easy for you people for much too long. You expect protection from the military, yet you don't pay for it. So things are going to change. When we get what we want, we are thankful. . . ."

The old priest's eyes were shining now and somehow he seemed to enjoy his newfound courage as he returned Kurochkin's stare. "What do you call what you just did to Maraydo's store?" The sweep of his arm included the owner, who was cringing in the shadow of the truck. "Or to poor Maraydo? He couldn't do anything to hurt you. Why beat him?"

"He refused to cooperate, Father. I had a shopping list of things I needed for my men, and he resisted." Again there was the hint of a smile on Kurochkin's lips. "Actually, when he tried to keep us from resupplying, we could have killed him. That's what the new directives authorize when anyone interferes. But we do have mercy. After all, we are citizens of the same country."

"And if I was starving to death, would you give back my chickens?"

"Father, if you were starving to death, I would give you back a chicken because I carry the same mercies in my heart as yourself. But if I gave back all the chickens, then my men would starve, and there would be no protection for you or your people.''

The priest shook his head in sadness. ''I can see things will be no different than they were back in Batista's day,'' he muttered more to himself than anyone else. Then he looked up at Kurochkin. ''Is this how you plan to supply yourselves from now on?''

''Only in the field, Father. When we are in the barracks, then of course we live on government supplies. It's only fair, isn't it?'' He turned to the one called Carlo. ''Get the men in the truck. We should be in Mataguá by nightfall.'' Then he looked back at the priest. ''Yes, Father, things have changed in Cuba—but it is all for the better. Our country needs less Marxism and more individualism. People need to survive on their own wits—like the military. You'll see,'' he said as he climbed into the cab of the truck. ''Duran will make sure things are a lot better in Cuba.''

As the truck careened around the plaza and headed in the direction of the next town, a well-aimed bottle was hurled from the back of the truck, barely missing the old priest.

In other villages and towns in the region—in Santiago de Cartagena, Gutierrez, and San Marcos; in Guillermo Moncada, Horquitas, and Mercedes; in La Sierrita, Topes de Collantes, and Muñoz—surprises of a similar nature were coming to parish priests and local mayors through the same medium, Spetznaz subunits in Cuban uniform. The message was short, but it was one that would spread quickly to both ends of the island nation. The transfer of power in Havana had not simply been a change of names in the upper echelon. A uniquely Latin philosophy, one that had haunted generations of Cubans, appeared to be surfacing: The people would be the ones to bear the burden. Juan Duran was a military man, and it would be the military who once again controlled the country. Whenever that had occurred in Cuba, the populace had paid a heavy price.

• • •

Paul Voronov ordered himself a dark rum with a fresh wedge of lime. When it arrived, he squeezed the juice over the ice and stirred it in with his index finger. He'd enjoyed the drink on a previous assignment in the Caribbean and it was something he'd been looking forward to since the day he was ordered to Cuba.

The first sip was always the best. The tangy lime combined almost sensually with the full raw flavor of the rum and intensified as he held it on his tongue. It seemed to explode when he swallowed it, like vodka, but the aftertaste was many times more pleasant. *Be careful,* he chided himself, *or you'll be compromising the operation before you ever sink your teeth into it.*

For an officer with his unique talents, this was much more than a simple behind-the-lines Spetznaz operation. His sergeants would handle the field strategy superlatively—they could develop a grass-roots hatred of Duran that would shock the new Havana leadership. It would be tremendously effective, certainly causing apprehension among even the educated classes in the cities who tended to remain aloof to the vicissitudes of government.

It was Voronov's responsibility to establish the necessity for a logical successor to Juan Duran, a concern that he pondered even now as he waited for his guest. No, he conceded, that was a poor way to consider it even in the privacy of his own mind. The person who took over when there was no more Duran would not—*could not*—be an obviously Soviet-sponsored individual. Arkady Bunin must stay completely out of it. That would be the kiss of death for Russian influence.

Rather, it had to be someone whom the Kremlin approved—in this case, Paul Voronov—and it would have to be someone who would understand he was beholden to the Soviet Union for his accession to power. *But,* and that was a critical word, he and his people would have to take control of the government on their own, with their own power structure, and do it when it became apparent that Duran was either too weak to govern or no longer alive. The latter option didn't really concern the successors, since Voronov knew that Juan Duran could not survive.

If he was able to do the job as he had been ordered, only a very few people in the Kremlin would ever know how the next Cuban leader achieved his position. It would all be a matter of timing. While Voronov would be comfortable in disposing of Duran at any time, the critical element was to install an initial discontent in the countryside and then couple it with uncertainty in the cities. At this still-early stage in Duran's government, the people could be influenced to believe just about anything. The man's actions to date had been erratic enough to make almost any story plausible. The loss of a relatively new, unknown dictator would make little difference. There was as yet no great love flowing from the masses to Juan Duran. They enjoyed his excesses, clamoring for outrageous displays, but they would withhold their admiration a while longer.

"Excuse me . . . Colonel Sanchez?" a deep voice addressed Paul Voronov.

Voronov looked up into a pair of flashing black eyes set in one of the handsomest faces he'd ever seen. Although he knew this man was in his fifties, there was hardly a line on his face and his thick hair was perfectly black—*like a movie star,* he thought. "Yes, sir." He stood and extended his hand. "Fernando Sanchez. I'm delighted that you accepted my invitation, sir." Paul Voronov had impersonated Spanish-speaking people in the past and was comfortable now in the role of an unknown military advisor to Duran.

"It was one that was certainly hard to refuse." Jorge Anaya's attire was as perfect as his features. The beige custom-fitted suit was certainly more expensive than any Voronov had ever seen in the Soviet Union, and the white shirt and tie were obviously silk. Anaya wore them like a second skin. "It seemed highly unlikely to me that one of

Juan Duran's advisors would want to discuss anything with me.''

Voronov smiled. ''General Duran hopes to expand his influence through every level of the government if his ideas are really to take hold—even in your own branch.'' Jorge Anaya's name had initially been mentioned by the Soviet ambassador, Arkady Bunin, during his emergency recall to Moscow. When he first contemplated contacting Anaya, Paul Voronov had agreed with Bunin's determination that the most logical place to look for uncertainty was in the Supreme Court of the nation. Where else would one find dissatisfaction with the means in which Duran came to power than with one of the justices? ''It is my responsibility to ensure that the judicial branch is comfortable with the future of the country.''

''Somehow I can't take everything you say at face value, Colonel.'' Anaya pulled back the chair that Voronov had indicated and sat down easily. ''I assume that's rum you're drinking?''

''With fresh lime.''

''The same,'' Anaya said to the waiter who had appeared beside them.

''I hope that you'll be comfortable with my first name before we've finished our discussion. I prefer being called Fernando. . . .''

''In government I have learned that using the correct title for an individual is often more rewarding than establishing a friendship,'' Anaya responded. ''I'm honest with everyone, Colonel, and I have no idea if I will want to begin any sort of relationship with anyone in Duran's government.'' He smiled easily. Charm had been as much a reason for Anaya's rapid rise in the Cuban judicial system as his intelligence. He was adept with both and surprised even his closest friends when he was appointed to the Supreme Court by Castro. Jorge Anaya somehow managed to be on the popular side of any judicial decision. Some even thought he was able to influence the cases sent to his court—others who knew that for a fact had been well rewarded.

It would be hard to disagree with a man like this one if he had just explained how offensive you were, Voronov decided. "That's just something we learn in the military, sir, when dealing with civilians. Many people today are uncomfortable with rank. I simply try to gauge people as quickly as I can. Perhaps I even understand people like yourself, who prefer formality, a little better. And I promise that what you hear from me this evening will be my own words—not words I've been ordered to say."

"You're trying to make me comfortable too quickly, Colonel. I think what will accomplish that is your willingness to tell me a little more about yourself, since you already know who I am. Why don't you try to do that and I'll enjoy my drink." Anaya had yet to take anyone at face value, but he sensed something about the man across the table that forced him to listen.

Paul Voronov's explanation of his background was perfectly viable, strong on duty to the military, stronger still in loyalty to his country. It was designed to appeal to a man of Anaya's intellect and position who would harbor an automatic suspicion toward the military. The judiciary was a separate but lofty element of the island nation's patriarchy. It had frequently been victimized by dictators whose legacy became a corrupted court that often sought, but always lost, political power. Repeatedly a justice of the court would be swayed by power. While they knew how to control elections and amass the necessary votes, they lacked the one element necessary to attain power in Cuba—firepower. They consistently lost to the military. When Fidel Castro, a lawyer himself, came to power, he installed an honest court that remained above the temptations of the past, and Juan Duran hadn't yet found the time to tamper with it. Jorge Anaya appeared to represent everything that was decent in Cuban jurisprudence.

"Colonel, it sounds to me as if your own career has paralleled that of General Duran."

"Until a few years ago, yes. I lack the training in terrorism . . . and I have never had the pleasure of being the guest of Qaddafi." Voronov had selected his words carefully as he dropped this hint of dissatisfaction.

Anaya paused for a moment, weighing what this unknown colonel had just said. "What did you say your specific assignment is now?"

"I'm the assistant to the military aide to General Duran."

"And you could substantiate what you just said?"

Voronov's offense appeared sincere enough so that Anaya's expression softened perceptibly. "The orders to Simferapol in the Soviet Union came through my office at the time. As far as his relationship with the Libyan, the prize possession on his desk is a photograph of himself and Qaddafi sharing a meal in a tent. Both of them appear in desert dress, and the photo is inscribed, 'To my brother in arms—may our goals bring us together in the coming years.' I can't bring the picture to you, but I can assure you of its existence." That was the seed. Now could he possibly infer that perhaps Cuba was on the road to becoming another Libya—perhaps even a satellite?

Jorge Anaya's questions became more probing. Though he tended to mask his concern as simple curiosity, both men understood that they would not be talking together if each didn't believe the other had a great deal to offer. The justice's insight into Duran's personality was uncanny. Voronov found that it became increasingly easy to paint exactly the picture he had intended of Duran, for it was precisely what Anaya seemed to expect.

"All right, Colonel Sanchez, let's get to the reason you called me. I took a chance coming here, but I'm certain now I can trust you. I guarantee that my bodyguard left at my signal."

"I appreciate your trust, sir." Voronov hoped desperately that his surprise wasn't evident. A tiny voice deep within his brain repeated the same message again and again: *You let your guard down, you idiot!* He'd seen no one, nor had he noted any sign from Anaya that might have confirmed it. *Be careful,* he reminded himself, *because you have found not only the right man but a very dangerous one.*

"Talk." The single word was enunciated softly, but it left no doubt that Anaya was used to giving orders and that he considered this colonel, no matter how close he might be to Duran, subservient to him. What didn't come through was that Anaya understood within fifteen minutes of their first meeting that this Colonel Sanchez was no Cuban.

"General Duran is in a very dangerous position. There are still a great number of people who support Castro—small enclaves, perhaps, but many of them still believe he is alive somewhere. The jails are loaded with political prisoners. The peasants are once again experiencing a military out of control, and I think the middle classes have yet to make up their minds about Duran. No matter how much he tries to entertain the people with his public trials and his unorthodox methods, they will not support him if they have any sense at all that they are to be his victims also—"

"Get to the point, please. I read the papers. I see the news on television. It's impossible to censor everything." Anaya had considered what he was hearing and understood immediately that not only was it sedition if the man across from him had been a Cuban, but this was a tremendous risk for anyone. Yet everything that this person was repeating was true.

"I am loyal to my country and have come close to dying for her more than once. But I also carry a great fear for her safety if something happens to General Duran, for there is no one to continue in his place. If our country became leaderless for even a short time—days, even hours—both the Americans and the Russians would have a tremendous opportunity to increase their influence."

"It sounds to me as if you memorized that last sentence, Colonel. Is that what you really fear the most?"

Oh, this Anaya was intelligent! There was no fooling men like him. He was absolutely perfect. *I owe Arkady*

Bunin a drink. "I'm neither a politician nor an ambitious man. What I would like to see—what other officers like myself would like to see—is someone who would take the office if, God forbid, something should happen to General Duran."

"Do you expect Duran's term to be a short one?"

"Who can predict something like that? The general most likely anticipates nothing of the sort, since there is no one in line. Maybe he wants that woman . . . that Cara Estrada. Who knows? That's a dangerous policy . . . wouldn't you agree?"

Anaya said nothing. He studied Voronov's eyes for a moment, then looked down at the empty glasses on the table. "Allow me." He waved to a passing waiter, indicating that they wanted two more drinks. Then he looked up at Voronov again. "You amaze me, Colonel, both for your bravery in talking with me like this and your stupidity in taking such chances. Just what do you think would happen to you if I was a Duran supporter?"

"Sometimes we have to gamble, sir. You must realize I didn't pick your name out of a hat. I think . . . I think it took me the most time to determine exactly who were the most patriotic Cubans. At that point I didn't think I would be taking a chance." Men like Anaya, intense men who often looked inward for their strength, were proud when others complimented their patriotism. Voronov knew how to seek out the key to each man's ego, and he also knew how to expose it.

"I don't want you to say another word until our drinks arrive. Then we will both sip and think before anymore is said. I want you to be absolutely positive that what you say from now on comes from your heart. I assure you that is exactly where my responses will come from." With that, Anaya sat back in his chair. Who was this man sitting across from him? It had become obvious from his first few sentences that he wasn't a native to the island. His Spanish was superb, almost perfect—too perfect for a native. It lacked the idioms, especially those that became second nature to a soldier. Each word was too clearly enunciated. But intuition also reminded Anaya that whoever this man was, there was something here for both of them.

When the drinks were placed before them, they each squeezed the lime into the glass. The men studied each other intently. Voronov licked the juice from his fingers; Anaya dried his on a napkin. They both swirled the rum first, sniffing at the aroma. Voronov took a mouthful and rolled it about in his mouth before swallowing, exhaling with a loud breath. Anaya took small, delicate sips and gave no visual or audible indication that he was enjoying his rum in the same manner. Each watched the other warily, becoming more aware of social amenities, of habits, of their position in life. Voronov couldn't have asked for more.

"You are indeed a soldier." Anaya broke the silence.

"How's that?"

"You demonstrate your pleasures to the world. Men who have seen too much death often exhibit such customs. They are impatient to get on with it all. We are two very different men, but we have much in common, including our concern about our nation's leadership. I think I understand you at least as well as you have gotten to know me. But I must think a good deal more. How can I contact you?"

"Don't. Can you imagine how people might talk if a justice of the highest court called a colonel in the presidential palace? I am sure even my apartment has been tapped. I'll be in touch with you in a week . . . after you've had the chance to think about our conversation. A man like yourself could become a great leader if anything ever happened to Duran."

When they parted company that evening, Paul Voronov muttered a silent thanks to Arkady Bunin. This Anaya was the perfect foil—though *foil* wasn't the proper word. He was a perfect . . . *candidate* was a better term. His ambition was the one personality trait he was unable to conceal.

The lust for power hung on men's sleeves for the world to view, but it shone like a neon sign in Anaya's case.

He knows I'm no Cuban, Voronov admitted as he swirled the ice in his glass before swallowing the last of the now-diluted rum. *He could have me in jail within the hour, but I would take a bet for any amount of money that won't happen. This Anaya understands people. He knows exactly what I'm planning, and he's going to hover on the edge to see if what I claim is happening will actually take place. The more he sees, the more he'll belong to me. Oh, that ambition, that old-fashioned hunger for power—it makes my job so much easier. The Honorable Jorge Anaya will be easier than even Arkady Bunin thought.*

Sergeant Kurochkin's foraging parties could not go unnoticed forever. While Paul Voronov knew from experience in other countries that the peasants would never complain to the army that they were being harrassed by army troops, he knew that eventually the authorities would become aware of the problem.

Peasants normally considered the military and the bureaucracy as their inherent enemy. It made little difference who was in power—the poor were always the easiest target. Since that was a way of life, Voronov knew that Kurochkin would manage to stay ahead of the military for as long as it took to establish a sound distrust for the new government.

But eventually word did reach higher authority. It was only a matter of weeks.

The initial complaint came from the priests who served in the countryside. Long used to such abuse themselves, their own hatred of the military kept them from speaking out to the authorities. But the sustained raiding by more than one party became too much. A priest in Horquitas, especially outraged by the damage to the store of a woman who provided him with both rum and well-concealed sexual favors, complained to his superior in Cienfuegos. Eventually the complaint received some attention from a colonel in charge of the various garrisons in the district.

Assuming that one of his junior officers had found a new method to supplement his income, Colonel Valenzuela decided to take a small party out to both halt the raiding and to regain the hearts and minds of the peasants. It seemed a fine way to attract attention to himself and earn his way back to the comforts of Havana.

Valenzuela passed the word of his personal crusade both to his superiors in Havana and to the priest who'd brought the problem to his attention. Havana promptly noted his intentions and filed them, unnoticed. The priest in Horquitas, overjoyed that a wrong might finally be corrected by the military, informed as many people as possible about the colonel's imminent arrival.

Kurochkin was overjoyed. Harassing innocent people was an unattractive job for Spetznaz. He took charge of preparing a welcoming party.

Colonel Valenzuela was enjoying the trip to the villages west of Cienfuegos. It was an area he'd never seen in the past and it made sense to see more of his district before returning to Havana. He rode in an open jeep ahead of the truck containing his troops. The roads became dirt-covered and dusty soon after he turned off the main highway to Aguada de Pasajeros, but the scenery was appealing to a man who had seen much too much of Cienfuegos.

The first blast was obviously the result of faulty cord, Kurochkin later determined, or the jeep would have disintegrated. But the second was perfect. The front of the truck reared like a crazed horse. One of the tires soared skyward, spinning like a top. Then the vehicle, still propelled forward by the rear wheels, arched to the right, dumping troops as it rolled into the dry gutter at the side of the road. The gas tank exploded with a roar, engulfing vehicle and men in flames.

Colonel Valenzuela peered back through the dust from the first blast. It had gone off no more than five yards behind, showering the colonel and his driver with dirt and stones. Neither of them had been injured. But they had both been terrified, and the driver had instinctively yanked the wheel to one side. The jeep's frame now rested on a rock, immovable. The colonel stared in horror as two of his men, human torches, raced screaming in his direction. He had no idea what to do if they made it to his side.

Kurochkin's men were killers, but they were sympathetic to how long it took to die. They shot the flaming men first before turning to the few others who had escaped the truck. There was never an opportunity to fire back at the Russians. The Spetznaz were much too efficient. They had been involved in similar ambushes in other countries. Those under attack always reacted the same, and the Spetznaz always dispatched their targets quickly.

The only individual to return fire was Colonel Valenzuela, who, when he recovered his senses, fired his pistol vainly into the undergrowth at the side of the road before he, too, died in a hail of bullets with his driver.

Within two hours there was no indication that any action had taken place on the dirt road outside Horquitas. Both vehicles had disappeared into the undergrowth and would never be seen from the road or the air. All traces of the fire had disappeared. The bodies were buried in a mass grave well into the woods. By the time Colonel Valenzuela would be classified as missing, rumors spreading through the Cienfuegos Barracks would discourage any more haphazard forays into the countryside without Havana's coordination until Sergeant Kurochkin and his troops had completed their mission for Voronov.

CHAPTER EIGHT

The two men glimpsed each other purely by chance as they passed on Avenida Salvador Allende. Their eyes locked—*I know you!* The shock of recognition was paramount at the instant, followed by: *Have I been compromised?* Fear, naked and devastating, pumped adrenaline through their bodies. No man—SEAL or Spetznaz—can ever remain totally detached from reality, yet both were aware that another man had seen through him instantly because his guard had been down. Both men, trained in totally different countries, had been warned of that ultimate traitor— ego, arrogance, overconfidence, whatever an instructor cared to call it. Men in exactly their positions at that very moment had died in the past because they had been either overly confident in their assumed roles or lost in thought when they should have remained alert. Too many times they also died ugly.

Paul Voronov retained the image of the other man perfectly for five more steps. *High cheekbones—were they Scandinavian, or slightly oriental like mine? Whatever, none of the features—the lips, the forehead, that distant expression on his face . . . that was it! No more Cuban*

*than I am . . . yet comfortable in the guise of a . . . what?
. . . Cuban businessman? A perfect Latin . . . so much
like me that he, too, is playing the game. Where have we
met each other? Or was it just a photograph?*

Voronov had taken no more than five steps since that
face shocked him, but the possibilities inherent in that
simple eye contact had raced across his mind. There had
been no response evident, no voice calling out, nor was
there the sound of a shot that would have indicated someone's search was over. He eased out toward the curb,
never changing stride, gradually turning his head until
anything of note would have drifted into his peripheral
vision. But the other had disappeared among the crowd.
Two more steps and the answer came to him. Paul Voronov
never forgot a face and now the answer was etched in his
mind—the American, *Ryng!* He felt as if a bullet had just
exploded through the gray matter of his brain. The Russian
continued down the street, oblivious of those around him,
yet afraid he would recognize another face.

Ryng was unable to breath. *Was this the way it was
when that slug hit you in the chest,* he wondered, *bursting
in your heart, knocking the air from your lungs?* If that
man had been badly disfigured, it would have made no
difference—those eyes would never change. They were
about the same size, and he knew the similarity was
evident in their thick necks and broad shoulders. But the
features around those eyes! Those high cheekbones, the
eyelids, the thin lips—they belied the fact that the man had
dark contacts to mask his blue eyes . . . just like Ryng! He
knew in an instant that particular Cuban colonel was the
most dangerous human being he would encounter—and he
knew instinctively that the man had also recognized him.

Keep walking, he said to himself, *keep walking. If his
job is to kill you, there isn't a chance in the world to avoid
it. Anything you try to do will just leave some innocent
people dead on the sidewalk . . . and you'll be a corpse
anyway if that's what he's after.* But there was no shot, no

bullet slamming him headlong onto his face on the sidewalk while a screaming crowd tolled his death. Five steps . . . and it came to him in a flash. *That arrogant face, the eyes that could cut through a man—Paul Voronov! The one who had escaped from . . . no, he didn't escape from me—he escaped from an army. Which of us has more lives?* Ryng turned his head just enough to conclude that the other man had also continued on his way. *Hoff told me there were Spetznaz here . . . but he never mentioned Voronov . . . that son of a bitch!*

Bernie Ryng would be the first person to admit that the few friends he had might be considered unusual, and he would argue until he drew his last breath that they were also the most faithful in the world. When Alf Hoff explained during their final meeting in Washington that Antonio Lynch was in Havana, Ryng didn't know whether to laugh or cry.

"I thought he was dead, Alf! Really. I saw him take four slugs from a machine pistol in Amsterdam a few years ago . . . knocked him right through a plate-glass window." He paused for a moment, staring off into space as he remembered the moment. "Yeah. If it hadn't been him, it would have been me. But he made the mistake, and they never gave him a chance." He cocked his head to one side and looked at Hoff with the trace of a smile on his lips. "Antonio . . . Tony Lynch . . . I'll be damned." He'd heard later that Tony'd survived, and he really had planned to locate him. But it was hard, double hard, to look up an old buddy who must be a cripple.

They'd been so close, as close as brothers, Ryng was sure, since they met in BUD/S (Basic Underwater Demolition/SEAL) training so many years before. If there was one basic message you got from the first day, it was that SEALs survived through teamwork. Everyone had a buddy. Nothing was ever done alone unless it was ordered. In the water they were swim buddies—one mile, two miles, four miles, fins, no fins, it didn't matter. Your buddy would get you through when you were ready to ring yourself out of BUD/S. Ryng had kicked Tony Lynch's ass through the obstacles almost every week. Tony was a terrific swimmer, but he never saw the reasons for obstacle courses: ". . . if I wanted to be a marine, I would have told the recruiter how much I loved stupid things . . . like crawling under barbed wire . . . or climbing that sillyass cargo net . . ." And when Bernie Ryng was ready to climb out of fifty-six-degree water after the third mile of the swim at San Clemente Island, it was Lynch who swam beside him, telling him what a chicken shit he was if he quit at that point . . . and left the best buddy he'd ever have.

"It's probably dumb of me to ask," Hoff remarked curiously, "but what the hell were SEALs doing in Amsterdam?"

"Terrorist problems. What else? Extortion in a way. A bunch of dissidents threatened to blow some vital dikes for some goddamn reason or other. The government didn't take it too seriously until a body turned up floating too close to one of the dikes that was threatened. When the autopsy indicated the victim died during some type of underwater explosion, they sent some divers down for a look. Imagine how surprised they were when a couple of explosive devices were located, just as promised."

"And they asked for SEALs," Hoff concluded.

"No one asks for us." Ryng grinned. "They intimate how serious their problem is and hope that Washington will decide to loan us. As far as the Pentagon is concerned, we're not for hire. No advertising. It's just when they really want to impress somebody that they imply that there is an organization within the U.S. military that might be able to help. The idea seems to be that the host nation—the one that needs us badly—is in big debt to Uncle Sam after we clean up their problems."

"The Dutch were happy?"

"They were ecstatic that we sanitized their dikes—

couldn't have been happier. But they got a little excited when we went after the source of their troubles. They couldn't seem to get it through their heads that the same problem would come up again if these crazy dissidents were allowed to set any more demolitions.'' Ryng grinned. ''That's second nature to a SEAL—don't solve half the problem if you can finish it completely.''

''That's how Lynch was hit?''

''It was his mistake. We couldn't blame anyone for that.''

''But you did take care of—''

''Scratch one group—to a man. That's why the Dutch got so excited. On the other hand, the problem was so well solved that we won't have to go back there again.'' There was no need for further explanation.

Lynch looked no different now as Ryng studied him over the beer bottles than he had the day he took those 9mm slugs, except he now looked exactly like a native of Havana—just like a chameleon, Ryng decided, no matter where he hung his hat. He was tall and slender, with slightly receding wavy black hair. His dark skin and pencil mustache were the same as always and his smile emphasized sparkling white teeth. The suit he wore was cut just like half a dozen others in the restaurant. Antonio had never known why his father used the name Lynch, since both his parents were Spanish. But he liked the name because he said it set him apart from everyone whose name ended in a vowel. And he was very much alive!

''I couldn't believe it when they said you were coming down here, Bernie. I thought you were dead . . . that day in Amsterdam when they surprised us . . .''

''Surprised you, Tony. They used that girl, the one in the car across the street from your position. Do you remember when she started screaming . . . and pushed open the door naked as the day she was born . . .''

''That's the last thing I knew.''

''Well, we got them. Her, too. When they carted you

away, they said there wasn't a chance. I hopped the next flight to Washington and cried all the way—then I stayed drunk for a week. They sent me down to Little Creek to sort out some special forces types who had orders to go through SEAL training. That's how the military makes you forget a lost love," he concluded with a wry grin.

"This is my first assignment since then. They wanted to retire me, Bernie. You see, this arm"—he patted his right arm as he spoke—"doesn't work too well anymore. So I learned how to shoot left-handed and got pretty good at it, too." He shrugged. "But they gave me my walking papers anyway, the pricks."

"So . . . what's all this . . . Havana and all?"

"I'm a civilian. I was assigned to Hoff. When the SEALs said good-bye, a friend of mine called Hoff and explained that there was a guy available with my background who'd been chased out of the service because of a bad wing. I talked to Alf two days in a row. The third day he took me down to the firing range to see what I could do. I went twenty for twenty on the targets he picked out. The rest was easy. I've been here for six months."

"Before Castro disappeared?"

Lynch winked. "I know where he is . . . or was."

Ryng leaned forward. "Well?"

"Shark bait. Old Fidel started to get a little religion near the end, enough so that he didn't want people to know he was still horny. But he was too habitual. Used to sneak out to visit a lady friend because he didn't want anyone to see her in the official residence. Duran knew about her and learned there was a schedule. They grabbed Fidel one night on his way for a little piece, took him down to the docks, and I'm told he was chopped up and fed to the sharks about ten miles out. The boat they used was back at the dock before sunrise and no one was ever the wiser."

"What about his bodyguards?"

"Same thing. There's two sick jokes going around. You take your choice. The first one among some of the higher-ups is that dozens of sharks turn up at the same place every night looking for another free meal—so everyone keeps turning down invitations to go fishing with Duran. The other is that the next day a fisherman spotted dozens of sharks belly up about ten miles off shore and reported that something horrible had poisoned them all.''

''Neither one sounds very funny to me.''

''You don't understand Cuban humor yet, Bernie. If you lived on the island long enough, you'd be a fatalist, too.''

Ryng smiled. Antonio Lynch really hadn't changed at all. He could see something funny in everything that ever happened. It had always been his way of hiding all the ugliness. ''So what have you done for me to earn your keep, Tony? Alf said you'd been doing a lot of digging since Duran took over.''

''Yeah. Presidential directive, I'm told. If there's one thing the White House hates more than Russians, it's Qaddafi—or any of his pals. When they got wind of all the time Duran spent in Libya, that got someone up there thinking. Then after Miami and New Orleans, that was the straw that did it. And I can guarantee there's more of those raids to come. Duran hates Americans like you wouldn't believe. Now that there's been demonstrations back home against our treatment of Cuba, there's sort of a carte blanche to do whatever he wants.''

''I read about those in the paper before I ever met Hoff. Duran must have some sharp cookies stirring things up on our own turf. All he had to do was mention terrorism on American soil and the campuses came to life.''

''Alf says it's more than the campuses this time, too. If people get so upset about an atom turning on their lights, imagine how they're affected by some guy who comes on like the next Messiah. Anywhere there's some left-wing sympathy, there's going to be a demonstration in support of the new Cuban government. And think of how many people fall for the fundamentalist preachers. He's going to keep yanking our chain until we do something dumb, then he's going to try to turn everyone against us.'' Lynch winked and grinned, tapping his forehead. "Smart, Bernie, so damn smart he's still a couple of jumps ahead of Washington. Just like a cat."

"Any weaknesses that you've seen?"

"If you consider being as stable, or unstable, as Qaddafi, I'd say that was a weakness. Duran's in love with himself, and then Qaddafi. Since I'm still supposed to be a noncombatant, I do a lot of nosing around . . . which I'm still very good at."

"And?"

"Another weakness, maybe more misjudgment on Duran's part. I've gotten religion, Bernie. I go to mass every morning, early. And I've found out that the Church is definitely not content with Juan Duran. It seems that Fidel decided that the best way to get back into the center of Latin-American politics was to make friends with the Roman Catholic Church, and his overtures seemed to be paying off. Then, bango! No more Fidel, and Duran turns everything upside down for the Bishop of Havana, who incidentally had Rome's support to open a dialogue."

Ryng's eyes reflected his surprise. "Where in the world did you pick up all that? Not from any parish priest?"

"No. But the parish priest has a buddy who happens to be a top dog in the bishop's office. Both of them have the same weakness for rum that I have." He nodded before Ryng could interrupt. "Yup, some people never change, Bernie. And I can assure you that rum still loosens people's tongues like it always did. What would you say if I told you that there are certain individuals very close to Duran who think he's soft as a fig?"

"Hoff must like to hear that."

"Haven't said a word to him because that doesn't give us any special opening yet. Hoff only wants to hear absolutes. But I have an idea how to get near Duran." He pursed his lips and winked again.

Always the same. Lynch still loved to tease. "Tell me about it."

"This is right up your alley. I might even have tried it if

I had two good arms. You're familiar with Cara Estrada, aren't you?''

''Duran's mistress?''

''More than that. His closest advisor. Just as smart as he is, I'll bet. But she's also got everything in order upstairs, and I think she's scared about Duran's stability.''

''The priests told you this?''

''Not really. They were just talking one night about how strange it is that she comes to mass. Never did before—a godless commie and all that. I guess she has to sneak out, but they said she shows up maybe five times a week. And—this is the kicker—she's taken up going to confession again.''

''What does she say there?''

''Bernie, these guys may be drinking buddies, but they're still priests. They're not about to relate what happens in the little box. But, I can tell from what they say to each other—that some days Cara Estrada is a very unhappy lady. I suggest that you get yourself some religion.''

They drank more beer and talked until Ryng decided to count the slips of paper on the table, one for each round. Six all told. ''That's it. My limit. You know me, Tony, never get drunk on duty. And one more will put me over the edge.''

''I never saw you drunk. The only times I ever hear of are the ones you tell me about. What makes you think you have to keep on your toes after just one day in town?'' Lynch had seen the look in Ryng's eyes when they first gave each other a big hug. And there'd been no doubting his caution as he glanced around the room before sitting down—or how he watched the door while they talked.

''There are heavy Russian types around.''

''Always have been—going on thirty years now.''

''No, not the run-of-the-mill. I mean Spetznaz.''

''That's a given, Bernie. Hoff must have told you Moscow wasn't any happier with Duran than we are. I knew there were one or more teams in country—Cienfuegos is the logical drop-off point . . .''

"No, this is different. I saw one on the street before I came in here. He was wearing a Cuban colonel's uniform . . . but I'd know Paul Voronov . . ."

"Ahh . . ." Lynch commented with a knowing wink.

"Correct. That means much more than just a little Kremlin concern. Voronov goes in only when there is an impossible job to be done, and always a dirty one."

"Do you think he might have recognized you?"

Ryng's mind recalled the image on the street as his gaze fell on Voronov . . . the other's eyes catching his for just an instant . . . *an instant of recognition*. No doubt about it! "Yes. He saw what I saw."

"Someone who wants to feed Duran to the sharks?"

"The question now, Tony, is how to make it look like the other guy did it."

Lynch appeared thoughtful before he cautioned, "It's not a contest between you and Voronov. Remember, we're supposed to make the successor government cozy up to us because the Soviets are the bad guys. If I was still a betting man, I'd say that Cara Estrada is going to be the key." Antonio Lynch had retained a vital lesson since Amsterdam—he was safer seeking solutions than ways to destroy—finally.

Later, by himself, Bernie Ryng's mind wandered back to another time when Tony Lynch was still so goddamn precocious. *Christ, what a team we were, though!* It had started at BUD/S when they pushed each other through Hell Week. A year later they'd found themselves together in Vietnam, just before U.S. involvement began to wear down. But there had been a need for SEALs right up to the end. There'd been some recon work, pinpointing enemy supply dumps for the B-52s, and they'd gone out together on intelligence runs. The latter meant bringing back prisoners, and Ryng and Lynch had drawn attention to themselves by delivering an NVA general to Saigon.

There were other times when they'd been on exercises together, but the best was in the Med. That had been a real assignment. COMSIXTHFLEET had gotten so pissed at Qaddafi when he sent those little pissant patrol boats out to challenge his carrier that he decided to destroy one.

"Bomb it . . . use missiles . . . I don't give a shit how you do it, but I want to see one less of those goddamn patrol boats at the pier in Benghazi tomorrow"—that was essentially how the admiral's orders sounded when they finally got down to Bernie Ryng. Cooler heads had prevailed. To take out a patrol boat with a bomb or a missile required an aircraft. Only the President could authorize such an attack, since it could be interpreted as an act of war.

The only way to accomplish what the admiral wanted was to be sneaky—make it look like an accident, whether or not the Libyans figured out how their boat blew up. The admiral's cool-headed chief of staff eventually prevailed, and it was agreed that a number of SEALs could solve the admiral's problem.

When the situation was presented to Ryng, who was CO of the detachment, his reaction was a simple question: Why a number of SEALs when two of us can piss off Qaddafi royally? The admiral knew enough about SEALs to let Ryng do it however he felt was necessary, as long as there was one less boat at that pier the next morning.

It wasn't the way Ryng preferred to handle an operation— there should have been more time for planning—so he rang up Tony Lynch in his stateroom and explained that he'd just volunteered. If you were going off half-cocked, the only man to have beside you in the water was Lynch.

They'd been picked up by helo from the deck of *Inchon* and flown over to listen to the admiral's harangue about "that asshole Qaddafi" before he explained exactly what he expected. An hour with photo intelligence followed. Then they were transferred to an attack submarine whose captain was purple with rage that a nuclear boat as vital as his should be used in an asinine effort to sink a lousy little patrol boat.

It was there that Tony Lynch's imagination moved beyond

the admiral's. "Would you feel better if it was more than one lousy little patrol boat? We're really very good at this kind of thing." He said afterward that he understood exactly how the sub's captain felt and that everyone should really get their money's worth.

The submarine captain had worked with SEALs before. He grinned. "Yeah. I really would feel a lot better."

There were no defenses against swimmers in Benghazi Harbor. There probably wasn't a soul in the entire city who'd ever considered such a thing—even when the Americans were exercising offshore. Why would anyone go to all that trouble for such a small target?

Ryng and Lynch had come in using SPUs, dragging the explosive with them. When they surfaced five hundred yards out in the harbor, Benghazi was lit up like a cruise ship. The docks were perfectly outlined against the lights, and Tony Lynch easily identified the depot where the patrol boats took on their fuel. One of the boats was close enough to the depot to make it look as if it all might be caused by the same blast.

Ryng moved away toward the patrol boat. If that survived, he'd never hear the end of it. He could hang up any chance of promotion when his time came. There was no one patrolling the piers that he could see, no lights on in the boat they'd selected. He set the explosive aft, near the fuel tanks. It would all seem natural.

He couldn't see Lynch, but he could almost predict each motion Tony made as he did his part. They'd rehearsed it all while the sub was working in as close to shore as the captain dared to go. Unless there was a glitch, everything would go up at the same time.

Tony rejoined him ten minutes later. They were back aboard the submarine in time to watch through the periscopes as both blasts erupted simultaneously.

"Captain"—Lynch motioned with one hand, his face still glued to the eyepiece—"is this worth all the trouble?"

The captain's smile broadened as he peered at the flames

rising over Benghazi's shorefront, blotting out the city lights. "I knew you guys were good, but I can't imagine how you can do something like that with just one blast," he said enthusiastically. "But the admiral's going to love it."

The admiral was overjoyed. He'd only seen a faint glow on the horizon from the flag bridge on the carrier, but the translation of the news from Libya the following morning made his day. It had been so perfect he'd even sent an official message to Qaddafi offering American assistance.

Yeah, Ryng murmured to himself as he drifted off to sleep that night, *it's wonderful to be working with an idea man like Tony again.*

Juan Duran was just like a peacock showing off a new uniform for his cabinet meeting. Once again it was one of his own designs. The high neck of the tunic had been borrowed from Qaddafi. Duran added broad shoulder boards covered with gold filigree for emphasis, and there were four new medals especially struck for him.

Castro's meetings had been informal, held around a circular table intended to invite participation from everyone. Duran had changed that format immediately. Round was junked in favor of rectangular so that members sat in order of their power, the strongest near the head where Duran was installed on a dais looking down on them. It was a symbol to anyone who remembered Fidel's boisterous sessions. Duran preferred to dictate rather than listen.

"They were landed in Cienfuegos, a few weeks ago, I understand," the defense minister answered irritably.

Duran glared at his intelligence director. "And you claim that not one person in your entire organization was aware of this."

"Not at the time." The man bristled just enough to show that he didn't believe he should be faulted for this one. "That ship was on a normal schedule. She'd called in Cienfuegos six times previously. Her cargo was always military supplies, and she always left with sugar. There was no reason to suspect anything—and there is still none at this point. . . ." he insisted adamantly.

"You're taking chances you can't afford—" Duran interrupted, halting midway in the sentence only because Cara placed a hand on his arm. He brushed it away but concluded less threateningly. "I expect you to furnish a written report of the incident with recommendations on how to avoid such breakdowns in the future. And I expect to see some heads roll by tomorrow at this time as an example to the rest of your people. Questions?" The expression on his face was enough to limit additional reaction from the intelligence chief.

"Where are they now?" Duran had turned to his chief of staff, Ricardo Nieves.

"They apparently drifted into the Russian barracks north of the city. There's a Soviet engineer battalion billeted on the Palmira road."

"What are they doing there?"

Nieves spoke up irritably. "We don't really know . . . probably training of some kind. They've kept quiet enough so that none of my people have noticed anything unusual—"

Duran's voice cut the air like the crack of a pistol shot. "Probably?" he bellowed. "You sit there as my chief of staff and say *probably*?" He half rose from his chair, leaning in the other man's direction with his palms flat on the table for balance. "You don't really know if that Spetznaz unit is in that camp . . . or in Guantánamo . . . or right here in Havana . . . or maybe in the countryside making you look as stupid as I think you really are." He scooped up some papers from the table and threw them in the direction of Nieves. Then his right arm rose slowly until Duran was pointing between the man's eyes with a shaking index finger. "You read those messages—those right there—and you tell me where you think those Spetznaz are. If you think what's happening in those villages near Cienfuegos is anything other than Spetznaz, then you don't deserve to leave this room alive." Duran's rage increased as he spoke, his entire arm shaking in anger. "I trained for months with those Spetznaz and I know exactly how they operate. Cuban soldiers are too stupid to accomplish what's happening out there." He shook his head sadly. "What do you think happened to that poor stupid colonel from the Cienfuegos Barracks . . . that ox and his sacrificial lambs who have disappeared?"

Once again Cara Estrada was beside him, a hand on his shoulder. This time she spoke to him so softly that not even the closest member of the cabinet could understand her.

Duran sat back in the chair, his face flushed. In a low voice he said, "I want each of you to go out to the next room and read those. In ten minutes I expect you back in your places with some answers as to how you're going to face that. I already know what I'm going to do, but I want to see if any of you can figure it out." In almost a whisper he concluded, "It takes weeks . . . just a few weeks . . . for a good Spetznaz team to control the peasants."

When the door closed behind the last person, Cara cautioned, "You can't allow them to witness outbursts like that. It's easier to intimidate people quietly than with noise. When you shout like that, they're afraid—but only for their own neck at the moment. There is more respect among men like that when you very quietly ask one of them to leave the room because he has displeased you, and then he is never seen again. You said that yourself not two months ago."

Duran looked down at his hands before nodding in agreement. "Qaddafi explained that to me. One night when we were camped at Assdadah, he was explaining how he controlled men." His face softened and he smiled as he reached over to pat Cara's hand. "It wasn't a conversation, it was a lecture. He did all the talking. I listened. He didn't even like to hear someone else when he was explaining political theories . . . or the psychology of commanding people . . . or even how to manage women.

You are, of course, correct, and I was wrong to express anger like that. I don't know why I lost control like that. It just happened.'' Duran rubbed his eyes. ''I simply can't condone stupidity. Maybe I should take a vacation.''

''Is that what you want to do?''

He studied Cara's face for a moment, saw that she was serious, and answered, ''Not at all. Not when Moscow and Washington think they're going to get rid of me and have their own way with Cuba again. How could I take a minute away from all this when they've offered me this challenge? Why, I'm going to have the Russians and the Americans fighting each other before they understand what happened. Before they understand what they're up against, they're going to find their people coming home in wooden boxes.''

''Why not just let them know that you're aware of what they're trying to do, or take your case to the UN? You don't have to do everything yourself . . .''

''But that's the part I want to do. That's where the fun comes in—beating them at their own game.'' Then his attitude altered completely, as if the curtain that Cara had opened moments before had suddenly come crashing down. ''I think that when my cabinet returns, I shall dismiss them all. They're going to have so many stupid ideas of what to do . . . and I don't have time to listen. I'll appoint people who understand how I want things to be done. But first I'm going to beat those Spetznaz at their own game. We can't catch up to them, but we can wait for them. Maybe,'' he concluded thoughtfully, ''they'd like to meet the real Scorpions. I'll have Major Gomes take a platoon of his best down there. If he can't take their squads one by one, then he'll find their base camp. When these Spetznaz squads return . . . we'll teach them . . . .''

Cara said nothing. Each day Duran's mood shifts became more unpredictable. She had no idea whether he really would remove these people, many of whom had supported him before coming to power. Their loyalty had recently been questioned more than she cared to remember, yet they were steadfast in their devotion to Duran. They were willing to allow him to increase his power as he saw fit, even if they were sacrificed in the process. Now he was going to personally challenge the killers who had been sent into his country to destroy him by playing their game. It made no sense to send in a platoon when he should ensure the job was done properly with a battalion—as many as it took to eradicate these people.

She was increasingly unsure of her own motives as each day passed, and even more confused by a growing realization that the only being Juan Duran could give himself to completely was—Juan Duran! There were too many nights when she found herself having to mollify him with sex because he had no more love to offer.

The intelligence director acted as the spokesman for a properly subdued cabinet when they filed back into the room. "We have a series of recommendations . . . now that we are aware of the information in these messages," he added. "If we might very humbly request, it would mean a great deal to us to be aware of such data before these meetings are called. Then we could give you the advice that you require—"

"I will make necessary information available in the future as I see fit." Then Duran's expression changed, displaying an affability that had been nonexistent seconds before. "It is difficult to read my mind. I admit that. I'll make an effort to disperse my plans more in the future. Now, how do you feel we should solve our mutual problem?" He had become the mirror image of cooperation.

Even Cara was amused by the ideas that had been hastily conceived by men who feared for their necks as much as their jobs. Some were simplistic to the point of incompetence, others overly sophisticated. None pleased Duran because the objective of each concept was to appease both the Russians and the Americans, and he had no intention of that.

"What we will do is eradicate the Spetznaz force," he announced. "Since my intelligence network has no idea how many of them are in the countryside and how many remain at the engineers' barracks, we will send out search-and-destroy units under Major Gomes. He was highly decorated for the same type of operation in Angola. He'll eliminate those teams in the villages—and our people will see real Cuban soldiers wearing the Scorpion badge when they do it." He indicated his most senior general with a wave of his hand. "By the end of the day, I want the Soviet engineers' barracks surrounded. No one leaves. The Spetznaz are on our soil illegally. Therefore, we will also destroy the barracks and everyone inside as punishment for this invasion. No survivors to tell tales . . . naturally."

Cara Estrada shuddered as she listened to the solution. They were in no position to challenge the Soviets in that manner!

Bernie Ryng was fascinated when Duran's decision was related to him through the priests. He would have thought that after taking Spetznaz training himself, Duran would realize that not even his crack Scorpion troops were up to handling the Russians. It would be even more absurd if someone warned the Spetznaz ahead of time—and that was exactly what he had Antonio Lynch do. The Russians would not understand the favor, but they would certainly be willing to make the most of it.

CHAPTER NINE

Cara Estrada paused outside the old church, staring up the stone steps at the massive wooden doors closed against the midday heat. She squinted against the sun's reflection, brilliant on the rough eggshell-dappled walls. Flies buzzed over a mongrel dog flopped in the shadows.

She was in simple street clothes with flat shoes and wore dark glasses. Pulling nervously at the black mantilla that covered her face, she slowly mounted the worn stone stairs. Father Allende's understanding voice seemed to float out to her as if she were dreaming. Not once had he ever criticized her. His tone remained soft, encouraging her to say whatever came to her mind, nodding whenever she hesitated. Yet . . . she was still outside . . . the voice was in her mind!

The last few days were fused together in her mind. There was no order, nothing coherent that could separate reality from dream. She retained the stark images of the victims mounting the steps to be judged at the New Plaza of the Revolution—always guilty, never mistaken for another. Under Juan Duran's system, the safest player in the game was the accuser. So many were taken away each day to die . . . some more horribly than others. And, too often now, the women continued to be stripped and beaten—yes, that had become popular, especially among the men who came out to watch during the midday break. Duran had solidified his support among that group.

Thank you, Father Allende, for your patience, for listening to me. There was no sound, no movement of her lips, just the silent thanks. Then, looking up at the outside of the heavy doors, she realized that once again it had all been in her mind. Father was in the church; she was outside. She hadn't been pouring out her heart to him at that moment . . . it was all so confusing . . .

The door always pulled open with remarkable ease considering how heavy it appeared. A rush of cool air washed over her face, followed by the pervasive musty odor familiar to old churches. It was so reassuring that she pulled the door shut as quickly as possible. As she proceeded across to the urn of holy water, her steps on the worn stone floor a hollow echo, the perfume of the candles burning near the altar tickled her nose. The scraping sound of each step seemed to emphasize an additional concern that she must discuss with Father Allende.

She dipped her hand in the holy water, made the sign of the cross, and moved slowly down the aisle of the empty church. There was no sign of Father Allende, so she stopped by the entrance to the front pew, genuflecting in a hurried motion toward the cross above the altar. Kneeling inside the pew, she lowered her head onto folded hands and began to mouth the prayers that had seemed so hollow to her as she was growing up. The words had never before meant a thing to her—mumbled only out of habit in the past. Now each word conveyed a comfortable message to her troubled mind.

Cara's head came around with a start as she sensed another person kneeling only a few feet away. It was Father Allende, his eyes shut as his lips moved with the same simple words she, herself, had been saying. She couldn't keep herself from staring as she waited for him to finish. Father was not in the mold of the priests she had known in her youth. He was still in his thirties, an intelligent, curious man who had once taught in a Jesuit school before requesting a parish of his own. Father Allende was popular with the few people her age who bothered to attend church anymore, and most had chosen his because it was in the Almendares district on the outskirts of Havana. There was little chance of being recognized by their peers in that part of the city.

He finished his prayers and turned to Cara, his usually smiling features set in stone. "I was afraid you might not come today."

"Why?"

"Oh, nothing special." He fumbled for the words. "One . . . one of the young men in the Ministry of Agriculture was seen coming in here a few weeks ago. He told me that he'd been questioned about it, and he hasn't returned since then. I guess I just thought you might be scared away."

"I am scared, Father, but not of coming here." The words astounded her, yet they were so easy to speak—and she meant them! It wasn't so long ago—less than a year, months even—that she had been planning the details of a revolution of sorts. That had been her strength, ensuring that the minutiae required in such a plan would not harm the objective. Cara Estrada, Duran's composer for Fidel Castro's overthrow, was now kneeling in a small church on Avenue 27 in the Almendares district months later, hoping that she could somehow make up for a horrible mistake.

"Why don't we talk in my office today?" His expression seemed almost haunted, and she noticed he wouldn't look in her eyes as he spoke.

"No, Father, right now I still need the security of confession." What she could not force herself to say yet was that she also required the confidentiality of the confessional, until she was sure that Father Allende could be wholly trusted. Even amidst the confusion of Juan Duran's erratic behavior, Cara's sense of survival remained strong.

"Of course I understand." What Father Allende couldn't say was that he had to violate her confidence eventually. He had been well counseled, though. One of his new friends, the one called Lynch, had suggested that he confer with the bishop. There had been no problem making an appointment with the bishop—strange, he thought now as he waited inside the tiny booth—just as Lynch had suggested. The priests who served the bishop would not listen to him beyond his explanation that through the confessional he was privy to facts that affected the security of the country. They agreed that he must speak to the bishop. The latter allowed the frightened priest to explain his problems, then explained in detail that Allende would not be violating any vows if what he had heard was also repeated outside the confessional. Father Allende returned to his church with renewed faith in his religion and his church's devotion to righting the wrongs that were tearing apart his country.

Now, as Father Allende waited for the woman, his mind strayed back to the man, Lynch, whom he had originally thought was related to Ché. His father had known Ché —Ernesto "Ché" Guevara Lynch had been his full name— when he was in the Sierra Maestre with Fidel, before those leaders had also become politicians. Father Allende experienced just a touch of pride, perhaps magnified a bit by the rum at times, when he explained how his father had fought with Ché, before asking Antonio Lynch if he was related to the great man. And he was just a bit disappointed when Lynch replied that there was no relationship there—sadly. The priest's thoughts were interrupted as the troubled lady began.

"Bless me, Father . . . for I have sinned . . ." Those first words were more difficult for Cara Estrada to say, for she did not really believe in sin, at least not in that form.

But this seemed the only way she could explain the problems that were weighing so heavily on her conscience.

This woman doesn't really believe she has sinned, the priest realized after a few minutes. *She is attempting to atone for the sins of others.* As he listened to her sad monologue, many of the incidents a repetition of what she had mentioned previously, the words of the Bishop of Havana came back to him: *"Our responsibility to the people of Cuba goes beyond that to the government. Liberation theology is an effort by religious leaders to reach a middle ground with the Marxists, but it is not a responsibility. When the people suffer at the hands of the government, it is our duty to respond to their needs. If you ever are certain that that woman—or anyone else who comes to you—indicates a need beyond that which you are able to offer, make this office aware."* Strange words, Father Allende thought, especially now that her troubled mind was relating a great deal that the bishop had anticipated during their discussion. Since the priest was definitely not a communist, he was in almost total sympathy with the bishop's objectives, and he knew now that he must follow those instructions.

"Stop!" The priest's words echoed like the crack of thunder through the tiny booth.

He saw her head, gradually drooping down to her chest as she spoke, snap around as if she had been struck. She could only see his shadow on the other side. "What . . . what did you say?" she whispered in astonishment.

"Stop." This time it was no longer an order. He repeated it softly as if afraid of his own sharpness. "I can't allow you to continue."

"Please . . ."

"No. You aren't telling me of *your* sins. They are someone else's. You are trying to atone for their sins. It can't be done . . . not here . . . not this way."

When Cara Estrada realized what he was saying, she experienced a moment of sheer terror. She couldn't trust the priest. She rose as if to go, turning slightly to assure herself that it really was Father Allende on the opposite side and not one of Duran's men. She released an audible sigh of relief as she recognized his black vestments and his familiar bald head.

The priest spoke to her as he had been asked the day before. "I will help you all that I can because what you have been saying goes well beyond the confines of the Church. You need help. You are in danger. There are people who can assist you, and I will arrange for you to speak with them." He emphasized this with the sign of the cross, as much for himself as for her, aware that eventually he, too, would be in need of confession.

Jorge Anaya considered his reflection in the floor-to-ceiling mirror. There were times when he'd imagined himself as the leader of his country, for he had no doubts that a man trained in the law was necessary to return the inherent rights of the people. A few of those now on the court were too old. The others were simply afraid of displaying independence and were willing to dispense justice as they felt the power structure in Havana preferred. Anaya had found that his boldness in dissenting from the party line—Castro's previously, Duran's now—had brought little criticism. Apparently the government preferred disagreement, as long as it was in the minority, for this allowed the trappings of the legal system to appear independent. He had even received verbal support from other quarters.

He hadn't been fooled by that Colonel Sanchez for long. While the man's story and his appearance were perfectly logical, the whole package just hadn't rung true—the way he spoke, a disturbing affectation on certain words, his too-perfect choice of idioms. It was the way a man would speak a second language that he had mastered in the classroom, but it was unlikely that a professional soldier would speak with such precision.

Anaya had an aide check out the name. There was a Fernando Sanchez stationed at Pinar del Río, but he was a major. Another, a young lieutenant, was at Manzanillo. There was a third, who had indeed been a colonel and stationed at the nearby Columbia Barracks, but that Sanchez had disappeared on the first day of the revolution. Apparently it was the latter's name that had been assumed. Anaya would know more after tonight, for he had made arrangements for Sanchez to be followed.

There were rumors, denied by the government, that became stronger each day concerning the presence of a new Soviet unit in the country. The purpose, Anaya had learned from more than one source, was to respond to the anti-Soviet attitude of Juan Duran. It was indeed possible that Moscow may have decided that their major Caribbean satellite was not well served by the new government. If they had determined that Jorge Anaya was a possible candidate to replace Duran, then he was indeed flattered.

He would certainly offer a more appealing presence than either Castro or Duran. The reflection in the mirror was of a handsome, proud man, one who appeared every inch a leader. Anaya had been very careful in outfitting himself this time. He'd been too casual at their first meeting because he had no firm idea of what the man called Sanchez would suggest. Now that they were again having a meeting, it called for appropriate dress. Supreme Court Justice Jorge Anaya wore what he assumed a man might wear to his own inauguration when he stepped out his door. He sensed the future was his to manipulate.

And when he returned that evening, the surface flush from the rum and wine they had consumed was compounded by an inner glow of pride. While Sanchez had yet to reveal who he really was or even whom he represented, it was quite obvious to both men that they had a mutual understanding of each other.

Antonio Lynch was capable of developing an intelligence network that would have astounded the professionals, if they had ever been aware of his talent. Large organizations like the KGB or the CIA depended on bureaucracies to establish and support their systems. Smaller countries too often had to create makeshift units combining their own people with pay-for-hire help, and the latter were only useful until a higher offer came from someone else. Lynch's system evolved through assimilation, and Bernie Ryng was one of the few who understood how efficient that could be.

Lynch's theory, if it could even be called that, was simplistic: There had never been a government without detractors. Isolate those who harbored the most hatred and one had a ready-made base; make those people believe that they were contributing to the eventual downfall of the object of their hatred and a network was established. If you didn't ask too many questions, these people were willing to dig for intelligence in their own way, which would have taken twice the time and manpower if coordinated by the professionals. For some strange reason that even Lynch was unable to explain, such a system also inspired tremendous loyalty—perhaps because each individual involved knew that every other was taking the same chances for the same reasons, a common objective. The CIA and the KGB were much too complex to provide such motivation.

Lynch located the Spetznaz group outside the village of El Naranjo, close to the main highway to Havana. While they had done a superb job as a Cuban Scorpion unit to antagonize the peasants in the district, they had done an even better job of covering their tracks. Cuban army units from the Cienfuegos Barracks had no idea where they were, only where they had been. But Lynch's network had been able to follow their progress, pleased that the Russians were accomplishing exactly what they had set out to do. Dissension was spreading rapidly through the countryside

When he came down the jungle trail, his bad arm hanging limply at his side, Tony Lynch was holding the halter of one of the saddest mules Sergeant Kurochkin had ever seen. Although its master appeared a victim of life's cruelties, this poor animal demanded increasing pity with each step. Its ears hung limply down either side of a scarred face. One eye was completely shut, the other as mournful as Kurochkin had ever seen. Its sad gray coat was covered with mud and its tail was tangled in briars. Each step seemed the last because of the weight of the woven baskets slung over its back.

"*Compadre,*" Kurochkin called out, "it looks like you both need to sit down for a time. Will you have something to eat?" Through every step of his training the Russian had been taught to be suspicious of anything new that came near him. But this pitiful sight had touched a tired man.

Lynch stumbled as he neared the clearing. Only a firm grip on the rope around the beast's neck kept him from falling. It seemed that the poor mule would collapse before its master. One of the soldiers rushed over to take the halter.

"*Gracias, señor . . . gracias . . . gracias,*" Lynch repeated as he shuffled over to sit on a rude bench in the clearing.

"That animal of yours looks like he's ready to retire. Why don't you let him have his final days in a pasture?"

"If I did, then I'd have to carry everything on my back." Lynch gladly accepted the food brought to him, eating as if it were his last meal.

Kurochkin grinned. "That's what we're here for, to see that the poor people get what they need." In the field he insisted on maintaining the charade to the end.

Lynch's expression brightened. "You really would find me another mule?"

The Russian nodded.

"How soon could I have it?"

"Oh, you're an anxious one."

Lynch gestured at the forlorn mule. "But look at him. You're right. He needs to rest. . . ."

"Then we'll find you another mule as soon as you've eaten your fill." It would certainly make an impression if they appropriated a mule from one of the middle class to give to this poor fellow. "You can come with me in the truck when you're ready."

When Kurochkin headed down the dirt road in the truck with Lynch, he explained that they would look for a farm that had more than it needed. Then they would simply choose whatever mule appeared to be a fit replacement. Although they weren't after the political support of the lower classes, this peasant could prove to be a useful tool to antagonize those who supported Duran's government. Kurochkin was enjoying himself as they passed down the dirt roads.

"You let your guard down, Sergeant. You'd be dead now if I was the enemy." Lynch's words were crisp and taunting.

The Russian's hands froze momentarily on the wheel. His foot eased off the gas pedal but never touched the brake. Slowly, as if expecting to see the business end of a gun barrel, he turned his head. The eyes that stared back at Kurochkin were bright and intelligent, a hint of amusement appearing at the corners.

"I'm not armed," Lynch said. "Why don't you keep on driving. I can assure you I don't need another mule. As a matter of fact, I had to drug that poor thing to make him pull at your heartstrings." The Russian still hadn't touched the gas. "If you prefer, we can pull over to talk. . . ."

Kurochkin found his tongue. "How did you find us?"

"I thought the first question would be who am I?" Lynch beamed as he added, "It really wouldn't be very smart to explain how I found you. Then I might not be able to do it again. And you can bet your ass you might have been very dead shortly if I hadn't decided to come out here and warn you."

"Warn me about what?"

"That Duran has sent some troops out here to kill you."

"People try to do that all the time. Some halfwit colonel, from Cienfuegos, I guess, came out with a truckload of his men. I suppose he was going to get a promotion for solving the problem before Duran even knew he had one. None of them fired a shot."

"I'd heard about that. But I wouldn't be so impressed with myself for killing off some troops who'd hardly ever heard a gunshot before," Lynch said with a grin.

Kurochkin found his wits and pulled the truck over to the side of the road. He turned to study the man in the passenger seat more closely. "As you can see, I remain very much alive. Anyone who has tried to kill me is very dead."

"The ones I'm talking about aren't your average troops. They're more like the Scorpions, the ones whose uniforms you're wearing now. The reason is because they're the real thing—the ones so highly decorated in Angola. And they won't be the type who serve themselves up for dessert. It wouldn't be some dumb attack. Ambush is their specialty. If you don't want to believe me"—he shrugged—"then I'll be on my way. . . ."

Kurochkin understood this man very well; he was almost as much Spetznaz as himself. "You're not making any move to leave."

"I expected that you'd listen to me."

"If these Cuban troops are really the Scorpions, can I assume they will try to operate in the same manner as we have?"

Lynch shook his head. "Like I would."

The Russian nodded thoughtfully. "And you are . . ."

"Voronov may tell you when you see him next."

Again Kurochkin's face expressed shock.

"In Havana. He was seen on the street. When he gets back, I'm sure he'll tell you that he knows a SEAL is in the country. He recognized our man."

Kurochkin looked down at the arm hanging loosely at Lynch's side. "And you, are you a SEAL?"

"No, not with this—I'm what they call support personnel instead. That's how I found you. We all have talents." He grinned at the Russian. "My specialty is finding Spetznaz."

Kurochkin ignored him. "Why are you warning me? What's your purpose?" he asked.

"We don't want to take the blame for what happens to you. That's simple enough. And we're in Cuba for approximately the same reasons you are." Lynch looked pensive. "Who knows what else? Some of the orders I get are pretty strange, but it's not my place to ask about them." He caught the Russian's eyes and held them for a minute. "There's no reason for me to stay around here any longer, is there?"

Kurochkin shook his head.

Lynch winked. "You can see that the mule gets a nice home." He opened the door and stepped down from the truck. "And nobody should try to follow me. If they do, I might not be able to save your life next time, Sergeant. Agreed?"

"You don't want to stay to see what happens?"

"No reason to. I already know how you operate. You'll do just fine." Lynch waved with his left arm. "Sorry our meeting was so short. But I knew you'd learn fast."

CHAPTER TEN

There were enough Miami television stations broadcasting in Spanish to reach almost anywhere in Cuba with the modern relay systems that existed. But Juan Duran's favorite news continued to be on an English station, one that included the network newscasts. Perhaps his preference was colored by the fact that Cuban expatriates ran the Spanish stations, and they tended to be predominantly hard-liners. The American reporters were generally liberal and sensitive to the Havana government. They possessed an understanding of Duran's intentions that oftentimes surprised even him. Guidelines—that's what they seemed to provide whenever he was in doubt about the Americans. Their analyses and predictions concerning Juan Duran were what he often utilized to establish policy toward the United States.

That evening he'd watched his threats—especially the not-too-veiled hints about Third World terrorism on the American mainland—considered in Washington by the Congress, and he was pleased to see their effect. With few exceptions, there were many who stated that American interference in the government in Havana would bring nothing but grief to Washington. Duran's challenges were in concert with an inconsistent policy ranging from indifference toward Havana to outright interference in Cuban affairs. Economic strangulation, military intervention, social isolation—it was a litany that must change now that a new face had appeared on the scene. Cuba's new leader had acquired a romantic following on American university campuses rivaling that of Fidel thirty years before. U.S. students were amused by what they imagined as David tweaking Goliath's nose.

Washington deserved it all, he decided with good humor. If his actions toward the United States could be deemed policy, then it was working more rapidly than anticipated. Duran had learned in the desert that the best way—the only way—to handle the giant countries was to antagonize them in public. Never do anything to them that wouldn't create headlines. But, above all else, make them appear greedy and brutal. Make yourself appear small but determined in the face of impossible odds. Attract sympathy to your cause—it doesn't really matter what the cause may be. Those attracted to it will be enchanted by emotion rather than reality.

And *fear*—there was still nothing more effective than good old-fashioned fear. The United States apparently had never been able to accurately trace those early attacks in Miami and New Orleans to Havana, at least not to the stage that they could get the American people to accept, nor had they been able to prove any of the other, smaller efforts—no more "Remember the *Maine*," Duran mused.

Duran's seeds of fear had been planted early. They germinated with surprising vigor. The new government in Cuba was not about to cower from the strength in Washington. They could, and would, strike back. Perhaps there was no chance of defeating such a superpower, but retaliation against years of humiliation was still possible. That was the idea Juan Duran was able to project across the narrow span of saltwater that separated these opposing ideologies. To date, it had been effective, more so in the United States than in his own country. Many of the Cuban people, especially early supporters of the new government, were still enjoying the holiday that was Juan Duran.

Even that evening, as Duran switched from one station to the next to hear the news from the United States, he was struck by his own brilliance. The American people, at least the students and certain liberal elements, were perhaps bored enough to look south for a fresh face and a cause. Considering their attentiveness, and sometimes their attention span, it seemed a perfect time for another foray to impress Washington even further.

He pressed the button on the speaker by his desk and asked that Major Pagos be sent to his office. Perhaps Captain Maceo would join Pagos this time? What might the two of them together be able to accomplish?

As he waited his thoughts momentarily turned to his Scorpion troops. Had he acted too quickly? They were his elite . . . the pride of the Angola conflict. The officers and men who had survived to be welcomed home as heroes had done their duty. Was it fair to send them out to take care of the Spetznaz after they'd already made such a great sacrifice?

Then Juan Duran realized what he was really concerned about. He'd been trained with the Spetznaz. He understood only too well how they operated, and there was a marked difference between the two groups. His Scorpions were combat troops, the cream of the Cuban military. Spetznaz were unconventional warriors who traded in stealth and ambush. The former captured objectives, the latter eradicated whatever stood in their way, generally without ever being seen.

Had his anger forced a too-swiftly made decision that would jeopardize his Scorpions? Cuba had no special forces equal to Spetznaz. After thinking more on the subject, he was about to issue new orders. It was sheer foolishness to force his Scorpion unit to play a game they simply weren't trained for. But Major Pagos was announced from the outer office, and the excitement of a new adventure on American soil whisked such concerns from his mind.

General Major Komarov had been dutifully impressed, even a little concerned, with everything General Dotov conveyed from Moscow concerning Paul Voronov. Unfortunately, the first and only visit the man had made to the Santa Fe headquarters upon arriving in Cuba confirmed what Komarov had begun to fear most—the man had little respect for authority and no regard for the chain of command. No matter how much he tried to prepare himself, the general simply wasn't looking forward to their next meeting.

As it was, Paul Voronov arrived at Santa Fe unannounced. Komarov looked up from his desk with irritation when his door flew open without the usual knock. "Your security clearances are a pathetic shame to our entire intelligence system, General."

For just a moment Komarov was caught completely off guard. Anger nearly brought him to his feet, but his reaction was tempered by years of discipline. He was damned if this colonel would have that satisfaction. The man wore no uniform. He was dressed like a native. Yet there was a look in his eyes, a don't-take-a-chance-with-me warning, that told Komarov to temper his reaction. "I realize, Colonel, that you are under direct orders from Moscow. However, since this is a military unit, I would ask that in the future you respect simple courtesies in line with the discipline I insist on from those military personnel assigned here."

"Stuff your military courtesies." Voronov's facial expression changed even as Komarov was speaking, eyes narrowing, repressed anger surfacing as he digested the inane words from the man behind the desk. "You're in no position to talk like that to me as long as you have men like this working for you." He threw a black-and-white photograph on the desk.

Komarov was taken by surprise. Instead of reacting angrily, he stared down at the photo. He saw a man who looked somewhat familiar and a very attractive woman he didn't know at all. She appeared to be extremely happy, sitting in the man's lap and waving at the camera. He was less excited, a look of what might have been surprise on his face. The table beside them was covered with beer bottles and glasses. The general glanced up at a glaring Voronov, then back down again at the photo. "So . . ." he began without looking at the other.

"Do you recognize the man?" It was a command demanding a response.

"I don't know . . . he looks familiar maybe . . ."

"Voloshin, Feodor. Cryptanalyst—Department K. A civilian employee of yours who learned his trade in the army. How about the woman?"

Komarov shook his head. "No. I'd recognize her. I don't have anyone who looks like that." Then his rank got the better of him. "Just what the hell . . ." He started to get up.

"Sit down, General. No need to be formal in my presence," Voronov snarled. "That's the source, the leak I questioned the first day I came here. No wonder Duran knows everything we're doing. You're broadcasting every move we make. That very attractive woman belongs to Duran's Dirección General de Inteligencia—what we call KGB in Moscow. And I'll bet you don't have to guess what she does best." Voronov was leaning over the general's desk now, his face very close to the other man's. "She does just what ours do. She screws for information, or, rather, she screws it out of our people. And you've got a singer there, General. For a little bit of strange flesh he almost had me and all of my men killed."

Komarov looked up at the man leaning over his desk. There was more than a hint of danger in those icy blue eyes now. Everything he'd heard about this Voronov was being confirmed. "Who took this picture?"

"Does it matter?"

"Do you know who took it?" Komarov asked more firmly.

"I did," Voronov responded with finality. "I put one of my men on this the minute I suspected the problem was right here in Santa Fe. It was easy enough to figure out. Even you or one of your own people could have done it if you'd been concerned enough. But then, General, your neck wasn't in any danger, was it?"

"Colonel, you're taking a chance . . ."

"No need to warn me about anything." Voronov continued to lean on the general's desk, staring accusingly at the man who ran the largest intelligence station outside the Soviet Union. "I'm well aware of my bounds, and if I get total cooperation from you from this moment on, you might just finish your career in the army. Now, before I kill that man, can you think of anything else pertinent to the situation?"

"That woman in the picture—" Komarov faltered. "What about her?"

"Dead. We left her body at the foot of the steps where she works. There was a message attached to her that said, 'This is what happens to people who spy on the Soviet Union.' "

Komarov paled. "Do you realize the trouble that will cause?" He shook his head. "Are you crazy, Voronov?"

"I wanted to make sure the message got through to the right people. You see, the body was timed to explode a few hours ago. I hope she took some of her compatriots with her," Voronov concluded nastily.

Yes, the general silently acknowledged, *they told me exactly what to expect, but* . . . "But . . ." he began, searching for the right words, "I was told to continue a covert operation . . . not to give them any hint that—"

"I was told the same thing, and I follow my orders until the situation alters itself. It changed yesterday. I received this wild message yesterday from our barracks near Cienfuegos that Duran had decided to get us out of the way. Because your security was worthless, he knew everything he needed to know about me and my team." Voronov's tone had begun to increase in pitch. "And his answer was to eliminate us. He's sent one of the special units out to ambush one of our own."

"He wouldn't take the chance . . ."

"Not only would he, General, but he's detailed his famous Scorpions. You know, I sort of wish I'd thought about that myself. He probably has similar plans for our other units, too. That is a superb way of weakening us in front of the Americans here."

"That's absurd." General Komarov was finally on his feet. "There are no Americans on this island."

"I can assure you there is at least one American SEAL here already, and I have no idea how many others there might be. No one can ever be sure about them." Voronov perched on the corner of the general's desk. He suppressed a tremendous urge to grasp the man by the throat. "You want to know how I learned there are Americans on the island? I can't see any point in keeping a secret from the man who directs Soviet intelligence in the Western Hemisphere." He paused to enjoy the look of pure hatred in Komarov's eyes. For the first time since he'd entered the office, his lips curled slightly to reveal a malevolent smile. "The Americans actually tracked down Sergeant Kurochkin's base. They didn't want me to think they had anything to do with any ambush—especially when I'd given them no reason yet."

Komarov came from behind the desk. "If your information is false," he asserted, pointing a finger at Voronov, "you're going to regret this intrusion for the rest of your life."

Voronov turned toward the door, dismissing the threat with a wave of his hand. "Do you care to see how Spetznaz handle traitors?"

Komarov was still attempting to gain lost ground. "If there is any proof of such activity under my command, I will personally—" But he was unable to finish, as Voronov stalked out the door.

The general's office was situated at the end of a long hallway. The occupants of the other offices were treated to the sight of Komarov trailing after a civilian, apparently muttering veiled comments under his breath. The general paused in the doorway of the head of the cryptanalysis section long enough to growl a not-so-veiled threat.

Voronov knew exactly where he was going because a proud Komarov had shown his guest quickly through the spaces the day he had arrived; now Komarov was hustling to catch up. Voronov pushed through a door at the end of another hall into a large room crammed with machines and electronic devices. Startled men and women, military and civilian, looked up in amazement as he strode by them with the general in tow.

The unfortunate Voloshin was one of the last to realize that the stranger was approaching him. By the time he looked up he recognized death bearing down on him. His eyes mirrored deep horror as he recognized the man who had photographed him the previous evening. He was unable to move, unable to breathe. Grabbing Voloshin by the shirt, Voronov dragged him bodily from behind his desk then bent him backward across it.

A powerful hand grasped Voloshin by the throat. "You do remember me, don't you?"

The terrified man saw the general stalking toward him. "I don't understand—" His voice died as his head slammed hard against the desk.

"There's only one answer I want to each of my questions." Paul Voronov's voice was level now, demanding, and the implied threat in his tone was as devastating as his grip on the man's neck. "You are going to tell everyone in here how you violated their trust." He backhanded the man once, his movement so quick it was barely visible. Blood sprayed from his nose. "If you lie, or even hesitate, the pain increases. Understand?"

"But—" Voronov's same hand came back across his face, wrenching his nose in the opposite direction. Blood poured down his chin onto his shirt.

"I am an expert at this," Voronov hissed. "I've made brave men betray their mothers, and you are a nothing in comparison. You're a sniveling wretch who tried to have me and my men killed. Now you have very little time to make up your mind. Either you die more painfully than I intend for you, or you explain to your comrades how a traitor operates." He glanced over his shoulder at his horrified audience. Each remained exactly where he had been when Voronov stormed into the room. "All of you, come over close, right here by me"—he indicated with his free hand—"so you can hear what Voloshin has to say."

Not a soul moved. Their eyes shifted from Voronov to General Komarov and back again. They were experiencing Voloshin's terror and that fear seemed to rivet them in place.

"You will order them to join us," Voronov commanded the general.

Komarov, after some early hesitancy in his office, had become a quick learner. The stories about men like this Voronov had made interesting listening in officers' clubs in the past. Quite suddenly such tales had become a stark reality. "Do as he says."

They slowly moved in Voronov's direction, careful to remain a respectable distance from the bleeding Voloshin.

"Did I take a picture of you last night?" Voronov snarled.

The man nodded, tears streaming through the blood on his face.

"Answer me. Say it." His grip tightened on the man's throat.

"Yes," came the gurgled response.

"Was there a woman with you?"

"Yes."

"Her name?"

"Camilla."

"And who did she work for?"

No answer.

Voronov twisted the man's nose with his free hand and was rewarded with a scream of anguish.

"Cuban . . ." the man screamed, "Cuban Security . . ."

"Internal Security!" Voronov barked.

"Yes . . ."

"And you told her whatever she wanted to know!"

When the hesitation was obvious, Voronov, his hand still gripping the other's throat, slammed the man's head against the desk. Then, yanking him into a sitting position, he moved behind him and pulled his right arm behind his back. Voloshin's face and shirt were bathed in blood. He whimpered softly. Voronov looked out at the gathering. They had obeyed the general's order, forming a wide semicircle but remaining as far away as possible. Their shock negated conversation. General Komarov had also remained in place. He'd known such treatment was common, even accepted it as necessary in many cases, but had never before witnessed it.

"Now we will start again," Voronov stated to no one in particular. Then he barked, "What did you tell this Camilla?"

Voloshin's head gradually dropped lower in silence, then arched back with agony as the snap of a bone echoed through the room.

"That was your index finger. The thumb will be next—or

maybe your middle finger, the one you used on Camilla so many of those nights. Correct?'

"Yes." The sound hissed through clenched teeth.

"Did you tell her whatever she wanted to know?"

"Yes."

"Did you tell her there was a Spetznaz team in Cuba?"

Silence.

Another bone snapped and Voloshin cried out in agony.

"Maybe I will break your wrist instead . . . or your arm. Did you tell her we were in Cuba?"

"Yes . . . yes . . ."

"And you told her about me?"

"I . . . I don't know your name."

"Oh, yes, you do. I was told my name was used. What is my name?"

Whether or not the others in the room knew who Paul Voronov was, it seemed evident that Voloshin had known it. His head popped up and he looked about the room in terror. "I did know . . . but I don't remember now . . . please . . . I don't remember . . ."

Voronov's movement was so quick that none of the people watching realized at first exactly what was happening. He had reached behind his back, extracted a concealed knife, and in the same motion cut Voloshin's left ear off. It had been so rapid, so efficient, that some of them weren't sure of what they had witnessed, until the ear bounced from the desk to the floor. Then the screech from Voloshin's mouth, the rush of blood down his neck, confirmed the act.

"Voronov. Colonel Paul Voronov, Naval Infantry. Currently commanding the Spetznaz team that you so willingly told her about. You even gave her one unit's approximate location. And for what? What did she give you in return, Comrade Voloshin? Do you want to tell your comrades what she gave you to become a traitor to your country?" The point of the knife was now at the corner of Voloshin's left eye. His arm was firmly pinned against his back.

"There's more pain for you. Much more. You were hoping perhaps you'd pass out from it—that you might escape this agony. There's no chance, Voloshin. There's not enough pain to allow you to escape the easy way, but just enough to make you aware of everything that's happening to you. Maybe your eye will be the next to go. Tell everyone here what you received from Camilla."

"Sex . . . sex . . . sex . . . ." With each word his voice grew softer as he fought the pain. His whimpering became deep sobs.

"Was it worth all this? Did you learn new tricks from her? All your female comrades would like to know what these Cuban women do that would make a Russian man turn against his country." Blood began to ooze around the point of the knife at the corner of Voloshin's eye. "Come on, you can feel your eye beginning to bulge. Do you want everyone here to see your eye pop out?"

"No . . . no . . . please, no no no no no no . . . ." As he tried to pull away from the knife, he could feel it cutting deeper. "NO," he screamed. "I'll tell you anything you want to know."

With that, Voronov let the terrified creature go, allowing him to slide from the desk to the floor. He looked at each of the people in the room before his gaze fell on General Komarov. "Now you see what a traitor is really like. That piece of shit on the floor"—he pronounced each word slowly, separately—"was willing to kill me for a little flesh, a piece of ass that any of you can enjoy almost any day of the week with each other if you want . . . but he was going to have me killed for it." Again he savored each word. "That's what Spetznaz does to traitors. Let him be a lesson to each of you."

No one, not even Komarov, moved. Not a breath was heard as they stared at Voronov and the bloody knife resting in his hand.

"Well, General, where do you execute traitors around here?"

"We . . . we've never had one before . . ." Komarov began.

"Well, since I want everyone who knew this Voloshin, this piece of shit, to see how traitors die"—he bent over and grasped the man by the collar, lifting his head a few feet off the floor—"this is as good a place as any." With a motion again almost too fast to see, Voronov's knife lashed out. There was a muffled gurgle as he sliced Voloshin's throat open and dropped the body to the floor with a thud. "Consider him executed. You were all witnesses to the trial." As Voloshin's blood spread across the floor Voronov growled, "Any questions about why the Spetznaz was sent to Cuba?"

Sergeant Kurochkin knew the direction the Cuban unit was approaching from, and after learning when they departed Santa Clara, he was fairly certain as to what time they would appear. To an outsider his prescience might have seemed magical. His own men knew that it was simply innate ability compounded by years of experience. Kurochkin was one of the early Spetznaz, chosen for their training when the theories on NATO front warfighting began to change from nuclear confrontation to overwhelming force. That's when concept changed to hard reality with the planners.

It was no longer a matter of jousting with missiles. If a conflict actually evolved with NATO, the Spetznaz would be the first to fight. While it was preferable for them to have enough advance warning to infiltrate quietly behind enemy lines before the first shot was fired, they could also be inserted into the zone by parachute.

They became the special forces, the cream of Soviet ground troops, designed to destroy command posts, lines of communication, and fuel and ammunition depots. Their mission was not strategic—they were committed to striking when least expected, maximizing the element of surprise, and disappearing. They were not in the habit of taking prisoners.

Kurochkin was accepted for training because of his intelligence and inherent pleasure in fighting. He displayed a natural talent with every weapon they might ever use, and actually relished hand-to-hand combat. When this enthusiasm was translated into injuries to his peers during training, he was promoted quickly. The army encouraged such initiative and went to extremes to commit men like Kurochkin to a military career.

He had seen action in every part of the world and was experienced in training indigenous troops for wars of liberation. Paul Voronov personally selected him as senior noncommissioned officer for the Cuban expedition. There appeared no need for additional officers. Kurochkin was more valuable.

So it came as no surprise to his men when Sergeant Kurochkin stole a farm truck the day before and drove the back roads to Santa Clara after learning that the Cuban troops would deploy from there. It was a process he had undertaken throughout his career, determining how his enemy would act by putting himself in their place. They already knew that his camp was halfway between Mataguá and Báez, and he expected they would travel to Mataguá on side roads to avoid attracting attention before deploying east through the jungle on foot.

Kurochkin covered the last five miles himself using one of the Cuban field charts. He layed out a likely track, then decided how *he* would have made the approach. The tracks rarely merged. He expected that the Cuban scorpions would utilize about half of each track. It was after he discussed the operation with his men, a habit that inspired tremendous loyalty, that he established the location for an ambush. Never allow the opposition to achieve surprise.

He was absolutely correct about their approach. His

timing was off by the extra half hour's nap that his men allowed him.

The Cuban point man was careless. He'd opened the distance between himself and the next man by almost forty yards. Conversely the others were too close to each other. Kurochkin disposed of the point with his knife. There was never a sound. The number-two man had no idea he had become point.

There was a depression where Kurochkin assumed it would be natural for the others to collect. He'd set his men on either side. When the point failed to respond to the clicks on the radio, which was now in Kurochkin's hands, the others made the fatal error of closing up. Kurochkin had anticipated their reaction exactly.

Kurochkin was the first to fire. He selected the one he assumed to be the officer in charge and killed him with a single shot in the head. Before the man's body hit the ground, the other Spetznaz opened up with automatic fire. The Cubans had no targets, nothing to fire back at. The initial reaction was survival—to dive for any possible cover, then move away from the scene before attracting more attention by returning fire.

Those who survived did ease off to either side. As they rose slightly to scramble into the undergrowth, they were torn apart by shrapnel from claymore-type mines that burst inward toward the gulley at knee level. There was only one man who appeared to have escaped. Miraculously avoiding injury, he crawled directly to the rear, remaining on his stomach as the mines on both sides of the gulley blasted into his comrades.

One of the Spetznaz raised his rifle. Kurochkin stopped him. "No. Let him go. We want someone to get the word back to Havana."

Then they moved down to dispose of the bodies. They collected weapons and ammunition before burying the Cubans in a shallow grave. There was no effort to hide the location. Any military person would know from the destruction of the vegetation by the mines that there had been an ambush.

Better to let the curious understand the ruthlessness of the Spetznaz. He knew Colonel Voronov would have insisted on that.

Juan Duran was unable to respond when Cara asked, "Do you wish to make some sort of statement for their families?"

There had been no one willing to report that the entire Scorpion unit was missing and presumed dead. That was why Cara Estrada had eventually acquiesced, for she was certain that Duran would have gone into one of his increasingly infamous rages if anyone else had told him.

There was a lump in his throat that prevented him from responding to her question without displaying emotion—an act he considered an inexcusable weakness. Better not to say anything than to choke on his words or, even worse, allow a tear to slip down his cheek.

Instead, after staring at her for longer than he intended, he shifted his gaze to the window. Then, as if seeing something that deserved more attention, he rose and walked over to look outside. Yet Cara detected his shoulders heaving as he sucked in deep breaths to regain control. Yes, considering how definite he was in presenting an unwavering image to those about him, it was a wise decision for her to give him the news about the Scorpions.

For Juan Duran, as he stood at the window seeing nothing beyond the image that moved through his mind in slow motion, the mental torture was almost unbearable. He saw a picture of death and suffering, of the last moments of each of the men he had sent out to do battle with the Spetznaz. It would have been an ambush—no doubt about that—and his vision displayed it from the perspective of each individual as he realized his own mortality. Juan Duran experienced each death twice, first as a Cuban soldier who realized he was about to die, then from the vantage point of the Spetznaz.

The vision revolved in a ghastly circle, eventually returning to the first death he had witnessed and observing each succeeding one from a new aspect. He had decorated many of these men himself and their familiar faces stared back at him in question. Each seemed to be searching for an answer to a question even he couldn't answer: Why had he insisted that they do it that way? It would have made more sense to—

Cara saw him shudder just before he slumped to the floor. Thank God she had been the only one to witness what he would be sure to consider an act of weakness.

CHAPTER ELEVEN

Havana is a city of contrasts. For the pre-Castro generation, those few new buildings of glass and steel represent a sterility once associated with the United States or the reconstructed post-WWII European cities. The younger people hope that new construction may presage a brave new world emerging from a tradition-laden past.

A bureaucracy that was unknown thirty years before spends its days inside the modern structures administering to the needs of a socialist nation. During the day too many Soviets walk the streets to please the older people, even though the Russian civilian and military personnel have been sent to improve the quality of life. At night the Copa still parades scantily clad showgirls across the stage in numbers that have changed little since the days of Batista. Such displays remain for the benefit of tourists, who bring much-needed foreign currency.

At various stages of his life Juan Duran resented these contrasts. The old architecture was a symbol of dictatorship and repression—the old-world influence of Spain. Yet the few modern structures that rose after Fidel Castro came to power were much too indicative of Russian influence. The older hotels and casinos, and even the office buildings that once housed the giant U.S. corporations, stood for American intervention in a small country unable to control its own destiny. Socialism was a welcome relief from dictatorship—until it became a communism paralleling the Soviet Union, and Moscow's influence became all-pervasive.

But the most deep-seated contrast, one that graduated into an uncontrolled malignancy, was between his own tiny nation and the giant to the north. The United States possessed immense wealth, an industrial and technical base with limitless possibilities, agricultural strength that actually had to be restrained by government decree to alleviate overproduction, and a beneficence flowing down to less fortunate nations that evolved into social arrogance, as far as Duran was concerned. The antithesis provided by Cuba was appalling—almost no industry, a complete lack of technical expertise, a single-product agricultural base, and a self-deprecating attitude bordering on servility. This gnawed at Juan Duran's soul perpetually, sometimes magnifying into irrepressible rages. Once again, this time as leader of his island nation, he was at a stage in his life when revenge became paramount, when there was no longer the possibility for rational thought.

Major Pagos had become the vehicle for Duran's revenge. The raid on Miami had been so successful that the major had become a hero in his leader's eyes. If any single individual could accomplish the impossible, it was Pagos. Yet even Major Pagos questioned the wisdom of his leader's latest target. Duran's response was an outright bribe—he offered a direct promotion to full colonel. Although it could not be refused and his ego had been properly massaged, Pagos had some anxious moments about striking a military installation. The security at Pensacola would be radically different from that at Miami International.

Bernie Ryng stared in wonder at Father Allende, then

shook his head no. What inner drive, or outside influence, was so powerful that it would motivate this parish priest to make such an offer? "No, Father. You have been requested to assist me in any possible way, but I can tell from your eyes that you were hoping I wouldn't go along with that idea. And I'd just as soon approach her without hiding behind the Church. Miss Estrada must understand that the time has come for her to appeal to some other authority than the Church. She's secure now only because she believes her words won't go beyond the Church."

The contact with Father Allende had been convoluted from the start. Antonio Lynch was the originator, of course, somehow able to charm even a parish priest. Lynch had given Ryng a short introduction to liberation theology as an explanation of why the Bishop of Havana would allow a priest such latitude. This unexpected opening was a relic of Castro's last days when he made serious overtures to reopen a dialogue with the Church. It was exactly what Rome had been waiting for. The bishop was given relatively free reign to negotiate with the Cuban leader.

But when Fidel Castro disappeared, all that carefully layed groundwork was erased. Juan Duran despised the Church and made it quite clear to those around him that involvement in it was a sign of weakness. The bishop maintained his silence in public, but the closest members of his staff understood how far he was willing to reach to bring the Church back into the mainstream of Cuban society. It was the bishop who willingly arranged for Antonio Lynch to establish the relationship with Father Allende once Cara Estrada's visits to his Church became known.

"I can assure you, sir," the priest replied hesitantly to Bernie Ryng, "that the only reason I offer the sanctuary of my Church is because of the orders from the bishop. In private he is quite adamant that I offer whatever you require." He appeared thoughtful for a moment before adding cautiously, "You look and talk like a Cuban, but there's something—I can't quite put my finger on it—that tells me you're not one of us.''

''Your bishop trusts me.'' There was no other response. If anyone ever became suspicious of his identity, it could be someone like Father Allende who would suffer. They could threaten a priest in ways they wouldn't dare with the bishop. Faith would only carry so far when a poor priest had no idea why he was being tortured. It was best that he be told nothing, other than to obey his bishop.

Father Allende nodded obediently. ''All right,'' he concluded with resignation, ''I appreciate the fact that you understand my position.'' Ryng had just explained that after meeting Cara Estrada inside the church—using her resurrected faith to establish contact—he would attempt to make future contact outside. Perhaps, he'd explained, it would take just this one time to make her understand; if so, he would not push Father Allende's faith any further. ''And I sincerely hope that we never meet again.'' The priest thoroughly enjoyed offering solace to those in need, just as he refuted the idea of influencing the future through people like Bernie Ryng. But he wasn't offered a choice.

When Cara Estrada arrived that day, she was visibly upset. There was no conversation. She asked immediately for confession. Father Allende thought to ask what was troubling her, but was unable to bring himself to do so. His first responsibility was as a priest. As he composed himself for what he expected might be an ordeal similar to the previous one, he considered his responsibility to Cara. Each day she came to the church, her anxiety appeared more acute. It seemed that confession served as an opiate for the moment, but its positive effects failed to balance the need for a larger dose of absolution each visit. Perhaps the presence of the stranger sitting idly in the last pew had been foreordained. After all, he had identified himself with the letter from the bishop.

The priest decided that today he would allow her to go on until she'd unburdened her conscience. Somehow he was sure this would be the last time either of them would experience together the unique relationship that was peculiar to the confessional. *Perhaps we both need these last moments*, he thought to himself.

Once she completed her litany of sins, Father Allende surprised himself by starting exactly where he had left off previously. "If you will recall our last meeting, I can not offer forgiveness for those sins that appear to be beyond the religious experience." His voice was heavy with emotion as he contravened what he truly believed in. But it was the bishop who had explained where that fine line was to be drawn as far as the Church was concerned. "Your personal sins will always reside here, with me, but those of a nation cannot be made to disappear within a confessional. You have come to me because you understand the difference between right and wrong, and it is necessary to right the wrongs of a government. Since I am a parish priest, not a politician, and I'm unable to help you in those matters, I have arranged for someone else to—" His voice faltered as he prepared to offer his repentant sinner to an even greater sinner, one who was outside the Church. But if the bishop insisted that it must be done and that it was an acceptable solution within the tenets of the Church and approved by Rome, then he had no choice. "—to assist you with these troubling problems," he concluded.

Even as he spoke Father Allende knew that these words coming from his mouth were wrong. He wondered how far this liberation theology would lead him away from the true Church. "He is here in the church now. I have been assured by the highest authority . . . the bishop—" he stammered, "that this solution is the only way . . . the only solution open to us . . ." His last words faded to a whisper.

There was no response from the figure on the other side. The priest found himself staring down at his hands. His fingers seemed to move independently of their master. Did they also feel that he was wrong? Were they performing a penance of their own to show that they had no part in this departure from what he originally understood the Church to be?

Father Allende looked up to assure himself that she was still there. Yes, he could make out her form. There had been no movement. She was in exactly the same position, her head inclined at the same angle, the mantilla covering her face so that it was impossible to determine what effect his words had made.

Neither of them moved, nor did it seem they were breathing.

Finally, "Did you hear me?" he inquired softly, surprised at the weakness of his own voice.

A breath. A muffled sob, equally soft. "I . . . I heard . . ."

"I haven't explained as well . . ."

"Yes, Father. Perfectly." A pause. "I understand." There was resignation in her voice. "The Church has political interests. Everyone has political interests." Another pause. "I just thought that perhaps you . . . someone . . . might help me escape. But there is no escape in this world that we've made . . . is there?"

"I'd thought . . ." *No*, he realized, *there is no escape for any of us*. "No," he concluded with finality. "I can make you feel better . . . spiritually. I can absolve the guilt you feel. But I can't help you escape. There is no way any of us can escape until we change what has made us guilty." Father Allende came to that realization at almost the same moment as the woman on the other side. He, too, would have a great deal to think about that day.

"Who has arranged this meeting for me?"

"The Church has made the decision," he answered, avoiding the question.

"The bishop?" she persisted.

"It is my understanding that it goes beyond him."

"Does the Church hate Juan Duran that much?"

"I don't know. I haven't been made aware. . . ."

Her voice was suddenly sharp. "If they tell you only what they want you to know, how do you know they're right? How do you know that someone else doesn't control the bishop? How do you know that tomorrow noon it won't be you and me being judged on that stage at the New Plaza?"

"I must have faith in something. I have faith in my bishop . . . in Rome . . . and I believe in justice, just as you seem to. That is why I'm asking you to talk to this man designated by the bishop. He will help us all."

"Where is he?"

"He's seated at the rear of the church. I will take you to him. . . ."

"I'll go myself, Father."

She was gone before Father Allende could respond. He'd planned on offering what he considered fatherly advice, not as a priest to a parishioner, more as a father to a daughter. But at this point he understood that she had just passed through another stage. She was so much more intelligent than the poor members of his parish who were quite satisfied to simply be absolved of their sins each week. She had come to him for answers. Finding some solace, but no answers, she would now seek revenge. And Father Allende knew the bishop not only understood that, but he had succeeded in making Allende a party to the seeds of that revenge. *No*, the priest said to himself, *there is no escape*.

When Cara Estrada saw the man seated in the second to the last row of the rough wooden pews, she knew he wasn't accustomed to being inside a church. He was dressed casually, like a native, but his legs were crossed and one arm was draped over the back of the pew. Those who frequented churches simply would never relax in that manner. This one looked more like he was waiting in a hotel lobby.

Cara Estrada walked slowly down the aisle, watching his eyes. They held her own for a moment, traveled the length of her body, then returned to her face as if he were able to determine what she was thinking as she approached. After the shock of listening to Father Allende, it was disconcerting. She was sure that was his intent.

Cara walked around the pew, passing behind the man, and sat down quietly at the far end, studying him in a similar manner, before saying, "Father Allende seems to think you can help me more than he can, but you're obviously not a priest."

"Hardly."

"What are you, then?"

"I don't think it makes any difference for the time being. You may not even like me. And if you don't, then I'll leave you alone and it's better that you knew nothing about me. Is that a fair way to start?"

"I don't have any choices, do I?"

"Not really. But I suppose you can walk away."

"Once I walk away from you, I have nowhere to go. Perhaps you don't understand what it's like when the parish priest feels it necessary to turn someone like me away."

"No, I don't." It was completely foreign to him. "I do understand what it's like to be alone. I do know what it's like to feel that the world's turned against you. And I have had some experience in trying to change things when they're wrong." He folded his arms and shrugged. "You really have no one you can trust and there's not the slightest reason to trust me either. But, since you're running out of people, and there are others who seem to think you should talk to me, I'm here."

There was a forthrightness about this man's approach that appealed to Cara. She would remain guarded about anything she said, but perhaps . . . perhaps . . . there was a little hope. "What do you want to know?"

"A great deal. But I don't think a church is quite the place to talk like this. It does make me a bit uncomfortable." He grinned. "I don't really spend a lot of time in places like this."

She smiled. "At least you're honest. You'd do a poor imitation of a priest."

"That's what Father Allende said. From everything I've heard about you, there was no way you were going to be fooled." His eyes became very serious. "I'm not here for that and neither are you. I have a place—a safe one, I guarantee you—where we can both feel more comfortable. Will you come with me? I promise you will be free to leave anytime you want."

Cara Estrada knew she was at a crossroads. Returning to the Church had been a simple way of cleansing her soul. If she had been found out at that stage, it would have been a matter of explaining away personal confusion. If she made the decision to talk to this man, there was no returning.

She closed her eyes and took a deep breath before murmuring, more to herself, "Yes, I'll go with you." Then she studied him for a moment before adding in a voice he could barely hear, "I have to trust someone." She didn't add that she had even considered suicide the night before because there was no one to turn to.

General Gibara had known Juan Duran for many years. He recognized the younger man's unusual talents early on, as well as his sometimes erratic tendencies. As a result, he'd anticipated exactly the opposite reaction from Duran as he interviewed the lone survivor of the Spetznaz ambush. He assumed there would be a display of uncontrolled rage as the youngster tearfully gave his report. On the contrary, Duran was fascinated.

"Our lieutenant insisted that we move into the bush as soon as we left Mataguá. He said that the type of people we were after would have lookouts posted near the roads, even the secondary ones. Our sergeant showed me on the map where we were going, since I was on point the first hour."

"Did you follow any trails?" Duran inquired with curiosity.

"No, sir. The lieutenant said that would be too obvious. Instead, he followed a stream for a while before we changed direction toward the enemy camp. Then we covered the natural low terrain of the land—that's what he called it. He wanted to avoid too much climbing because we should be as fresh as possible when we set up our ambush."

The young soldier relating the story looked exactly like the soul survivor of an ambush. He had been found wandering in a daze near Mataguá, weaponless, his uniform torn, his body covered with cuts and bruises. But most importantly, he was speechless, unable to explain what had taken place. Medical treatment and a night of fitful sleep at the Cienfuegos Barracks had been necessary before he could be brought to Havana.

"Could you show me on a chart where you went?" Duran asked gently, looking into the youngster's eyes. He'd seen ambushes before, both as a perpetrator and a victim, and he understood the exhilaration on one side and the pure, uncompromising terror on the other. The soldier had experienced combat in Angola as a member of an elite unit, but he had never been ambushed before. Duran understood what was taking place in that terrified mind and empathized as the young man was forced to relive the experience. So far, Juan Duran was the only person who had been kind to the soldier; before his arrival, the others had shouted and screamed as if he had been the cause of the ambush. Even General Gibara had threatened him with a court-martial when he broke down the first time. But Duran was patient because he understood exactly how the Spetznaz operated—he had been one of them.

Duran smoothed a chart across the table and motioned the soldier to come over beside him. "Now I'm going to trace what I think is the probable path your lieutenant decided on, and you tell me when I'm wrong." It wasn't difficult. Part of the Spetznaz classroom training involved charts, both estimating the enemy's path of advance and establishing your own, setting it so that no one else could ambush you.

"Yes . . . yes, that's it." The soldier's hands were still shaking as he leaned on the table. He watched in astonishment as Duran's pencil followed almost the same path, correcting him only once when he forded a stream and moved up a grade. "No, my lieutenant said that stream was too wide and the far side was perfect for ambushes."

"Good." Duran smiled at the soldier. "That's the way we want to train our people. Now, I'll bet that you were hit about here . . ." He circled a position on the chart that was logical for the Spetznaz, not so probable to people who were unfamiliar with their tactics.

"I . . . I think so . . ."

"How many men were lost again, General?" Duran asked over his shoulder.

"Nineteen. This is the only survivor we've found. There was a flyover, and we think we located the position, but there were no bodies."

Duran smiled bitterly. "Not if they can avoid it." He turned to the young soldier. "I know how you feel. I've seen their work before. Did they have mines set up on either side of the area?"

The soldier opened his mouth to speak, but there were no words. Duran put his arm around the man's shoulders, patting him softly on the back like a child. He remembered even the toughest soldiers recoiling in terror when they were given no option to fight back. To General Gibara's amazement Duran, who had been raving over an insignificant error the previous day, led the soldier over to a couch at one end of the room. "Here, sit down. I know exactly how you feel. It's terrible to see your friends die. I've had the same experience myself." He sat down beside the man, rubbing his back softly like a father sympathizing with a son. "I wouldn't bother you if we didn't really need to know the details. Do you think you can speak to me now, or would you like to wait a little longer?"

"I remember there was no warning. All of a sudden . . . there was automatic weapon fire. But . . . but none of us were firing back." He buried his face in his hands, his muffled voice breaking as he continued. "We were just trying to find out where they were, I guess. You can't shoot at someone you can't see. Our unit has always been on the attack in the past, never—" He paused and looked down at the floor. "A few of the men just dropped right where they were . . . never raised their rifles . . . never knew . . ." He cleared his throat. "They . . . they didn't have a chance . . . none at all. Some ran to the sides . . . looking for cover . . . I heard my sergeant shout about a defensive perimeter . . . and that's where the mines were, I guess the ones you're asking about. I almost ran there myself. But I saw what happened." He began to shudder. "The whole bush seemed to explode. Everything came at them—dirt, brush, trees, just everything. It tore them apart. One of them—I can't even remember who it was—just disappeared. I saw his arms and legs and head disappear . . . then he just wasn't there. . . ." His head fell to his chest as he ended his sentence.

Juan Duran's arm was around his shoulders, hugging him now. Duran was talking so softly that Gibara was unable to hear the words. It reminded him of a man talking to a hurt and frightened child. Waiting until the soldier grew calmer, Duran asked, "Do you know why you were able to survive?"

"No. They were shooting at everyone. I was at the rear." He looked at Duran, his eyes wide as he relived the terror of the ambush. "I didn't run . . . believe me . . . I was afraid they'd shoot me if I started to run."

"Go on. I believe you. You were right."

"I worked back on my stomach . . . toward a rock . . . and then there were some trees . . . I just got farther away . . ."

"And you never fired a shot," General Gibara added with contempt.

"Please." Duran's eyes spoke for him as he stared back at the general. "At such a time it would have been foolish to shoot, to draw attention to yourself like that."

"I guess they never saw me. It was over so fast." His eyes were on Duran for support. "It couldn't have been more than seconds. All that noise . . . and then nothing. Not even any screaming. They were so . . . so torn apart . . . never a chance. I don't know how they missed me."

Duran looked up at General Gibara. "They didn't miss him. They sent us a messenger." He rose and walked the short distance back to his desk before speaking again. "I will accept the blame for this. I should have known. There are times when—" But he never finished the sentence, dismissing those in the room with a wave of his hand.

In Angola, Major Pagos had performed his duties with a flair that earned him both early promotion and medals uncommon for such a junior officer. It was in the remote villages of Afghanistan, however, that he attracted Juan Duran's respect. The Mujahideen were brave fighters who constantly held the Russians at bay, controlling them with their indigenous method of guerrilla warfare. But they were unable to ferret out spies within their own element who revealed both their hideouts and their weapons caches. Based on his reputation alone, Duran sent for Pagos when the Soviets proved unable to contain these guerrillas with a modern army. Pagos, working under Spetznaz instructors, produced a personal reign of terror that forced the Mujahideen to alter their strategies. At the same time he created a permanent place in Duran's heart for himself as one of the foremost Cuban terrorists.

But now Major Pagos, leading Juan Duran's latest raid, was scared. It wasn't a fear of the unknown. Rather, it was prompted by what he didn't know. In the past he had been involved in terrorist operations against guerrillas. Their strengths and weaknesses were common knowledge. Now he was facing a security system established by a professional military on their own soil.

Pensacola was the training command for navy pilots. It was the type of installation that Duran felt was suited to

Pagos's abilities. His success at the Miami airport had so impressed the Cuban leader that he yearned to produce another pyrotechnic display. Exploding aircraft and burning fuel provided a better picture for television than anything he could imagine, and Pagos was a master at creating such diversions.

But concept and reality were two entirely different elements. Duran's purpose was to create a diversion of sorts, to captivate American opinion as his predecessor had more than thirty years before. But he must make it appear that he and his tiny nation were retaliating against heinous oppression from Washington. He had already released a series of statements, first blaming the United States for fishing in Cuban territory, then for sinking three Cuban fishing boats, and finally for shooting down a Cuban aircraft that was in international airspace. More accusations would follow, but this seemed satisfactory to start. His purpose was to stimulate dissent in the United States, especially on college campuses. He had learned in the tent at Assdadah that words were almost as effective as bullets, and he'd said enough that the U.S. President would think twice before striking back. Duran wanted Americans to feel that his concept of retaliation for American sins might possibly be justified.

The reality of a terrorist attack on Pensacola was not quite as easy, as Major Pagos was learning. There were guards around aircraft mooring areas, guards by the fuel and ammunition dumps, even guards patrolling empty hangars. This was completely contrary to his intelligence reports—Cuban agents in Florida had indicated limited security coverage. There was no reason to protect pilots in training as if they were aircraft carriers, Duran had claimed, because security was saved for the major bases. The concept sounded reasonable at the time.

Pagos peered from the shadow of a hangar. The main fuel terminal was surrounded by guards. There seemed no easy way he and the three men with him could possibly get close enough to set their explosives. What the hell kind of intelligence existed around here? It had been as easy to gain access to the base as he'd been told, but it ended there. Each man was still burdened with the heavy packs they'd brought in with them. There'd been no chance to get anywhere near the helo concentration, which had been a secondary target. There were armed marines everywhere.

Once again Pagos saw a repeating message flash across his mind's eye: *You were expected, sucker*. It had first occurred to him as they entered the base and almost stumbled across a marine patrol. A chill ran down Pagos's spine as the flickering warning became a signpost. Could one of the intelligence sources here have blown the whistle? Or could there be someone back in Havana who learned about the operation?

He gave a signal to drop back behind the hangar. He needed a secure space, for no more than a minute or so, to use a covered flashlight. He'd come here for a purpose and he was going to complete the mission. Each man carried close to fifty pounds of plastic explosive and they were exhausted. If there were only one way to complete the assignment—prepare the explosives now—then that's what they'd do, then get them as close to a target as possible.

Fuel was the primary objective to serve Duran's purpose. Even if they weren't able to blow anything else, towering flames would appeal to the television audience. And an avgas fire would also provide the distraction for them to escape. "Whatever happens," Duran had counseled just before departure, "don't get caught."

Don't get caught, Pagos thought. *What about don't blow yourself into tiny messy pieces?* One of the first lessons in this profession was not to set the detonator before the explosive was in place: *Don't run around with equipment that is ready to blow!* But that's exactly what he was asking his men to do. They were going to have to go against everything they'd ever learned as gospel fact and prepare the explosive, then wait for a chance to get it in

place. They had been selected for one very simple reason—
they were his finest. That meant they would do whatever
he asked. Because Major Pagos's one weakness, if it could
be called that, was a loyalty to such people, actually
giving these orders brought deep pain.

Their preparation was as fast and efficient as if it had
been daylight. They could have accomplished it if they
were blind. Light was only for an emergency. There was
no possibility of using wires—too easy for a guard to
chance upon one—and timers were out of the question.
This would have to be done electronically within line of
sight. Nothing would come easy this night.

Pagos crept back to study his targets again. He wanted
to attach one piece, the largest, to the valves of the fuel
pumping station. The second and third were to be placed
by a hangar containing training jets. The guards appeared
to be moving about freely, saturating their area coverage
rather than limiting them to individual sectors. Occasionally a group of two or three would merge for a short
conversation. A few moments later they would move off to
an area they hadn't covered previously. It was at that
moment, as Pagos studied their habits, that he noticed their
eyes sweeping back over the previous area before moving
into the new one. It seemed almost as if they were anticipating someone rather than guarding a particular area.

That would be the first item he would report upon
returning. This was a special patrol established for a specific purpose. They were waiting for someone—*it appeared there was an intelligence leak in Havana!*

He sent two of the men to set their explosives by the
hangar. Pagos would handle the pumping station himself.
Done properly, the blast would fracture pipes carrying fuel
under pressure to the main valves. There should be no way
to shut them off after the blast. Duran would enjoy his
television tomorrow! His third man had the single automatic weapon and the responsibility for providing covering
fire if they were seen; the others carried only pistols. This

last man would also activate the detonators if they got into trouble. There had to be an explosion, regardless. Duran preferred dead heroes to prisoners who could talk.

Each of them wore camouflaged clothes. Their faces were blackened. Pagos moved out parallel to the fueling area. He'd been no more than a shadow in his other operations, even Miami—but there hadn't been security like this at Miami! He remained in the shadows, halting every few feet to study the marines. He knew he was almost impossible to see if he was still, less so when moving low. The worst would be crossing that single short section of runway because he would be outlined against the concrete. The piping meant safety. Once there, he'd become a shadow again.

Pagos froze as two of the marines appeared no more than twenty yards ahead. They seemed to merge for just a moment, engaging in a few words. It was enough time. Pagos skittered across the concrete and merged with the maze of piping.

Only moments were required to set his charge. There was no time to do it perfectly. But the plastic would do the job, even half-assed. It wasn't the most efficient he'd ever set, but there would be no satisfaction for Duran if Pagos decided to be a perfectionist.

Now to get the hell away! But what about the others? He peered back into the shadows. If they were there, they were doing a hell of a job of staying out of sight. Then, just as he was about to turn back toward the marines, there was just a flicker of movement. The two others had rejoined the third. The mission was almost complete. It was so close now. He was the last. They were waiting for him; then they could set off the detonators. And Pagos had ordered them to set off the detonators if there was the slightest hint of trouble.

Once again Pagos studied how the marines covered their areas. It was no different than before. The two nearest him headed away from each other, scanning a new area, one looking directly at the path of concrete Pagos had to cross. He waited. Then, retracing their steps, the marines moved toward each other, once again ready to merge, to talk, to be looking at each other for a second or more—rather than in his direction!

That would be it. Only seconds before they turned away again, but that was enough time. He waited, held his breath. Now! Staying very low, almost moving on all fours, Pagos went. Twenty yards to safety. That was all.

"Look!" The voice was a thunderbolt.

"Halt!"

There were no other words. But there was the crack of gunfire, a single shot, then automatic fire. The night was exploding in sound. And at that same instant Pagos felt a thump between his shoulders, perhaps a second just below the first, and knew he was falling, rolling. Probably that scream was his.

As he went down he saw the flash of gunfire from the shadows where his men were waiting. No . . . no . . . they'd given away their position . . . for him . . . before they set off the explosives. He'd told them, "If there's any shooting, blow everything!" Major Pagos's last thought as he smashed facedown on the concrete runway was, *Did they blow it before they were hit?*

As quickly as the gunfire had turned the night into horror, there was total silence. Flashlight beams cut through the shadows, toward the hangar, toward the form on the runway. The marines moved as they'd been trained, one by one, well separated, toward the bodies. The one on the runway was sprawled on his belly, facedown, arms and legs spread out. The first one prodded him with his rifle. Nothing. They rolled him over. The exiting bullets had torn him apart. No chest, no threat. Those in the shadows near the hangar lay awkwardly entangled. They'd been too close together. The automatic fire had ripped into all three at once.

"How about the ones you got over there?"

"Dead, Captain."

"They Cuban?"

"Who knows? They're just dead."

"Hey, what's this?"

"Don't touch it. Wait until the captain takes a look."

"What do you make of it, Captain?"

"Jesus Christ!"

"What is it?"

"Don't touch it. Just get on the horn and call EOD [Explosive Ordnance Disposal]. Tell them these have to be the Cubans. Christ, they must have been setting explosives."

"Hey, Captain. Remember you said that intelligence report—the one about Cubans planning to bomb the base—was probably a lot of bullshit?"

"I was wrong. Got EOD yet?"

"Yes, sir. Someone's rallying them."

"Christ, was I ever wrong. They were trying to blow the avgas."

"What makes people so crazy they'd try something like this?"

"I don't know. Maybe it's that guy in Havana."

CHAPTER TWELVE

Pagos's failure should have been obvious to Juan Duran that morning when he arose, because not a soul had ventured near his suite. But he was entirely alone at that early hour and still brooding over the fact. Cara had argued with him in the evening. They'd shouted at each other, shrieking uncontrollably. He remembered grabbing her by the shoulders and shaking her until she left in tears, saying that she'd sleep somewhere else that night. A half-empty bottle of rum in the sitting room reminded him that Cara had taken only a single drink; his head was a sad witness to the balance. But his biggest mistake over that ten-hour period came when he turned on the news that morning.

Now, glaring down at the men around his conference table, Duran remembered his own helplessness as he'd stared at that television set in stunned disbelief. He'd known at the time that he would be able to repeat almost all of the newscaster's words verbatim. The others had obviously seen the news, too, or at least heard about it, but he wasn't about to let this moment slip away.

''I can tell you exactly what I heard—they were the first

words of the day: 'Early reports from Pensacola, Florida, relate an amazing attempt to sabotage this military base, which is the main training center for new navy pilots. Around two o'clock this morning marine guards opened fire on and killed four terrorists who were attempting to blow up the main fuel supply and a hangar containing jet aircraft used for training purposes. Although early reports remain unsubstantiated, the explosives were apparently in place. Only the quick action by marine sentries averted disaster. Early indications are that there had been some warning concerning this raid, although navy spokesmen have yet to comment. The four terrorists have been tentatively identified as Major Esteban Pagos, Captain Ferdnand Maceo, Sergeant Romulo Frontera, and Sergeant Alvaro Centella, all rumored to be members of the Cuban military. There has been no response from Havana.' ''

Not a man at the table looked up. Not a voice was heard.

''NO RESPONSE FROM HAVANA,'' Duran's voice boomed. With a wild kick his chair went over backward. ''Of course there's no response because there's not a soul at this table who has brains enough to respond.'' He took a breath and leaned forward on the table. ''Dog shit! That's what you all are—dog shit. Outside of the people in this room, there were only a couple of others who knew about that raid, and they have been with me from the beginning. One of you''—Duran's hand swept around the table, his finger pointing at each one of them—''is a dog shit traitor . . . so low that I—I—'' Duran sputtered, searching for the proper words to express his anger. His eyes flashed with a hatred never before seen by anyone in the room. They were evil eyes, killer's eyes—a madman's eyes, one of those at the table thought to himself. Those eyes fell on Ricardo Nieves, his chief of staff. ''Speak!'' Duran ordered.

Nieves looked up at his leader. If he had any doubt beforehand, there was none now—this man was mad. ''I was not aware of the details. All I know is what you explained in this room. I wasn't even sure who you were sending. The U.S. must have had their names beforehand. They wouldn't carry identification on any raid. I would think—''

''I'm not interested in what you *think,* or what anyone at this table thinks.'' Duran's fist slammed the table. ''We are infested with traitors.'' He pounded out each word. ''And I want to see each one of them on that platform on the New Plaza. I will personally whip the flesh from their bones. Then''—he wiped his mouth with the back of his hand—''then I will . . . I'll reduce that Pensacola . . . to sand.''

The intelligence advisor had hesitated before, but somehow he gathered enough courage to say something to make sure that he was free of suspicion. ''I don't know how the Americans could have their names. They weren't supposed to carry any identification—''

''Of course they're not,'' Duran barked. ''And they weren't. Pagos had been at this much too long.''

''Then how—''

The question only brought more pounding on the table. ''The Americans didn't identify the bodies, you idiots.'' Duran's complexion, which had graduated to a high flush, now complemented his wild eyes. ''They knew . . . before Pagos even got there . . . they knew when they were coming and they were waiting for them.'' He reached across the table and grabbed the intelligence chief by the collar, popping buttons off his neatly pressed shirt. ''Your job is to know about spies. Maybe you're the one who told the Americans. How do I know . . .'' he screamed, half dragging the man from his chair, ''how do I know it isn't you?'' His voice peaked in a high-pitched scream.

''Please, please . . .'' Nieves was at Duran's side, grasping his shoulders beseechingly. ''This is a staff meeting. *You called us here.*'' He was pleading now. He'd been with Duran many years—they fought side by side in pitched battles. He had come to revere his leader more than any other man and had never questioned his own undemanding loyalty until recently. But now he was frightened. The past few months had made it so much more difficult for him to manage the staff as their leader grew increasingly unreasonable. But this was the first time he had actually threatened physical harm to any of them. "You are probably right about a traitor in our midst . . . but, please, we must discuss this rationally."

Duran turned his head just enough to stare at Nieves. There was a flicker of recognition. Then he looked from man to man at the table before his eyes settled back on the terrified intelligence chief. The man's ludicrous attempt to maintain his decorum and his balance by grasping the edge of the table had become a losing effort. Very slowly Duran released his grip on the man's collar. Then he folded his arms, once again studying each man intently. "All right, we will talk about it." He enunciated each word separately to clarify that he was giving up nothing.

As soon as Nieves had settled back in his chair, Duran eyed him with a withering glance. "Talk."

"I would as soon offer my neck today as accept the idea that anyone at this table has turned against us." He was the only one willing to hold Duran's stare. "We have worked together much too long, you and each of us. It is too soon for adventurism. Wouldn't you agree?"

"I would have until today," Duran snapped. His head throbbed with a combination of rum and anger.

"I still believe it to be true," Nieves answered humbly. "I would like to suggest that we try to single out those who knew of the operation." He looked around the table before adding, "You told me of this just the day before yesterday. I know of only one other here who was directly involved." He nodded toward the senior general at the table. "Of course Carlos"—he indicated the intelligence chief—"knew of this because he helped with the planning. Did anyone else here know of the raid on Pensacola?"

The intelligence advisor glanced about the table as if he

were standing before a judge before murmuring softly, "I swear I know nothing about what happened. I arranged the contacts in Florida to analyze security at Pensacola, and I helped with the escape plans, but I swear I never discussed this . . . even with my own staff. . . ."

"I served with Carlos in Grenada," Nieves responded, turning to Duran. "He saved my life. I believe enough in his word that I would stake my life for his, right now."

Duran grimaced but said nothing.

"I will ask one more time. Does anyone know which of us here might have had knowledge of the details of this operation . . . or the names of Pagos's team?"

As his eyes traveled from one man to the next, each one shook his head negatively. Duran followed his gaze, intimidating with his scowl.

"What I would suggest is that each of us write down on a sheet of paper the name of anyone we think may have had knowledge of or been involved in some phase of the operation. Is that satisfactory?" he asked Duran. The burden of fear seemed to lift as Nieves gradually calmed his leader. He had regained control of the meeting.

"Do you expect me to do it also?"

"It would mean a great deal to us, although you are certainly free to decide whatever you feel is right. For myself, I think if everyone here were to cooperate, it would ease your own burden."

Silently they jotted names on the pads of paper before them. It was done quickly, since only three of them had known directly of Major Pagos's venture, and the rest would only guess the name of someone junior to them who might have been aware. Duran watched for a moment before acquiescing to what he finally agreed was sound logic, but he hesitated when the others passed their sheets around to his chief of staff.

"Would you prefer to go over these?" Nieves asked Duran.

"It will be easier for me to listen to you," Duran answered, handing his own list over.

For the better part of an hour the few names that had been suggested were discussed. As the time passed and Duran became an animated participant, the others also began to take part in the discussion. For any number of reasons they were able to discount most of the names almost immediately. Eventually they argued over two individuals, neither of whom seemed to have the reason or the ability to compromise Major Pagos. As they neared the end of their analysis Nieves noted that Duran was becoming increasingly nervous, drumming his fingers, chewing on the pencil he was rolling across the table, and licking his lips as if he were about to speak.

"I'm afraid we've exhausted this idea," Nieves ventured to Duran. "I'm sorry. I thought it might help clarify—"

"You have contributed more than you know," Duran said through clenched teeth. "You have helped each of us through a difficult morning. You have prevented me from doing something very wrong in a fit of anger. And"—he paused, looking down at his fingers still drumming the table—"you have given me the time to think rationally. There is one name I failed to include on my own list." He looked at the general who headed his secret police unit. "Would you see if you could locate Miss Estrada and have her brought here, please. She left my suite last evening around nine. And, please, bring her directly to me."

The men at the table stared back at Duran in disbelief. Shock registered openly on their faces as they realized that there was absolutely nothing sacred—no one above suspicion—in Juan Duran's government. He had just named his mistress, the single human being closest to him for years, the woman that each of them revered as if she were a goddess, as the one he now suspected of being a traitor.

• • •

Since that single brief moment of recognition Paul Voronov and Bernie Ryng had each attempted to put the other from his mind. That they were in Havana for similar reasons was obvious. Neither had anticipated the other, but a profound sense of respect from their experiences a few years before in Panama made them cautious.

It was important to avoid each other. That was a certainty. It was as if they could read each other's mind in that regard.

Voronov accepted the fact that eventually their paths would cross. But there was so much to be done in the meantime that he could only hope that the singularity of the objectives of both his country and the United States— the end of Juan Duran's reign—would bring the solution nearer to completion before they met again. His intelligence network indicated at this stage that the United States had not inserted a SEAL unit of any size. But how many were there? More than one, obviously. He'd never heard of them operating with less than two. But how could two men accomplish what Voronov had been ordered to do?

The Santa Fe center would report if there was any indication of a U.S. effort to reinforce Ryng. So Paul Voronov had determined that the wisest decision was to know where his opposite number was and whom he was involved with; but he could not bother himself with worrying about the American. Eventually they would again come face-to-face.

Ryng's reaction was much the same. The Soviet effort was different from his own, aggressive in nature from its inception, but their goals were mutual. *What the hell,* he decided, *perhaps Voronov will lay enough groundwork to make it all that much easier for me.* It was wishful thinking and he didn't hold much faith in the possibility, but he preferred that the Spetznaz unit draw attention to itself. Let the Cubans concentrate on the Russians as long as possible.

Bernie Ryng had been making use of a small dingy apartment in a rundown section of the Nuevo Vedado district, not too far from the Havana zoo. After his first night there, he'd teased Tony Lynch that the monkeys must have slept in his bed while their cages were being cleaned. But it was supposed to be a secure place in an unfriendly environment. It was the same place he decided to take Cara Estrada.

They had talked through much of the night into the following day. At first Ryng had been convinced he was using a turncoat to unseat Duran. But as Cara explained her life with the man, his willingness to listen gradually evolved into respect for a woman who had been forced to make decisions that most people never encounter in their lifetime.

Cara Estrada was a naive young girl when she journeyed from her home in Bayamo near the foothills of the Sierra Maestre to register at the University of Havana. She'd come from the same province that had nurtured Fidel Castro in his youth and was infected by his revolutionary spirit like so many of her age. The university boiled, as always, with radicalism, and that was how she'd met Juan Duran.

Even Ryng could understand how she'd fallen in love with Duran as she related his involvement in campus politics. Fidel Castro was his hero, too. Even before he enchanted her with his stirring rendition of "History Will Absolve Me," she had heard all of his supporting speeches before groups dissatisfied with Castro. Duran was tall and handsome and brilliant, and he could change the attitude of a rabid, taunting crowd with his oratory.

Cara told of living with him in city apartments with no running water, in a sleeping bag on their pilgrimage in the Sierra Maestre, in a tent on the Isle of Youth, and finally in the presidential palace. Not until they moved into the palace did she understand fully that her Juan Duran had disappeared. But, she said, it had been a gradual process. That she was sure of.

Perhaps it began when he fought in Angola, or even

when he was sent to Russia. But there was no doubt he was a different man when he returned from Libya. If the man she had fallen in love with years before failed to return from that tent at Assdadah, the man she respected certainly vanished among the high ceilings and vaulted hallways of the presidential palace.

"Falling out of love," she said, her eyes telling as much as her words, "is not something you do overnight— not after the years we spent together. Even Juan, himself, doesn't fully understand what has happened yet; at least he hadn't two nights ago. He still assumes that Cara Estrada, and everyone else around him, will continue to obey as he changes. But he no longer understands who lives inside his body."

"Do you agree that he's crazy?" Ryng inquired softly. Her reaction was as important as her answer.

"I don't agree with anything," she snapped. "But he started out as a Cuban patriot—like all of us—and somehow he has established a new level of patriotism that excludes anyone who fails to agree with him. He doesn't see it. There is no one who dares to tell him . . . even if he would listen." She was beyond tears at that point, but the sadness in her voice was more a lament for a lost prince than for Juan Duran.

Ryng considered the woman who had spent a good part of the previous night revealing her soul to a man she'd only just met. When he challenged her sincerity at one point, her reaction had been simple. She shrugged her shoulders, looked him in the eye, and said, "My soul was released to you by Father Allende. It wasn't my choice. And the authority for that decision came from the Bishop of Havana. Since I have nowhere else to turn and no one else to trust, what would you do?" Then she smiled. It was a warm smile, one of the most beautiful he'd ever seen. "If it's allowed me to make peace with myself, perhaps it doesn't matter who you are."

There was so much sweetness in the expression that

overspread her face that it was difficult to imagine this was the woman who had inspired Duran to overthrow Fidel Castro. She had charmed the doubters, brought the fringe groups to Duran's cause . . . yet she had also carried a weapon and fought alongside the men. And he also knew that she made no effort to halt the slaughter when Castro had been deposed.

"Yet you all went along with the killing when Castro was overthrown?" It was a dirty question, Ryng knew, but he'd been waiting for the right time to pose it. There were so few women who ever rose to her position in any government—he was more curious than anything else. All revolutions required victims; it was just a matter of the number required.

She studied him closely, then asked, "Why do you ask if you already know the answer?"

"I need to hear what you have to say."

"Of course people die when a government changes like that. Most of them deserve it. That's not a Cuban phenomenon. And if you have heard that I planned much of it, you are absolutely correct. Castro had become surrounded by corruption. So many took advantage of him . . . and they would have done the same with Juan. Cuba's better off without them," she concluded bitterly.

Cara Estrada's story was one of crushed dreams—from the loss of the only man she'd ever loved to the loss of her country—yet she continued to display a power and determination that Ryng admired. No wonder Duran had won her. But would he ever know what he'd lost?

Tony Lynch pounded on the door with a vengeance meant to convey his sense of urgency. He was surprised to see a door creak open instead at the end of the dingy hall. An old lady peered out from her apartment, glaring through rheumy eyes at the source of so much noise, and shouted something unintelligible at him. He smiled and gave her the finger. She screamed a series of obscenities in his direction before slamming the door. Lynch renewed his hammering.

"Who's there?" a voice called from beyond the door.

He recognized Ryng's voice. "Lynch."

The door opened a crack, still on a chain, just enough for Ryng's eye to peer down the hall beyond his visitor before he dropped the chain. Satisfied, Ryng's finger eased off the trigger and he slid the pistol back in his belt. "It's all right," he called into the other room. "It's a friend of mine."

Cara Estrada entered the room hesitantly, sucking in her breath in shocked recognition when she saw Lynch. "You . . ." she uttered, her eyes growing wide.

Ryng glaced from one to the other with amusement. "I didn't realize the two of you had become such good friends," he said to Lynch.

"I couldn't take the chance of saying who my friends were, just in case she ever had a change of heart. With the type of people she hangs with, the lady could have blown the whistle on me."

"You seem to turn up in some very strange places, Mr.—" Cara's eyes had narrowed as she realized how deep Tony's contacts ran in the Havana community.

"Lynch. Tony Lynch, Miss Estrada. I've learned through experience that if you look like you belong, hardly anyone ever questions you."

"And you do seem to end up in some very strange places, at least for an American."

"Believe me, I've been in Havana for so long I really feel like a native these days. But that's not why I came here, Bernie." Lynch scanned the room quickly. "No television, I see. No news, then. When was the last time you were outside?"

"Haven't been out yet today . . ."

"Then you didn't hear that they bagged four Cubans at Pensacola last night, trying to blow the place?"

Ryng's face relaxed into a grin. "I didn't know whether

they might not use more than four of them. But I'm happy to hear there was a welcoming party.''

Tony Lynch looked hard at Cara Estrada, then back to Ryng. ''I was wondering if you weren't the one who blew their cover. You still have that touch with the ladies, don't you?'' Then his expression changed. ''Lucky for you—not so lucky for her, I'm afraid.''

''That's why you're here?''

''I figured if Duran didn't know where she was, then you were the only other answer—''

''Juan?'' she interrupted.

''I got a little secondhand information no more than half an hour ago that he ordered the police to pick her up. There was a special meeting of Duran's staff this morning, probably right after he heard about Pensacola. Unfortunately for Miss Estrada, he must have put two and two together.''

She said nothing, her eyes on Ryng.

''Do you have any idea how many others were involved in that raid on Pensacola?'' Ryng asked her.

''Very few. Normally there was always some data transmitted to us by locals in the strike area. Then a security analysis was done here. A few of his closest staff would review the plan, but most of it was done by people like Major Pagos. He had a great deal of faith in his own ability. He said too many people confused the issue, and he also believed that the less people knew about something, the better the chances for success. Those others on Juan's staff who were involved probably helped him come up with my name.''

''Do you know if you have any enemies on his staff?''

''Enemies? I doubt it.'' She smiled unhappily. ''But no real friends either, I can tell you. That's become a man's world now. You see, everyone is welcome to the revolution in the beginning. We were all equal because we were all willing to die for the cause. But once Castro was gone and Juan Duran took over, a power structure emerged—

and those kind of men don't like women being equal to them. I was his mistress. That made them forget who did all the planning in those early days when Juan Duran was becoming famous overseas. They were all jealous because they couldn't sleep with him." She looked at Ryng grimly, the corners of her lips turned down in disgust. "I think some of them would gladly have climbed into bed with him if they could have. And they were jealous of me because I was there." She stared down at the floor and shook her head sadly. "But, no, no enemies. They respect what I accomplished for the revolution. They wouldn't turn against me now."

"Duran's orders are to bring her directly to him," Lynch said.

"He probably wants to get me up on that stage of his at the New Plaza," Cara remarked. She looked at him cautiously. "How do you know you weren't followed here?"

"I'm careful that way." Lynch grinned.

But the fear was evident in her eyes. "How long have you been in this place?" she asked Ryng.

"A few days."

"Do you know who else lives here?"

"In this rat trap? I haven't bothered to find out."

"How do you know that one of them isn't one of the CDR?"

"What's that?" Ryng asked.

Lynch looked as if something had just bitten him. "The CDR is the Committee for the Defense of the Revolution. They're everywhere. They control every block in this city. It could be the guy next door, the one who runs the local store, your brother, even the old lady down the hall . . ." he added wistfully. He nodded at Ryng. "Yeah, the lady down the hall. If she doesn't like what you're doing, she just contacts the police and they come around to ask why you're making so much noise . . . especially banging on the door of the stranger who just moved in a few days ago—"

Ryng watched silently while Lynch knocked calmly at the old lady's door. No answer. Then he pounded on the door. When there was no answer, he pushed it open very softly and disappeared inside. In a moment he was back in Ryng's room. "Let's move. There was food on the table in there, still warm. She left it to go tell someone she didn't like my attitude." Lynch shook his head with disgust. "I should have used some common sense. I was so goddamned anxious to make sure you kept this lady out of trouble. We've got minutes, nothing more, the way these guys operate. What do you need to take with you?"

"You know me, Tony, always packed for any occasion," Ryng replied, moving into the adjacent room. He returned with the miniature radio he'd been using to contact Key West. "All I need is this," he said as Lynch headed down the hall.

"Let me check the street . . . just to be sure," Tony called over his shoulder.

Cara, who had remained quiet for the past few moments, placed a warning hand on Ryng's arm. "If you go anywhere around this city with me, you're inviting them to grab you, too. Everyone knows who I am. They don't have any idea who you are right now."

"Without you, there's no way I can get close to Duran," Ryng answered. "I'll take the gamble. He has to see you before he does anything rash, in case he decides his friends might just be jealous enough to want you out of the way."

Tony Lynch never made it to the street. He rebounded up the stairs, reappearing suddenly, gun in hand. "Too late. One of their vans just pulled up outside. Got to get out the back, my friends."

"The window's the only way," Ryng said.

"Then take the window. What's out there?"

"Rooftop, one floor down."

"Good. No alley for them to cover. Now move it. Try to hit the street before they send someone down to the next block. I'll cover."

"Where do we join up . . . if we lose you?"

"Father Allende's. That's the only safe place I can think of. Move it. I can hear them on the stairs."

"Don't do anything dumb this time." Ryng began to lower himself from the window in the back room. "I'm getting used to you again."

"My aim's as good as it ever was," Lynch shouted back. "Just takes a little longer to reload."

Ryng released his grip on the sill, dropping easily to the roof under the window. Cara followed, landing in his arms. Then they began to inch their way through a maze of television antennae and clotheslines across the roof.

Ryng heard the explosion of Lynch's gun three times before he saw Tony dropping from the window. Junk crisscrossed their path to the back street—clotheslines with flapping sheets, more antennae, potted plants, piles of refuse—and the going was painfully slow.

Lynch caught up as Ryng halted at the edge of the roof. "Three shots—two stiffs. So there have to be more of them somewhere."

"They're fast, Tony, maybe too fast. Or they know something we don't," Ryng said, pointing down the street where a police van, siren howling, was inching along through the traffic-jammed street. "You know this area better than me."

"Why don't you let them take me. They wouldn't dare to hurt me," Cara said. "That's all Juan wants right now. He doesn't even know who you are."

"Forget it, lady. You're our ace in the hole. So what do you think we should do now, Tony?"

"I think we hit the street with our feet moving. Up here, we're delightful targets." He pointed at a car parked below. "That's our first step. Me first—you cover," Lynch said as he leapt down to the car's roof. From there he jumped lightly to the street and moved toward the approaching police van, using the other cars as protection.

"There's no room for two of us on that car together," Ryng said. "Go. I'm right behind you."

Cara jumped without hesitation, barely touching the car roof before hopping easily down to the hood and then the ground.

As Ryng landed on the car he saw three men in police uniforms appear around the opposite corner, guns drawn. So much for covering Tony, Ryng saw.

He pulled Cara down behind the car and drew his gun. The odds had just turned on them. Ryng waited, pistol cradled lightly in both hands, his mind churning over his options. There was no sense in shooting at this range, not until he had a good chance of hitting the first one.

The Cuban police charged carelessly up the street, more intent on cornering Cara Estrada than worrying about their own fate. Ryng raised his gun slowly and took aim at the chest of the closest one. He could hear Lynch's gun barking to his rear. This was not the way it was supposed to be. *What happened to my covert operation?*

Then Ryng, his finger slowly tightening on the trigger, stared in astonishment as his target halted in midstride. The man's arms flew skyward at the same second that his body seemed to be hurled backward. There was no sound, no indication of his fate, as the body plunged into the gutter.

And there was also no time to think as Ryng's sights automatically fell on the man to the right. He squeezed the trigger twice and watched his target crash headlong through a plate-glass window.

Ryng's eyes were already on the third man before his barrel swung around to the body, and it was just in time again to see this one twist halfway around before crashing to the street. *What the hell? Don't stop to ask questions . . . just go . . . get her out of here! It's Cara they want. There's an open path ahead!*

Ryng looked behind. The police van had mounted the sidewalk, crashing through a storefront. He could see at least three uniformed men, all firing in Tony Lynch's direction. Ryng's gut reaction—*back up Tony*—lasted less than a second. Cara Estrada, the key to Juan Duran, was crouched at his side.

Time was precious. *Get your ass in gear. Move!*

Ryng grabbed Cara's hand, pointing down the now empty street. "Stick close. Do what I do. Stay low."

"I was in the mountains, remember? I carried a rifle just like the others. Just like your friend there." She turned and pointed at a man running low in a zigzag pattern. "That one shoots well."

It was impossible to identify whoever it was as he stopped, dropped to one knee, fired in the direction of the police, then began his run again toward Lynch. "Do you know who that is?" asked a bewildered Ryng.

"Not that one. But the way he moves, he's military."

"Come on. Do just what he's doing. There may be more ahead." Ryng pulled her to her feet. "Come on. We'll have to worry about Tony later." They raced down the street and dodged out of the danger area. Cara led them on a crisscross path to Father Allende's church.

Less than an hour later Tony Lynch caught up with them, looking as if he had taken no more than a brisk walk. "I think the nature of our mission has changed somewhat."

"We also have a benefactor. He looked as good as the old Tony Lynch."

"He's as good as the current one, but only because he has two good arms."

"Who, Tony?"

"Your life might have been saved, certainly for the first time and more likely the last time, by the Spetznaz." Lynch's grin spread from ear to ear.

"Talk to me."

"Settling a debt, my friend. Don't ask me to explain how he looks at it. You sent me out there near Cienfuegos to warn Voronov's boys that Duran was gunning for them.

But that's all I can figure. He didn't stop to exchange the time of day. As soon as it was clear, we went our separate ways.''

"Do you know which one it was?"

"His name is Kurochkin. He's a sergeant, most likely one of their senior ones. Very close to Voronov. Believe me, he didn't say anything. He wanted to get out of there as fast as I did.''

"I wonder why he was there," Ryng remarked.

"He was following one of us. More likely me. He wouldn't have hung around all night waiting for you. I probably brought him along as a tail, but I don't know what he was after, unless he figured I'd bring him to you.''

Cara injected her own idea. "What about me? Why couldn't he have been after me? For the same reasons as you. Juan is set to wipe out the Russians and they know it. Maybe they know that I'm with you . . .''

"And yet he was willing to bail us out," Ryng said.

"Or her. Maybe he was just making sure she didn't end up with Duran.''

"That sounds better than your first idea, Tony. I never heard of the Spetznaz paying a debt without looking for something in return.''

Lynch was silent for a moment before concluding. "Kurochkin was leading one of the teams out raising hell in the villages, trying to drum up a little hatred for Duran. If he's back around here now, that means Voronov has them closing the circle around Havana already.''

"They wouldn't do anything without having a replacement for Juan," Cara said. "It wouldn't make sense for the Russians to take over here. The army wouldn't stand for it.''

"You're right." Ryng looked at Cara. "If you feel Duran and his power structure may have turned against you, Voronov must have you in mind to back up someone else. Tony, I'm going to talk to Father Allende for a few minutes. I want him to put up Cara. She'll make up a list of the people who might be possibilities to move into Duran's place—people who are acceptable to all sides, the ones who don't make waves.''

That evening Bernie Ryng was in direct contact with Key West. The original plan wasn't following the proper path at all. The Spetznaz were moving close to Havana too soon. They never did that unless they meant business. There had to be someone ready to take Duran's place, but Ryng wasn't prepared for that alternative yet. He couldn't let Voronov move before he did or it would end up with Americans fighting Russians in the streets of Havana.

His only option at this stage was to bring in the SEALs. They'd been waiting in Key West for his call.

CHAPTER THIRTEEN

The Soviet Spetznaz units, simply by their ability to disappear into the countryside, confounded the Cuban military. The elimination of the small unit from the Cienfuegos Barracks, followed by the ambush of the much more professional Scorpions, focused attention on the defense of Havana. It was obvious to Juan Duran that no Spetznaz would tarry in the countryside waiting to be caught. Their goal would be Havana, and it seemed as important to prevent them from entering the city as to search the surrounding provinces.

Duran was alternately enraged by the loss of a section of his most elite unit and immersed in his plans to harass the Americans. His moods varied to the point that his closest advisors would check with each other before talking with him. There was no longer a Cara Estrada to serve as a buffer. It became difficult to determine exactly what he wished of them. At one moment his single desire would be to surround the Spetznaz forces—and his rages increased each time he learned that they had slipped away from one more apparent trap. Hours later he would be involved in the intricacies of inserting terrorists in American cities.

The map of western Cuba was marked with Spetznaz sightings, Spetznaz atrocities, Spetznaz disappearances, whether or not they actually took place. What was evident to each cabinet member, even though not a one would put his fear into words, was that Duran was absolutely correct about their movement toward Havana. The locations and direction were often erratic, but there could be no doubt that the capital city was their goal.

There were occasional skirmishes with claims of minor victory by the Cuban army, but not once did they produce a Russian body as evidence of their claimed victories. As Duran pointed out more than once to his chief of staff, very few of these contacts were reported during the day, since the Spetznaz enjoyed contact in the dark. That was because most of Cuba's troops were oriented to daylight combat. And when night contact was reported, Juan Duran knew his enemy well—if any Spetznaz had been hit, his comrades would never have allowed him to be taken. No, it was more likely that Cuban troops, spooked by the darkness, often experienced firefights with shadows. The Spetznaz always picked when and where they would fight.

Fedor Kurochkin ran—or, in his mind, he saw himself as running. He imagined himself moving at full speed through the streets of Havana, the crowds separating to allow him passage, automobiles pulling to the side for safety's sake. It was the netherworld of a dream when the sleeper is struggling to awaken.

But he still was unable to get to his destination as fast as he wanted, no matter what his mind projected! He was losing the struggle. The distance was expanding with each step.

His strides seemed to increase—six or eight yards before a foot landed each time—and then he found himself leaping over the cars. It was truly a marathon, though he wasn't bringing word of a victory. He was carrying critical intelligence to Paul Voronov that could very well be the seeds to chaos. *Cara Estrada had chosen the enemy camp!*

Kurochkin's decision to lend aid to the enemy had not been an integral part of his training, nor was it an act he had undertaken in the past. It had been extremely personal, a decision made at the instant, more duty to another human being than logic. When he trailed Lynch to Ryng's hideout, there had been no thought of whether or not he might kill the other man, given the opportunity. Quite simply, Spetznaz training was based on superb conditioning, following orders instantly. It meant never giving the opposition an extra second, a moment one may later regret. No different than his compatriots, he was a professional killer who enjoyed his work.

It was the recurring vision of the slaughter near Mataguá that had led him to assist Lynch. It was difficult for anyone, even a Spetznaz, to wipe a picture from his mind of human beings totally unable to defend themselves as their bodies were literally torn into shreds. On the positive side, Kurochkin and his men were alive—the Cubans had done the dying. Tony Lynch had been the single individual who prevented a reversal of that situation; the alternative had been live Cubans while Kurochkin and his comrades were torn to pieces. The Russian sensed a debt, a personal one perhaps, but he nevertheless owed his life to one man. His decision came to mind only at the moment he realized that Lynch might soon be killed by the Cuban secret police who were already moving around behind the building.

The thought was simplistic: *I cannot allow the man who saved my life to be destroyed by literally the same people he saved me from.* Those weren't the exact words that ran through Kurochkin's mind, but they were close enough as he considered his actions on the way to see Voronov. It hadn't been duty and it hadn't been instinct—and Kurochkin was uncomfortable with himself as a result. He knew that he would think about it late at night in the days to come.

When Kurochkin told Paul Voronov that Cara Estrada was with the Americans, the Soviet colonel was speechless. In all the Russian's dealings with Jorge Anaya, never once had they considered the possibility of anyone close to Duran moving to the American side. Cara was scheduled to die along with her lover. She'd been an integral part of the revolution and she was revered by the people. The possibility that she could be beyond their reach was a shock to both the Spetznaz colonel and the Cuban justice.

"That woman is already a saint in the eyes of the people—an Evita," Jorge Anaya said. "She is to Duran what Ché was to Castro. The legends continue to grow about her deeds."

"I thought Havana was a man's world . . ."

"To the generals and the hangers-on close to Duran, it's still a man's world. But to the people, the peasants, Cara Estrada stands for the revolution as much as Juan Duran. All the time he was out of the country making his name in places the average peasant can't find on the map, she was busy. She would appear at the rallies to speak when even the military was sure none of her kind would show up. Her appearances were never long, but they were always enough for the people to boast about to their friends the following day. She wrote for the newspapers, but what she put on paper was in the language of the poor man so that he could understand. None of her work ever made it to *Granma* or any other of Castro's big papers." Anaya paused to look more closely at Voronov. "You've never seen her, have you?"

"Photographs . . ."

"No, I mean face-to-face. She is a very beautiful woman; not beautiful in the sense of a movie star, but beautiful when you see her eyes. When she dresses for formal occasions, she can be as beautiful as Evita was, but in a much different manner. It is something that is hard to understand if you have never known a peasant's life, because she stands for something those people can identify with. She smiles with them, she cries with them, she fights with them. Juan Duran is a hero, but one they have come to fear. They love Cara."

The anger Voronov was experiencing remained hidden until Anaya— ". . . they love Cara . . ."— finished his speech with an emotion that showed even he felt something for the woman. Obviously she touched every level of Cuban society. That misconception on the part of Soviet intelligence now loomed large in the Russian's eyes.

Paul Voronov called Sergeant Kurochkin back to him that same afternoon. "How many of your units would be able to function at one hundred percent if they had to go tomorrow morning?"

Kurochkin considered his options. "I can have all three ready to move by then." Spetznaz were considered capable of operating for extended periods behind enemy lines without concern for the fatigue that affected regular units. These professionals were recruited from cocky volunteers who were sure they could become part of this special force, yet were surprised when no more than one in five were selected. This hard core were those few who thrived on mental and physical excess. "But I'm not sure I could guarantee one hundred percent," Kurochkin continued. "They could all fight to their maximum, of course, but they've been living off the land for more than two weeks now."

Survival was natural for Spetznaz troops, and the rigors of living in a strange country had little effect on them. Divided into three groups shortly after landing in Cuba, they relished their assignment, performing their mission with a flare that left chaos in their wake.

Kurochkin had led his unit on an eastward feint, away from Cienfuegos, before turning back to move toward Havana through the central towns. The second had gone northward toward Sagua la Grande, turning just before reaching the sea and moving through the coastal villages in the direction of the capital city. The third had pushed toward the Caribbean, accomplishing their goals in the towns of Horquitas, Yaguarama, and Real Campiña, before crossing the main highway between Santa Clara and Havana and wreaking havoc in the southern villages of Matanzas province as they also headed westward.

The peasants had no way of knowing the Spetznaz weren't really a part of Duran's army, foraging under the orders of their new leader. They were outfitted in Cuban uniforms, their leaders conversed in Spanish, and they left identifying marks at every location to indicate they were part of the Cuban military. Once a protesting villager found himself on the receiving end of a gun butt, or saw one of his goats or pigs slaughtered before his eyes, there was little chance of convincing him that foreign troops were the perpetrators.

Communications were poor enough that it would take a month or more before Havana's reeducation process could begin in the countryside. By then, Paul Voronov anticipated that his efforts would have culminated in a new government. It was a perfect example of special forces applying the modern Soviet strategy: strike rapidly and achieve the objective before the opposition has the opportunity to recover, a late twentieth-century blitzkrieg applied to a Third World culture. It was especially effective with Spetznaz troops under Paul Voronov.

But Sergeant Kurochkin was concerned as he expanded on his force status. "My own unit was the first to arrive and they've rested for three days. I'd recommend they be used right away. Group B has been in camp for twenty-four hours at least, and I'd like to give them another day if there's time. The others just moved into position outside Tarara and they're still in the process of establishing security." That meant they hadn't slept for twenty-four hours; no Spetznaz rested until the entire unit had established a secure camp. Once that was accomplished, those off watch could sleep soundly without fear of attack. It had been proven time and again in countless operations around the world that four solid hours of rest accomplished a great deal more than two days of grabbing catnaps.

"Fine," Voronov answered. He understood intuitively

when each unit would be ready for assignment. "I want you to select a few of your best men to operate independently in the city with you. You know who are the best on their own. Cara Estrada will be the key to what we do in the next few days. You have to find her."

Kurochkin waited silently. The expression on Voronov's face worried him. It wasn't really confusion he saw, but more a look of puzzlement. The sergeant had always followed orders without requiring explanation of their purpose or the end result desired. That was why Voronov had selected him originally. But Kurochkin's response to orders had always been based on the absolute confidence of his superiors, especially Colonel Voronov. This hint of confusion was reason for concern, reason enough so that he finally said, "Do you want us to eliminate her once she's been located . . . or simply bring her to you?"

Voronov frowned. "I'm not sure." He studied Kurochkin and recognized the concern in the man's eyes. "You see, I'm not absolutely sure yet whether she's turned against Duran. Maybe she could be infiltrating the Americans . . ." But his voice trailed off as though that were more than he could imagine. It didn't make sense. That American— the SEAL called Ryng—wouldn't be fooled by something like that. She had to have gone over . . . but why? Had Ryng learned something Voronov hadn't? "No, I can't imagine that. No, Sergeant, you don't have to kill her at this stage. I just want to know where she is, who is with her . . . every move she makes. Once we learn that, then I'll decide what to do with Miss Estrada."

Alf Hoff surprised himself. Normally he was a man who made instant decisions. Instead, he found himself reviewing each of his options after receiving Ryng's message. Wouldn't it make sense, he questioned himself, to clear each request through the Pentagon? A serious mistake on Ryng's part could end a lot of careers. But if Hoff did go across the river, each of the other services would want to involve their people. Even though the creation of the Special Operations command was intended to avoid that competition, the branches would instinctively revert to service loyalty. They'd want their own units inserted if for no other reason than to justify their own existence.

No, that wasn't the way to go, Hoff decided. This Ryng was the ultimate SEAL. He made it clear over lunch that first day that he operated best with his own kind.

That was part of the mystique of the SEALs that evolved in Vietnam and had been nurtured by their experiences since then. No matter where one or more SEALs were, their brothers were somehow in touch. If a SEAL unit wasn't involved in a covert operation somewhere in the world, then they could be found training indigenous troops in another country. It made little difference whether it was an East Coast or West Coast unit that went into action because there were so few SEALs that word traveled quickly. Yet these elite of the elite, steeped in well-earned pride, kept their adventures to themselves. They knew where other units were sent and often what they accomplished even before they pulled out. It was enough to know they were the best in the world. They could work with army or air force units when it became necessary, but they didn't have to like it—not when they were the elite of the elite.

Alf Hoff understood that.

Hoff analyzed the locations on the map designated as landing zones by Ryng. The first was Santa Fe, the Soviet intelligence complex west of Havana. The second was due south near the Caribbean village of Batabanó, and the third was east of Havana near Alamar, again on the north coast. Each had one aspect in common—they were within easy access of highways leading directly into Havana. Hoff appreciated the rationale—SEALs made it a habit to arrive when least expected, and it was obvious Ryng meant to have them in position before either the Cubans or Voronov had any idea of their presence.

The hell with it, Hoff reasoned. *What can they do to me? If Ryng does what I think he can, I'm a hero. And if he fails, they can't do any more to me than they would if a combined operation blew it.*

There were specific names and phone numbers in Ryng's message, probably the ones he refused to provide during their last meeting. Hoff remembered the exact words Ryng had used: "You don't want to know them, Alf, not unless I decide we need them. They wouldn't respond to you unless they were sure I was involved. You're not a SEAL. When the time comes, I'll let you know who, I'll let you know how, and I'll give you the exact words that will let them know it's me. Don't worry about the navy. They'll approve." It was supposed to be as easy as that . . . if your name was Ryng.

Alf Hoff had met a lot of people who probably would have killed, literally, to be like Bernie Ryng, but none who ever matched his reputation. "You'll work together well," Hoff remembered being told. "He wouldn't want your job and you'll never want to try his. Once he's in country, he needs a program manager in Washington; you need a superman." And they'd been right. No one had ever taken charge of an operation like this.

And now it was up to the program manager to support his superman.

Hoff followed the instructions. He called late at night, ". . . because that's the way we work . . ." Ryng had said. It wasn't kosher to contact them at their duty station because the main phone lines simply weren't secure. It was preferable to just tell your man to mount up in the middle of the night. SEALs knew the equipment would be ready wherever they were sent. The wives and girlfriends accepted the reality of those calls, Ryng explained. That's why they were lucky enough to be hooked up with a SEAL.

And that was it—kiss the wife good-bye, take a last peek in at sleeping kids, and out to the car. "And they always come home just the way they left,'' Ryng added, ''quietly. No one but the wife and kids ever misses them. No one's ever wiser. It's our job,'' he added wistfully.

Hoff's calls moved from the Atlantic coast to the Pacific.

''I don't know any Hoff.'' He would add Ryng's message and then, ''Tell Bernie we'll be there.''—Charlie Rand.

''Ah thought he'd forgotten where mah tired old ass was. Mr. Hoff, y'all let Bernie know we won't let him down.''—Tom Loomis.

And a wife who answered, ''We don't know any Hoff . . .'' He added the message as quickly as possible. ''Honey . . . honey . . . someone who knows Bernie is on the line.''—John Turner.

''Has anything happened to Bernie? He's all right, isn't he?'' ''Yes, he's fine.'' ''If you're a friend of Bernie's, you're a lucky man, Mr. Hoff. You just take care of him until we get there.''—Tom O'Leary.

''Gawdamn . . . gawdamn . . . I thought I was gonna be an instructor in one of those rookie schools for the rest of my tour. Mr. Hoff, if you were here right now, I'd give you a great big kiss.''—Harry Lang.

It was a strange sensation. There was never a moment's hesitation. Each man responded immediately to his request to be at the staging areas in twelve hours. There were no questions. Bernie Ryng would never ask unless things had reached the critical stage.

Signals went out to a freighter meandering through the Caribbean, its cargo—high-speed, thirty-six-foot Sea Fox boats for delivering SEALs—hidden under camouflaged tarps. The SBU (Special Boat Unit) transferred to Key West from Little Creek shifted to full alert before Hoff finished calling the SEALs. The same message was copied by the DDS (Dry Deck Shelter) equipped submarines trailing their antennae for the midnight transmission. They were a diverse collection, but they had all worked together before. They were SpecOps units—Special Operations.

Message understood.

Jorge Anaya couldn't remember when he'd been so elated that early in the morning. Paul Voronov, the one who had called himself Colonel Sanchez the first few times they'd met, had dropped the masquerade. His reasoning was simple. The Russians couldn't live with Juan Duran. They saw their thirty-year investment in Cuba going down the drain. Coupled with that, their precarious foothold in Central America seemed more tenuous. Their entire strategy in the Western Hemisphere would have to be drastically altered if Duran continued his policies.

"I can trust you, Señor Anaya." Voronov didn't ask if he could trust the man sitting across the table. Instead, he made a declaratory statement. There was no room for dissent. "I'm sure of that." He smiled and waited for the other to agree.

"You can, of course." The hook seemed to have been taken. "But I must know why I should trust you. A justice of the Supreme Court could be accused of sedition for having dinner with a foreigner these days." He sipped at his rum thoughtfully. "Times are not easy in Havana," he continued with a knowing grin. "We are living in a troubled world."

Voronov smiled inwardly to himself. Anaya appeared ready to agree to almost anything he proposed. Ambition attached invisible strings to certain men so that individuals like Voronov could control them like puppets. Jorge Anaya was ready to dance. He was repeating those time-worn phrases to avoid his own conscience. "Yes, it is a very troubled world, Señor Anaya, and I am going to help you change it." Again there was no room to disagree. "You apparently have known for a while now that I am not Colonel Sanchez. Yet you were willing to go along with me because you saw I sincerely wanted to see Cuba returned to the people as much as you did."

"Why would a foreigner want that?" Anaya was surprisingly comfortable with himself. His willingness, or curiosity, to listen to Voronov in no way lessened his self-confidence or pride. He understood that an objective could be obtained through this man. In the end, perhaps there might even be a question of exactly who was using whom.

"You had me followed after our second meeting," Voronov stated without responding to the question.

"Yes. It was obvious you weren't a Cuban."

"A lot of people believe I am."

"A lot of people fail to listen." Anaya leaned forward as if it were now his turn to assert control. "You make a good Cuban, but not a perfect one. Any man who had achieved the rank of colonel would have served his entire career under Fidel's generals. Security was very tight in the days you would have been a young officer. No foreigner could have wormed his way into the forces in those days." He drained his glass before adding, "There are only two types of colonels in our army now: those who are loyal to Juan Duran . . . and yourself. The rest are dead."

"Do you know who I am?"

"Does it matter?"

"I could be preparing you for a turn on the stage at the New Plaza right now . . . as a traitor to Duran."

"Duran's methods aren't that sophisticated. There's no entrapment in his makeup. He simply decides—loyal or disloyal—and then he executes. He wouldn't have wasted someone like yourself, or so much time, if he wanted to kill me."

Voronov couldn't help liking this Anaya. He exuded a confidence that was unusual in such a position. Normally a man would be guarded in speaking with a person he knew to be scheming the overthrow of the government. "You aren't concerned with who I am?"

"I am most concerned. You managed to elude my people, the ones who were trailing you. On the other hand, that means you not only anticipated I would have you followed, but you are also highly professional." His eyes held Voronov's and there was no smile. "I plan to use you as much, if not more, than you will use me. Therefore, I see no reason to be concerned. You're Russian. I fully understand why we're sitting here." He stopped abruptly and stared at Voronov as if he had just taken control of the conversation.

Paul Voronov could think of nothing to say for the first time since he'd met Anaya. He sipped at his drink, stared back at the Cuban for a moment, then poked at the ice in his glass. "My name is Paul Voronov."

Anaya remained silent.

"I am a colonel in the naval infantry, and I am currently on assignment with the Spetznaz."

"I had heard you were on the island, Colonel. Or, rather, I had been told that the Spetznaz were making life very difficult for our military. I didn't know your name before and it means nothing to me now. When I learned about the disruption in the countryside, I assumed it was either Soviet or American. Our military is much too disciplined to do such a thing, even though our peasants don't know that. After our second conversation, I was quite sure of why your men were doing what they were."

"How did you determine I was Russian rather than American?"

"I didn't. You just told me." Anaya smoothed his mustache. "I am aware that your objective is to disaffect the people from Duran's charm. It's not difficult to assume that both superpowers were disturbed when Duran began turning toward confrontational situations. He is a disciple of Qaddafi. Neither Washington nor Moscow is in a position to accept this abrupt change in Cuba at this time. If the people in the countryside turn against Duran, which is certainly the case in the past few weeks, then either country could use covert means to install a government friendly to themselves."

Voronov nodded to himself, slowly turning an ice cube with an index finger. "And it made no difference to you which side was involved?"

"It makes little difference now who assists me in returning the government to what it should be," Anaya concluded.

"That doesn't sound to me like a justice of the court speaking," Voronov countered with a nervous laugh.

"That's right. You hear a Cuban speaking. If you read our history books, you will find that most everyone has felt free to interfere in our government. I look at you as a means to achieving an end, Colonel. If it happens, fine. After Juan Duran is gone, then we begin to skirmish over who controls Havana." There was no expression on Anaya's face. "The objective *is* to change the government. Correct?"

A surprised Paul Voronov looked over his shoulder and signaled for two more drinks. "You are like me in many ways. I hadn't realized that until just now. You're a whore who enjoys the work." *This Anaya is a judge, yet he has no moral values beyond himself!*

"I am a whore who enjoys the end result. I am also a patriot who is willing to join hands with the devil to achieve that end result. You control me, Colonel, just as you intended. But we have just reached the stage where you also have to depend on me. I think you are close enough to moving that you would be lost without me. So let's be honest with each other. And you may start by explaining exactly what will happen to Duran."

Voronov's expression changed from disbelief to humor as he studied Anaya's face. *Score one for the Cuban*, he said to himself. *He tried to turn it around. He really wanted the upper hand*. Over a pleasant dinner Voronov gradually eased Anaya back into the position he'd planned.

What Jorge Anaya had accomplished was more simplistic than he realized. He had gained some grudging respect from the Russian—more than he had before, less than he thought—and he was sure he'd asserted himself as a leader. But he failed to realize to what extent he was still under Voronov's control. Anaya had become so involved in his own lecture on Cuban patriotism that he had buried the blind ambition that had committed him to the Russian.

Jorge Anaya failed to appreciate the nature of the Spetznaz or a man like Paul Voronov. Nor was he able to realize there was now no chance of turning back.

Not until Paul Voronov explained how Anaya must confer directly with Juan Duran did Anaya comprehend his irrevocable position. And only when he returned to his chambers did he understand the thin line he had chosen to walk. Juan Duran was still in complete control of Havana. He was still conducting the daily ritual at the New Plaza to the delight of the city's lower classes. He shuddered at the final instructions—that he must confront Duran when Voronov considered the time critical.

The next twenty-four hours terrified him as he sat behind his desk staring at the leather-bound volumes on the shelves. Never before had he been manipulated in that manner. From what he had considered a position of superiority only hours before, he had literally become a pawn. Whether or not this man would succeed, Jorge Anaya found it hard to believe that he might have chosen the wrong side. This Voronov—he was fantastic!

CHAPTER FOURTEEN

The nuclear submarine *John Marshall* had departed Charleston the previous week. Her movement had been duly noted by Soviet satellite. The normal alert was delivered to naval headquarters in Moscow, then relayed to scouting units off the U.S. coast. There was no effort by the Americans to hide her departure because senior officers ashore knew she would be closely watched.

John Marshall had served her country admirably as a Polaris missile submarine. Upon retirement she was selected for conversion to an attack boat configuration. However, it was eventually learned that these giant undersea craft were unable to adapt well to such a role. She was then designated for Special Operations, along with her sister ship, *Sam Houston*. Her huge bulk, once designed to house ballistic missiles, would now carry something almost as deadly—SEALs.

A Soviet submarine fell in astern of *John Marshall* soon after she dove. That was normal operating procedure. The Americans did much the same off the Soviet coast. It was a sound method of intelligence gathering in addition to providing superb training for their crews.

She headed south-southeast, paralleling the Bahama chain. The first indication for the Russian submarine that this might not be a standard trailing exercise was the detection of a second submarine, then a third, both American, moving into the area. *John Marshall* then turned east, accelerating to maximum speed. The Soviet submarine matched her, as did the two newcomers.

Initially the telltale signature of the target was easy to track. But it soon became evident that the other two were merging with *John Marshall*. Soviet sonar began to experience difficulty separating the individual sound signatures. Temperature changes bent and altered sound patterns. Depths and speeds changed until the Russian captain found his sonarmen confused by the sound saturation. The Americans' purpose was obvious.

There was no way to tell exactly when *John Marshall* went dead in the water. But there was no doubt when the chase ended twelve hours later and the two other U.S. submarines went their separate ways that she was no longer in the vicinity. Late that night, during his normal transmission period, the Russian commander reported what had taken place. By then it was much too late to search for the American sub. Her projected track had her racing across the Atlantic at high speed. The two logical assumptions available to Soviet intelligence were that the United States was either planning an exercise involving special forces in European waters or that an actual mission was under way. In either case, regaining contact with her would involve a great deal of luck.

John Marshall remained absolutely silent for four hours after the sound of the other submarines had disappeared to the east. Her sonarmen listened intently, waiting for the slightest hint of another Russian submarine in her vicinity.

Nothing. There was no indication of any Soviet activity.

The huge submarine once again came to life. Turning

southwest, she increased speed and set course for the Silver Bank Passage between the Turks and Caicos Islands and the Dominican Republic. The following day she turned west, paralleling the coast of Haiti. That same night *John Marshall* streamed an antenna to send her final position report before dashing through the Windward Passage off the southeast coast of Cuba. Once in the Caribbean, she passed south of the Caymans, then turned northwest toward the Yucatan Channel. Thirty-six hours later she hovered off the Cuban coast west of Havana. It had been a circuitous passage but a successful one. The Soviets had no idea where she had gone and no indication that American SEALs were now in position near Cuba's capital, according to Bernie Ryng's plan.

The Russian intelligence system had also been misled by a series of exercises a few weeks before off the Virginia capes. Navy SEALs operating from their high-speed Sea Foxes had combined with the marines for a series of landings along Cape Henry. The exercises were standard and attracted little attention from Soviet satellite or land-based sources. As a result, the Russians lost count of the thirty-six-foot boats long enough for them to hustle up Hampton Roads under cover of darkness. They moved on past the naval piers, ducking under cover at the commercial shipping docks in Portsmouth. By the following morning, they were snuggled under tarpaulins on two civilian freighters. To comfort Soviet intelligence, plywood replicas of Sea Foxes appeared back at their normal docking area in Little Creek the following day.

A few days later a back-up force of five Sea Foxes was nestled under camouflage netting at Key West. The second freighter made port briefly in Jamaica, ostensibly to pick up cargo, before getting underway for a Gulf Coast port. She would be dallying approximately ninety miles south of Batabanó, Cuba, when the anticipated signal came from Ryng. The freighter also carried forty SEALs who were most anxious to put their Sea Foxes over the side.

• • •

Father Allende was surprised with himself, even elated. Not only was he lying, he was enjoying it. There was no way he could be sure of who the man questioning him might be, but he'd sensed this was not a friend as soon as the man opened his mouth. He was no Cuban, not with that precise Castilian pronunciation. Nor was he a civilian. Although his eyes were black and his skin was dark, he possessed a certain hardness, almost an undercurrent of violence, that was uncommon to the average man. And he was so well muscled, yet light on his feet like a boxer, that the priest understood he was talking with a dangerous man.

The stranger was looking for Tony Lynch, though he claimed not to know the name. "He's an old friend of my brother, from a long time ago. They lost contact when my brother went to work in Santa Clara. Now my brother is very sick and I have promised my mother I'll find some of his old friends."

"You can't remember this young man's name?"

"That's why I was hoping you could help me, Father. It's been so long that I no longer remember. I was just a little fellow when my brother went to Santa Clara. But I can describe him." He went on to describe Lynch fairly well. "And he had a bad right arm. He could barely use it."

"Yet you can't recall his name," Father Allende said thoughtfully. "I'm not sure I remember someone like that recently . . ."

"But another friend of mine said he saw this fellow at mass in the last week or two." The man was growing nervous, shifting his weight from one foot to the other. "If I had a picture, I'm sure you'd recognize him."

"Do I know your brother? If he was ever in this parish, I'd certainly like to be able to visit him. If he's as sick as you say, I'm sure he would appreciate hearing about the others in this church that he once knew. . . ." Father

Allende was actually enjoying himself, toying with this fraudulent individual who was trying to extract information from him. It was exciting.

"Father, I really have very little time." The eyes narrowed slightly now and exasperation was evident in his tone. "I know for a fact this man has been seen here . . . and I owe it to my brother . . ."

"Would you like to come inside . . . out of the sun?" Only a few moments before, one of the young men who helped to clean the church had told Father Allende about the stranger wandering back and forth outside. It was hot in the sun. "It's much cooler inside. Maybe you could tell me more about this individual." The reaction was instant. Nothing seemed to bother men like this more than being invited inside a church.

"I really have very little time, Father. Perhaps I can make my point a little clearer. There are very few people like the man I've described, *with a bad right arm*. He's been seen here too often to be a stranger. I am told that he's here a great deal more than just to attend mass. Let's be honest, Father. He comes here to see you."

"You may be right about the arm, I suppose," Father Allende answered, still very pleased with himself. "But as a priest, I tend not to notice other peoples' infirmities. We are all God's children—"

The Russian's hand shot out, grabbing a handful of the priest's cassock. He yanked Father Allende close and growled. "I really am out of time. This man has been seen in your company too often for you to play with me anymore. You're not in a position to lie to me."

"Please, you're mistaking—"

"There's no mistake, Father. You can give me his name now and you can tell me exactly where he is, or we can go inside. I don't want to hurt you," the stranger added menacingly, "but if you give me no choice, I'll find what I need to know my way." The grip tightened until the cloth around Father Allende's neck began to cut off his breathing.

"I don't understand. Perhaps it's another church . . ." It seemed necessary to buy as much time as possible. Cara Estrada was inside and she had been wandering about just before he came out to talk with the stranger. Certainly, in the end, it was she whom they wanted. He hoped that she would know enough to remain hidden if anything serious happened. This man was dangerous.

The stranger made no response. He simply moved up the front steps of the church, his hand still gripping the cassock at Father Allende's throat. The priest found himself being dragged bodily up the stairs and past the heavy wooden doors of his own church.

The Russian's orders were to locate the Estrada woman. The fact that she might still be with the American who had saved his life made no difference to Kurochkin when he sent his man Valenko, to the church. The debt had been repaid the day before. Although he remained afraid to tell Colonel Voronov what he'd done, he would no longer have any compulsion about killing the man with the bad arm. Orders were orders—his personal debt, which he still had trouble understanding, was settled.

Father Allende stumbled as he was hauled bodily into the church. The Russian released his grip and the priest fell to his knees. Struggling to regain his footing and composure, he glanced up just as a heavy fist came down between his shoulder blades, knocking him to his knees.

"Now, Father, we have no time left for games. I'm not the type of person to hurt people who aren't trying to hurt me. But I no longer have any choices." The stranger paused, wondering why he was explaining all of this. He'd never been in the position of interrogating an innocent person before. "Where is the man I'm looking for and what is his name?"

"I can't tell you . . ."

This time a closed fist caught the priest in the ribs with a blow that knocked him sideways. Father Allende was slammed into the side of a pew. He was surprised by his own voice as he shouted out in pain and shock.

That was the sound that attracted Cara Estrada. She had almost come into the open when she heard them enter the church. It had been that close. Peering through a drape to one side of the altar, she was shocked to see Father Allende slowly rising to his hands and knees, gasping for air. The other person, a large man with cruel eyes, reached down and grasped the priest by the nape of the neck and lifted him halfway to his feet. Although she could not hear the words the man spoke to his victim, she was sure that the priest was trying to protect her when she saw the man slam his victim to the floor.

Cara Estrada was not affected by the threat of physical harm. She had been willing to accept that gamble for many years. There was no doubt she could handle herself. Whenever she encountered a man who sought to protect her, she lashed out with an anger that shocked everyone—everyone but Juan Duran. He understood what motivated her more than she did herself.

Juan Duran was also the only man capable of drawing out the woman beneath the brilliant revolutionary. He was the one to fathom that underlying fear that even Cara was unable to see. Duran sensed that it was an aberration in an otherwise sturdy makeup; he saw that she feared the unexpected. She could face death bravely, as long as she saw it. *It was the unknown, that something lurking in the background, that she couldn't understand*. It was a phobia, but it was just as threatening to Cara as the childhood monsters that lurk under the bed.

The first time she'd experienced real fear—raw, gut-wrenching, unreasonable fear—had been when she was a student at the University of Havana. She knew Juan Duran, perhaps had even fallen in love already with his image, but he barely paid attention to her. He was already a student leader, head of a movement to remove the power of the secret police. Cara Estrada determined that the quickest method of attracting attention to herself was to move to the front of the march that would start at the university and end with a rally at the Plaza of the Revolution.

What she could not understand at her age was that Duran and his associates knew that they would never reach the plaza. The police would never allow such a victory.

The procession had barely reached the major intersection at the Castillo del Principe when the police appeared from three separate directions. There was no warning and there was no hesitation on the part of the police. They used water cannons and dogs to herd the students into groups where they were clubbed by the police.

Cara was terrified. She had heard stories about such brutality but had never seen or been part of it before. There seemed nowhere to run. She was surrounded by students shouting in fear, while those on the periphery screamed in agony as they were clubbed to the pavement. The water cannons corraled them into tight groups. She was unable to move. Then the fearsome sound of snarling dogs came to her ears.

It was only later that she would remember what had happened. It was fear, pure fear, that she felt. The crush of people forced her one way, then another. Twice she almost lost her footing, and she knew that if she fell, she would be crushed underfoot. But she was totally unable to respond.

Unable to understand the senseless brutality or the panic that ensued, Cara lost control of her senses. She had to react! It made no difference whether those around her were her friends. She struck out. She created a space between herself and the crush of humanity about her. It was senseless when she thought about it later, but it was purely a reaction against the unknown. She had no idea why she was surrounded by this chaos, nor could she comprehend why she was there. It was more frightening later to remember exactly what had taken place. She knew only that her ability to rationalize, to comprehend her situation and react accordingly, had been lost. That, in itself, was more terrifying than the danger she faced that day.

There was one person who saw her strike out, and he came to her aid. Juan Duran, experienced in such demonstrations, recognized the beautiful girl who he had indeed noticed on the campus. Even though the police were clubbing their way into her group, she seemed to be clearing a space for herself without a care about those around her. She handled herself magnificently, he thought, and he bulled his way through the throng and grabbed her hand.

Cara had no idea she had been rescued until she found herself sitting under a tree on the grounds of the nearby hospital complex. Juan Duran, the one she had admired from a distance, was cradling her head in his lap and smoothing her hair with his hands. From that moment on, there was never another man in her life.

And from that same moment Cara Estrada also understood that she possessed a hidden weakness she was unable to cope with. It was the first time she'd ever experienced such a feeling and her reactions terrified her. She never encountered a similar situation in the ensuing years, even when she was handling weapons. She eventually understood that her experience had been extremely unique and that her deep-seated fear could quite possibly be a one-time affair. She dreaded the possibility it could appear in the future.

Now, when she saw the stranger beating Father Allende, she sensed immediately that she was the cause. She had no idea who the man was or whom he represented, but she immediately experienced a fear of the unknown—he . . . they . . . whoever . . . someone was after her. If it was Juan, she couldn't imagine him sending someone who would beat a poor priest so brutally. Although . . . in the last few weeks . . . No! Perhaps it was Juan's police—but even they would be under orders to avoid something like that. Of course the priest would say nothing, but he was also unable to stand up to the pummeling for long. The burly man would certainly search the place when he realized the futility of gaining anything from Father Allende.

There was no place to hide in the church—and a strange sensation was overtaking her.

Ryng had given her a gun for a moment such as this. She tiptoed, as if she might be heard above that commotion, to the tiny room off Allende's office where a cot had been set up for her. The revolver was underneath her single change of clothes. She hesitated as she weighed it in her hand. A shudder coursed down her back, but it was generated by that fear of the unknown. She had used guns many times before and had no more objection to using them than any other soldier. Yet now there was no reason, only . . . fear!

But who might she be firing at? Could this really be someone sent by Juan? She didn't recognize the man . . . and she was sure she knew every face in his secret police. Her hands went to her face in frustration, and for a moment tears welled at the corners of her eyes. Indecision was a close relative of fear. *God, oh, God, oh, God . . . what should I do?* She couldn't just walk out there and shoot him. The fact that she was capable of doing that was clouded by the fact that she had no idea who that man was. The unknown . . . the unknown . . . the . . .

Cara ran. Gathering a light windbreaker off a hook on the wall, she . . . escaped. She jammed the gun in her pocket and raced out the rear exit of the church. Looking to her right, she saw a car parked at the end of the alley. She turned left and ran . . . into the arms of Major Ibares, one of the senior officers in Duran's secret police.

Ibares was as surprised as Cara. "Miss Estrada, I—"

She twisted her shoulders violently from side to side to shake herself loose. There was nothing unknown here. She knew Ibares. He tortured people . . . he was the enemy . . . he was trying to sneak up on—

Squirming frantically, pounding her fists in his face, clawing with her fingernails, Cara escaped the grasp of the surprised major.

Ibares reached inside his jacket. She reacted instinctively. This she understood. Danger. He had to be going for a gun. Cara fumbled for the revolver in her pocket. It seemed to be caught. Without a moment's hesitation she squeezed the trigger, one . . . two . . . three separate times, shooting through the jacket with slow precision.

The initial expression of surprise on Ibares' face was replaced by one of wonder as the first bullet bored into his stomach. It was a small caliber and Ibares did not fall or reel backward. He remained in place, his hand pawing at the hole in his belly. The second and third shots were higher, striking him in the chest and neck. Ibares frowned when the final bullet hit. Then his eyes rolled back in his head and he slumped face first onto the dirt.

Cara stared at the body jerking reflexively at her feet. Her hands fell to her sides. Death was a function of life that she understood. She'd reacted as efficiently in numerous situations in the past. But this was only one threat. The other, the one that had sent her racing into the alley, was still real. The shots must have been heard inside the church. That man, the stranger who was beating Father Allende, would know they came from the alley . . . from her . . .

She closed her eyes, squeezing them tightly together, before instinct told her that she must escape. Then she bolted up the alley, pausing at the street just long enough to see if there was anyone coming from either direction. Then she turned right, running as fast as she could from something she did not understand.

Who was that man in the church?

Juan Duran was wearing his third uniform of the day. Another of his own design, this one emphasized oversized green-and-gold epaulets displaying five stars surrounded by lightning bolts. They were mounted on well-padded shoulders to enhance the effect. There was also gold piping on the uniform blouse that tended to crack when he sat at his desk. As a result, he remained on his feet, pacing about the room nervously. The expressions on the faces of those who entered the room reinforced what Qaddafi had promised—lesser men were always impressed by the power of the uniform and tended to obey more readily. After all, he had learned in the tent at Assdadah that he must expect absolute obedience. It was his due.

Major Ibares' death had been reported to him an hour before. The church, of course, had been immediately searched. In addition to the fact that it was probably Cara Estrada who had been using the small room adjacent to Father Allende's office, the report also detailed the beating of the priest. There was no evidence that Ibares had ever entered the church. Therefore, the police concluded, someone else was also looking for the Estrada woman.

Duran's chief of staff, Ricardo Nieves, and his intelligence minister were the only others in the room when he said, "Wouldn't you say the Americans were responsible—" But he never had an opportunity to finish.

"I don't think they had anything to do with it," the intelligence chief responded curtly. Major Ibares had been one of his favorites. "You, yourself, gave the orders to bring her in when we were discussing the failure at Pensacola. You suspected she may have been the one who provided information to the Americans."

"Enough," Duran barked, turning his back to them. He wondered if they could tell he was nervous. He'd slept little the previous night . . . but that shouldn't have brought such an outburst from the intelligence chief. He was one of the group that had been so subdued at that morning meeting.

Nieves also had no qualms about speaking up. "Major Ibares never entered the church. His driver said that he'd been out of the car no more than two minutes when he heard the shots. That's when he saw someone he thought was Miss Estrada running from the alley." He was equally tired and had decided moments before he entered the room that he was going to assert himself before the situation became any more chaotic. Any man who would change uniforms as Duran had that day and then actually allow his comrades to see him in the clown costume he now wore had to be struggling with himself. "We can't allow hatred of the Americans to influence us. We are down to one choice—the Russians. And I think the Spetznaz are a perfect choice."

"I agree," the other responded. "We can't let prejudice cloud our reactions." They'd both agreed before coming in that somehow they had to gain Duran's attention. The man was exhausted and increasingly irrational. The travesty of the morning's meeting was impossible to dismiss. "It is time we admit that our problems are right here in Havana and that both the Americans and the Russians are actively involved in subverting our government."

Duran turned to face them, studying his intelligence chief. For so many years the man had followed dutifully, obeying orders. It was only recently that he seemed to be rebelling, contravening authority. And Nieves had been loyal for so many years . . . why now . . . why when they had finally achieved power?

"Miss Estrada murdered Major Ibares, in cold blood. His gun was never removed from its holster. He was following orders to bring her back to you . . . alive." The intelligence chief assumed he might also be dead before the end of the day if some sense of order wasn't returned. "I believe you were correct when you assumed she might have gone over to the Americans. I also believe the Russians understand how valuable she is and that they were the ones who assaulted the priest in an attempt to find out where she was."

There were no words that would come for Duran. He folded his arms and paced from one end of the room to the other, his brows knit. He wanted them to believe he was in deep thought, desperately hoped that something would come to mind to challenge them. Yet somewhere deep inside he was sure they were correct. He knew the Russians had inserted Spetznaz in the country . . . but he couldn't find them. Now they seemed to be . . . in Havana! How? Why? And where were the Americans? "Where are the Americans, then? Who are they? If you think you know so much about them, why haven't you found them?" His voice was as high-pitched and intense as at any staff meeting, but the look in his eyes vacillated between authority and concern.

Never since the day he first met Juan Duran had Nieves seen this symbol of power waiver. There was good reason, he admitted, for confusion. "There had been nothing obvious. We stumbled on the Russians soon after they arrived in Cienfuegos. . . ."

"And where are they now?"

The intelligence chief looked to Nieves for support before replying, "We are aware of each village they passed through."

"And not once did the army catch up with them," Duran bellowed.

"Twice they did. Both times they were ambushed. These Spetznaz disappear into the countryside—"

"You didn't answer my question."

"They are near Havana."

"And," Duran concluded, "they are going to make more trouble, aren't they?"

The intelligence chief decided that he might as well say exactly what he had planned before he entered the room. "And if they find Miss Estrada, there may be no limit to the amount of trouble."

"Then you have no choice, do you?" Duran asked.

Nieves stared back curiously. Had they succeeded?

"Issue the orders. I don't need her alive, then. Bring me her body."

• • •

Paul Voronov listened intently to Kurochkin's report before finally interrupting. "You say she had already disappeared by the time Valenko got to the back door of the church?"

"He saw nothing, only the Cuban's body. Since he was a major and there was an intelligence insignia on his pocket, we assume he was fairly senior. Valenko had to go back through the church, since there was someone from the Cuban's car running down the alley."

"Isn't that just like the Americans, hiding someone in a church," Voronov mused. "The question seems to be, Who's going to get to Miss Estrada first?"

"I'm not quite sure where to look for her next," Kurochkin said. "I have a man watching the apartment the Cubans raided before, but she's too smart to go back there."

"I have an idea and it may be completely wrong." Voronov stretched to work the kinks out of his muscles. "The Church has been very unhappy since Duran came into power. I wonder if perhaps this type of sanctuary Miss Estrada enjoyed wasn't approved by the bishop in the first place. There's almost nowhere she can go in Havana . . . except to the Church again. Have as many men as necessary keep an eye on the bishop's residence. See if they can't locate her trying to hole up there." If he could just find the American, Ryng, through her . . .

Kurochkin hesitated before broaching a new subject. "As far as the neutralization teams you requested, I have four men from my team and two from each of the others available now. You said tonight was as good as any to start."

Paul Voronov continued to thank his lucky stars that he'd been the first to recognize Kurochkin's talents. Mid-level officers were fine in the regular military units, but when Spetznaz were in the field, NCOs like Kurochkin were superb. They didn't waste their time preparing lists of questions—they functioned. "Our friend Jorge Anaya

prepared this list for me," he said, handing it to the
sergeant. "I'm sure he didn't understand exactly what we
intended. Why don't you divide this among your people,"
Voronov said, as if he were handing over a grocery list.
"Wait until after midnight. No witnesses. I want Duran to
understand what real fear is. And I want everyone else to
think that maybe their leader is back to his old tricks
again—making people disappear."

"If there are witnesses . . . like wives or children . . ."
Kurochkin hesitated. That was the only part that ever
concerned him. The necessity of eliminating witnesses was
obvious, but he preferred that neither he nor his men
involve themselves in that aspect without direct orders.

"Be as brutal as Duran was. Remember, that wasn't so
long ago. Cuba has become used to this over the years.
Her people bleed each time the government changes. They
understand that when the other side takes power, the losers
must suffer. To people who lost friends or loved ones
when Duran took over, it was just yesterday. When it
looks like his secret police are wiping out another level of
the bureaucracy, there's going to be both fear and retaliation. That's where our Mr. Anaya comes in."

Voronov knew that Jorge Anaya would be upset when
he awoke to the news the following morning. Nevertheless, he would still be alive and in an appealing position.
So many others would be among the missing, and there
would be scores of terrified people wondering if they were
next. By then, it would be too late for Anaya to back out.
Voronov would make sure of that.

The Spetznaz were familiar with this type of operation.
It had been accomplished in other countries in the past,
more recently in Angola and Afghanistan. In any sort of
change in government, particularly when opposition was
anticipated, the upper strata of leadership had to be
eliminated.

It did no good to remove just the executive level. Any
effective leader, military or civilian, would have created a

succession of strength beneath him. That was why assassination often created civil war—those who planned to effect a takeover would find the successors to the murdered leader ready to challenge them. Afghanistan was a perfect example of allowing such a horrible mess to happen. A leader had been removed, but his underlying support remained powerful. Neither the indigenous army nor Soviet troops could effect a total change. It became a war on both the civil and religious level, where there were no winners.

Paul Voronov meant to avoid that problem in Cuba. The leadership was tagged to die, but he also intended to eradicate the second and third levels of the power structure. A properly stratified system could survive that, because potentially strong leaders should be available even at the lower levels. Yet Voronov was willing to bet that Juan Duran had neither the time to have effected that likelihood nor the popular support.

Sergeant Kurochkin had succeeded in such efforts in the past, and Voronov had confidence that he would accomplish the same now.

Jorge Anaya had never found it necessary to question his unique ability to analyze other people. It was a talent he'd recognized in his youth. Even in primary school it allowed him to be in the right place at the right time. All of the schools he attended in the 1950's were parochial, and the nuns appreciated young Jorge Anaya, who always stayed out of trouble. In the upper grades Jorge became president of his class. He knew how to appease the right boys to attract votes. And when he entered the University of Havana, he remained silent and observant the first term, learning exactly how the student body operated. The campus had been activist even before Castro attended, and the students ran their own government independent of the administration. Once Anaya understood which organizations represented power, he was able to dismiss the weaker groups. It was at this stage that he also added a superb sense of timing to his understanding of people. If his success had been unconscious in his formative years, his approach was now very well choreographed.

His life was so well planned, his moves so strategically carried out, that he now sat in stunned silence in his library as an hysterical newscaster related the events of the past eight hours. Duran's intelligence chief, *dead*! His foreign minister, *dead*! His secretary of interior affairs, *dead*! His chief of propaganda, *dead*! General Carlos . . . General Tarnas . . . General Huera . . . General Cholas . . . *all dead*!

No, when Anaya made some phone calls, he learned they weren't necessarily dead. They were missing. Quite simply, when morning came, they failed to respond to the normal security checks. In General Cholas's case, he had been at home the entire night and his wife was missing also. The propaganda minister had last been seen with his mistress; both had disappeared. Secret police vehicles had been seen near some of the locations . . . yet the intelligence chief, who included the police in his domain, was missing also. Even though the television station was run by the government, they'd been unable to contact the second-in-command at police headquarters. The lines were dead.

It took little time for Anaya to match the names announced on the news with the list he'd given to that Colonel Voronov . . . that Russian who had been only too willing to drop his masquerade as one of Duran's military aides. The missing people were those Anaya considered the most critical to Duran's power—*yet he had marked those he deemed necessary to his own success*. The intelligence chief was a murderer, the propaganda chief's morals were lower than any alley cat—they were better off dead as far as Anaya was concerned. *But General Cholas!* He had been in charge of recalling the reserves in an emergency, and Anaya felt certain he would have to call them up for a few weeks. And General Huera had definitely been a patriot, neither a Duran supporter nor a friend of the Soviets. Anaya had imagined Huera as his chief of staff!

Obviously this was only the beginning. Duran had yet to come to his senses and declare a state of emergency, but that would come in time, certainly later in the morning. But how many people critical to Anaya's retention of absolute power would disappear before he could clarify the problem to Voronov? Otherwise there would be complete chaos before the end of the day.

And then he began to comprehend how the mind of the Spetznaz colonel was operating, and a feeling of helplessness coursed through his body.

A single Spetznaz unit was designed to be a most efficient killing force. Operating in hit-and-run fashion, they could paralyze multiple objectives more quickly than the enemy could react. Paul Voronov, agreeing that the military's high state of readiness had never declined since Duran's revolution, determined initially to smash headquarters operations with his individual Spetznaz teams. Kurochkin's team was to eliminate the air force command, for no one, not even a special forces unit, could function for long if their enemy controlled the skies. The other two were in charge of neutralizing various army command posts. The navy would be last, for they were not considered a serious threat in the next forty-eight hours.

Paul Voronov knew that as long as the Cuban military remained in a state of shock, his Spetznaz could eliminate the power structure with little opposition. Therefore, he had never established the necessity for secondary forces should his first encounter difficulty. But there was a singular element that he had never really anticipated.

Shortly after midnight, as the Soviet assassination teams were carrying out their assignments, the American freighter lolling south of Batabanó moved inside the Canarreos island chain. Cuban radar and countermeasures gear had been effectively jammed prior to Ryng's orders reaching the freighter. That equipment remained useless until after she had once again turned southwest, at which time she reported engine and electrical problems and requested a course to steer clear of Cuban waters until she could effect repairs. She had never been close enough to create concern ashore.

The freighter never stopped; there was no need to create suspicion if an alert radar operator happened to be on duty. With way still on, four Sea Foxes were hoisted over the side, and ten SEALs and their equipment dropped down into each one. The little boats were so low in the water that their radar profile was negligible. It was a calm night and they were able to maintain a speed of almost twenty-five knots as they raced shoreward with their deadly cargo.

An hour and fifteen minutes later they stopped a quarter of a mile from the shore east of Batabanó, just long enough for the SEALs to escape from the Sea Foxes' cramped quarters into their rubber boats along with their weapons. Outfitted in camouflage, their skin darkened, they paddled ashore within yards of their assigned landing zone. While scouts scoured the area to establish a secure perimeter, the boats were buried in the sand near the tree line.

Tony Lynch had acquired a map designating the storage areas for the Cuban reserve forces. The Batabanó reserve unit was assigned four ancient trucks, and Lynch was sure that the SEALs would find at least two that were operable. A team of four men moved out ahead, locating the Batabanó motor pool on the outskirts of the village. In half an hour they had acquired two open vehicles and were underway for the outskirts of Havana, headed for the camp occupied by Kurochkin's Spetznaz team.

Sergeant Kurochkin had established his camp in an un-inhabited area outside of Managua, a little town south of

Havana, a few miles from the major highway into the city. To the west was Lenin Park, Fidel Castro's answer to Copenhagen's Tivoli, which drew a constant stream of citizens from the entire western end of the island. Kurochkin's reason for being near the park was simple: In the event of serious trouble, it was the perfect place for his men to melt into a crowd until they could effect a rendezvous.

It wasn't a true camp in the military sense. There were no tents or campfires, and access was almost impossible unless a trained individual was actually searching for it. Any Spetznaz encampment for such a limited period of time always became a merger of man and his environment. Detection was almost impossible. Protection from the elements was effected by camouflaged tarps overspread with foliage. The Cuban climate negated the need for side covers of any kind. There was no cooking, therefore no smoke. Nor were there specific sanitation facilities; that would attract bothersome insects, animals, and even curious human beings. The purpose was to provide a secure base where half the men could rest while the other half protected them. It would require exceptional people to breach it, if such a chance existed.

Harry Lang was one of the SEALs specifically designated by Ryng for his exceptional talents before he left Washington. Lang had seen action in the latter days of Vietnam and had made his name by ferreting out enemy camps seemingly impervious to ground or air search. His ability to detect booby traps, underground tunnels, and jungle hideaways was part sixth sense and mostly "the finest nose in Vietnam." No unit he had ever been with had become the victim of an ambush.

When the trucks appropriated by the SEALs neared the town of El Volcan, Lang directed his officer-in-charge to turn into a dirt road. It was barely a passable path meandering through the lush undergrowth toward what appeared to Lang to be the vicinity of the Spetznaz camp. Tony Lynch's intelligence had been extremely vague. His trackers had followed Kurochkin's team into the general area. When the Spetznaz failed to emerge, it was assumed a field camp had been established, at least until Voronov issued further orders. That was good enough for Harry Lang. He ordered the trucks to stop before they could get within hearing distance.

Lang moved into the darkness by himself.

At that time of night the Cuban countryside was at its quietest. Most of the night creatures had completed their hunt. Even the bugs seemed settled. If anything was disturbed at that hour, the sound would expand rapidly until anything alive would know that something, or someone, was disturbing the predawn tranquillity.

But nothing moved. Harry Lang merged with the night as if liquid black had become a second skin. He moved at a speed that would have surprised the quietest of hunters. But Lang had done this many times before. It was what he was best at. He was hunting men, and he knew that if any of his quarry became aware of his presence, he was an instant corpse.

Lang moved like a cat, rarely touching as much as a leaf. After twenty or thirty yards, he would stop, remaining absolutely immobile until his senses understood everything about him. The slightest hint of movement, even a noise inaudible to the average man, was enough to keep him frozen like a statue. It was the manner in which he had survived in half a dozen other small wars since Vietnam.

It was Lang's sense of smell that eventually drew him toward the Spetznaz camp. Though the first hint was nothing specific, he could sense a subtle change from the earthy aromas of the undergrowth. There was barely a breeze, yet it was enough for Lang to determine the origin of this new man-smell. He knew he was very close when the aroma of newly turned earth came to his nostrils, followed closely by sap from freshly stripped wood. The Spetznaz wouldn't be foolish enough to cut wood for cooking. More likely homemade booby traps. They'd learned their lessons well from the Mujahideen.

Lang moved off parallel to the assumed campsite. His ears were attuned to any sound that would identify guards patrolling the camp's perimeter. But it wasn't a voice from a human being that told him he'd found the first guard. It was a man pissing that revealed his position.

Again Lang moved away, circling around what he assumed was the center of their camp. This time it was an indistinct sound, similar to that of a man quietly clearing his throat, that keyed the location of the second guard.

That was enough. He knew where two sides of their camp existed. No need to search further. Spetznaz were trained to establish small, superbly protected camps with guards generally no more than a hundred yards out on the perimeter. Very quietly containing his pleasure at once again accomplishing what he did best, Lang moved as fast as he safely could back to his own unit.

He'd memorized the chart on the freighter, and he'd ticked off his starting point before moving out alone that night. Now he was able to locate the Spetznaz camp precisely, based on the number of steps it had taken him to return.

There were no high points around the spot the Russians selected, nor was there a stream. It had been purposely chosen to avoid ambush and to challenge the logic of anyone who would assume camps were always by water. As they considered their options for trapping the Spetznaz at dawn, a radio message from one of Tony Lynch's contacts reported the beginning of the disappearances of Duran's people. No one needed to tell the SEALs that it was obvious the Spetznaz would be on the move shortly. There was no longer the luxury of time to effect the perfect attack.

They divided into four elements. Half a dozen who relished the fine art of booby traps headed toward the western side of the Spetznaz camp, the one with easiest access to Lenin Park. The other three groups would close from the remaining sides. They moved through the dense undergrowth with a caution combining haste and the knowledge that their enemy was too often an equal. No one ambushed a Spetznaz unit on a mission like this one, not when they scattered a guard force in every direction. Their most logical plan, their only one, really, was to drive the Spetznaz in a single direction—and trap them before they could anticipate the purpose.

In the Spetznaz camp Sergeant Gurashev watched nervously as his men consumed cold rations. First light was breaking to the east. The guards sent out for relief had been ordered to compress the perimeter until they could serve as point men for the unit's movement in about fifteen minutes. The trucks they had appropriated the previous day were hidden near a rarely used dirt road two miles to the west. Following normal precautions, it would take approximately forty minutes before they would board the trucks. Gurashev was timing their arrival at an army HQ at about the time breakfast would be served in the dining halls. Voronov had explained to each of his sergeants that word would already have spread concerning the assassinations. Although a heightened state of readiness would be in effect, there was no military base that ever postponed a meal. It was the hour that men would be farthest from their weapons.

SEAL point men disposed of three of the four Soviet guards silently. The fourth heard his attacker and managed to squeeze off a burst from his automatic weapon before he died.

Gurashev had been in similar situations in the past. He had seen the army head off away from the sound of firing only to be decimated in the opposite direction. Spetznaz were taught to think first. Three men were sent out to scout the remaining sides.

All three returned with the same message: It was absolutely quiet on the perimeter. *All right*, Gurashev reasoned, *then it makes more sense to force them to come in to us*.

The SEAL commander, "Big John" Preston, understood why there was no reaction. He was sure the Spetznaz had established effective fields of fire before one man was allowed to rest the previous day. He passed the order over the radio for each team to move toward the center, one man at a time. It would be suicidal to move together.

SEAL and Spetznaz—shadows, specters, creeping, barely breathing, halting, absolutely motionless, listening, creeping cautiously—neither side could detect the other. Each man seemed to blend with the foliage in the shadows of first light. They waited for that first sound, that first visual, that first hint that the enemy was close, for then he was a dead man. They waited for anything that would help to prolong life. Every lesson they'd ever learned was employed by each individual.

It was the southern flank that finally exploded. Lang remembered distinctly that a Soviet AK-74 was the first sound he heard before every man opened fire. The crash of automatic weapons filled the air. Hot metal ripped away the jungle mantle. A flash of gunfire was a target. And just as quickly as targets seemed to appear, they were gone.

Grenades exploded where the Spetznaz had been, but Lang was sure that by that time there wasn't a soul within thirty yards of the blasts. The initial firing was anything but accurate on either side. They had found each other. They had an idea how big each force was. They knew what weapons were fired. And they had learned what the other side could accomplish. The Spetznaz assumed they were surrounded on three sides, if the enemy force was any good.

Gurashev sent three men out to probe the northern flank. Once again the jungle exploded. Two returned. It was no different to the east. The logical solution was to move in the direction of Lenin Park. Only there could his survivors eventually have a chance of rejoining their comrades.

The SEALs understood that Gurashev had made his decision. There was only one direction he hadn't tried and it was the one Lieutenant Preston had anticipated. If Gurashev was planning to move that way, then they would help squeeze him in that direction, just like the cork in a popgun.

The SEALs commenced harassing fire while the eastern team pushed inward with care. It was effective. It reinforced Gurashev's decision as he prodded his Spetznaz westward. When one of the SEALs hit a hidden trip wire, Gurashev was assured that a number of them went down in a hail of shrapnel. But the SEALs to either side of the center closed in a pincer movement, increasing their fire. It was definitely not a retreat and the Russians were forced to continue the course they'd originally planned. They were protecting their flanks as they moved toward the distant Lenin Park in a leap-frog fashion.

To Harry Lang, it was like herding sheep. The Spetznaz were moving efficiently with minimal losses, continuing to assume their escape route was the only logical course. SEAL losses, other than from the booby trap, were minor. They met covering fire with harassing fire.

Sergeant Gurashev remained confident until the final moment. He realized his mistake only when the jungle erupted in front of his men. It was a classic ambush, one he would have attempted had he been in the Americans' position. He expected them to cover the final side, but he hadn't considered they'd had enough time to lay a trap. His men ran directly into claymores that had been set to cover a wide front. The hail of metal came waist high, cutting down more than half of his troops before they could retreat.

There was no other direction to go. Gurashev knew the SEALs were closing in from three sides. To stay there was to invite a concentrated fire until they were all dead. It was a slim chance, but some of them might possibly escape if they charged directly ahead. He used hand signals to spread his six remaining men, then gave the order to move forward.

It was no longer a matter of the SEALs concentrating fire on a mass. Each Spetznaz was on his own. They had to be taken separately, and one by one they went down until only Sergeant Gurashev remained. The SEALs had orders to take only one prisoner. They drove the surviving Russian until he was out of ammunition. Then Gurashev found himself facedown on the jungle floor with a boot in the back of his neck. He would have preferred to die.

The first of the three Spetznaz units had been negated.

For longer than he could remember Juan Duran listened to Ricardo Nieves without interrupting. *Is this how Fidel felt?* he wondered. *Did he really understand what was happening? Or did he think there was a chance once his forces were marshaled?*

"You have placed the military on alert," he assumed.

"As soon as I received the first call."

"Have you been able to capture anyone yet?"

"There's no one to capture. Everything was done at night . . . before there was any indication. Now there is nothing . . . no one. There are no soldiers attacking, no planes in the air, no tanks moving." He shrugged with frustration. "No announcements from anyone. Only the television and radio seem to be aware of what has taken place. I don't know how they learned, but they are broadcasting as if the orders came from here. . . ."

Duran wheeled about in anger. "Absurd." He had yet to put on his first uniform of the day. He passed about the room in a silk bathrobe with general's stars woven in gold on the shoulders. "You say that police vehicles were identified by some of the locations where my people disappeared?"

"But the individuals who reported this were unreliable. Mostly drunks about at that hour of the night. And General

Mora is one of those missing. I hardly think he would order his own men to kidnap him.''

''The reserves. I'll need the reserves to help restore order. . . .''

''General Cholas is also missing.''

Juan Duran blinked. His eyes were shut for but a fraction of a second. But during that brief moment he imagined himself on the platform of the New Plaza, and he saw someone coming before him to strip the shirt from his body.

It was Cara Estrada!

CHAPTER FIFTEEN

Cara Estrada, desperate for even a fleeting sense of security, pressed her shoulders against a chipped plastered wall in an alley near the residence of the Bishop of Havana. Her legs trembled with exhaustion. Her heart pounded, threatening to burst through her chest from a combination of fear and fatigue. She closed her eyes, squeezing them tightly to hold back tears of frustration. *Not now*. If she cried, she was sure that would be the end. It would absorb that last ounce of strength she was saving . . . that bare reserve that might bring her into the sanctuary of the bishop's residence.

After killing Major Ibares, Cara had panicked. But it was not because she had just shot a man. The threat in the alley was short-lived, but that within the church—the senseless beating of poor Father Allende by that stranger—was still real.

She'd run!

In retrospect she wasn't sure what had provoked her flight. There was no goal in mind when she bolted from that alley. She simply knew that she must escape an unknown and terrifying force that was willing to beat an innocent priest to gain access to her.

Cara could not remember everywhere she had been during the day. At first she'd limited herself to the alley-ways and empty streets. Then, realizing how easy it would be to spot her alone, she drifted cautiously back to the more crowded streets. It seemed logical to lose herself among the people.

But the soldiers . . . the police . . . those were probably the ones who would be looking for her. And for some reason there seemed to be so many more of them as the day lengthened, and all heavily armed. Certainly Juan had alerted his police to find her by now. And the people who came after her in the church—one wasn't even wearing a uniform. How could she escape from someone she didn't even know?

But they all knew . . . they knew exactly what Cara Estrada looked like!

Most everyone in Havana knew what she looked like! Madre . . . *how are you going to escape, Cara? Look at all the people staring as you pass. They know who you are. They are the ones who have always loved you. But see how they look at you now. That questioning look on their faces, that curious expression around the eyes when they seem to say to themselves, "Can that really be Cara Estrada? Can that woman rushing by in those old, wrinkled clothes with her head held so low really be the most powerful woman in Cuba? What is she running from . . . ?"*

Wasn't that what they were saying to themselves? Or was her imagination playing tricks on her?

No. She couldn't stay on the crowded streets. There was no way she could lose herself there, not Cara Estrada! Whoever was chasing after her would surely see people turning to point at her—"Isn't that Cara Estrada?"

Get away from the busy area, she told her legs. *Go out where there are trees . . . less people . . . less chance of* . . . She eventually found herself on the Calzada de Puentes

Grandes near the botanical gardens. Cara was unaware of how she had arrived there, just that she recognized she was near the Nuevo Vedado section. And then she was resting on a bench in the shade of some trees . . . with no one around to recognize her and point her out to the people who must be chasing her.

It seemed to Cara that time must have stopped. The future, which she'd so recently held control of and hoped to influence, was bleak. It had only been a few days since she'd made the decision to get away from Juan Duran. The man she had once loved, always respected, had become a shallow creature twisted by the power he craved, no longer caring for those same people he claimed to love. Then she'd run from the safety of Father Allende's church . . . because there was no haven there either. She'd run from the crowded streets and she'd run from the empty streets without understanding why she was running.

But had she run fast enough? Had they been able to follow her? Were they just now preparing to corner her on this bench under the tree in the botanical gardens? . . . Was that where she was? Yes, she was certain of that. It had seemed the safest place to hide. The only other place she could think of was when she had been with Ryng. Yet, even there Juan's secret police had found her.

She knew she couldn't stay in the gardens, even though the singing of the birds and the cool shade were peaceful. Her stomach was churning . . . perhaps some food would make her feel better. And certainly there would be people who worked in the gardens who must pass through before sunset to make sure everybody was out. They'd know who she was, too!

In the end, when she finally willed her legs to move, she saw a discarded hat in the bushes and pulled it down over her eyes. Then she tore at the sleeves of her shirt, until they were frayed, and smeared dirt on her slacks. Perhaps people would turn away from her if she looked like one more drunk wandering the streets.

And that was how she turned up across the street from the Bishop of Havana's residence. She'd experienced another bout of depression in the process, imagining herself wandering aimlessly forever. But she seemed to regain partial control of her senses as she stared at the familiar building across the street. That residence represented protection.

The idea had originally been mentioned by Father Allende. When, if it ever took place, the overthrow of Duran became a reality, then the Church would certainly honor the concept of sanctuary. There were enough known dissenters, people who understood implicitly that Duran's rule had corrupted itself, that many would be seeking asylum of some kind until it was safe to establish a new government. It didn't matter at this stage who would emerge as a new leader. It was more important that a base of real support would exist as soon as it was safe for them to reappear.

The Bishop of Havana had let a number of people in strategic positions know that his Church would offer sanctuary. While there was always the chance that certain elements within the government would disregard it, the Church had established renewed strength from the moment Fidel Castro had made his overtures. Cuba had been a strongly Catholic country. Communism had set the Church back in the sixties and seventies, but religion had never died. It had simply waited for that day when Fidel acknowledged that the Church had changed over the years as much as he had. Duran had been unable to crush the resurgence that continued even after he achieved power.

She had turned against her best friend, her lover . . . or had he been the cause? Had she attempted to bring the real Juan Duran back to reality? Cara was no longer sure in her present state. Father Allende, the one who had offered kindness and a place to rest without requiring anything in return, had been smashed to his knees in her last glimpse of him. Tony Lynch, the man who had brought her to

Allende in the first place, was a mystery to her, a ghost who seemed to appear when least expected. And Ryng—he said she had nothing to fear from Juan—was as much a mystery as Lynch. But he was also the most powerful individual she had ever met, and he represented such a positive force in comparison to Juan's precipitously falling star.

Cara eased to the corner of the alley and peered across at the bishop's residence. The street was empty. Strange . . . this time of the evening the people were usually crowding the streets. But as she considered this oddity she realized that she'd seen very few people in the last hour or so. Coming from the botanical gardens had involved traversing the alleys and side streets and they, too, had been almost empty. Even the stores and corner stalls were closed. Only now did she also realize that there had been relatively few times that she'd had to pull back into the shadows to avoid a car, and those had been police or army vehicles!

What had happened today? It couldn't have been because of her. Was there some kind of curfew?

A police car was parked at the curb in front of the bishop's residence. *Madre!* There was no way she could get to the door with them right in front of it. Had they been there when she looked only a few moments back? Her mind must have been a blank then, for she could not recollect when she'd last glanced across toward the building and, when she did, had no idea of what she'd seen.

Despair flooded her soul once again, but this time she recognized it for what it really was—a paranoia she could control. She had to if she was to survive the day. So far her instincts and inner strength had provided the balance that kept her going whenever that ùnknown fear arose to strangle her reason.

Maybe she should just take her chances, move around the alleys until she was behind that police car and then make a dash for the front door. There might be a chance, just a small one . . . *No*, a tiny voice commanded from the back of her mind, *wait!* It was a command that had to be followed. There was still a semblance of logic somewhere in her body. *Wait. You're safe right where you are for now. Don't move . . .*

It was instinct again! Pure and simple. She was unable to move a muscle because . . . there he was, with another man, both dressed in Cuban army uniforms, coming down the street in her direction from a car that had been parked in the next block. There was one that she recognized for some reason—but what was it? He was much bigger than she realized, or maybe she'd never noticed his size. But she recognized that face for some reason, and there was no doubt she had come in contact with him.

When? . . . where? . . . how?

She remained frozen in place, unable to command her body to move. Why, if they crossed the street, they could come right over to her!

Reason slowly returned, but it was momentary. One fright was replaced by another, but this time it was physical and one she could identify. A hand clamped firmly over her mouth, and before she could react, Cara was being dragged deeper into the alley.

Terror pulsed through her body. A surge of adrenaline forced her to grasp at the hand. But her captor was amazingly strong. She was being hauled backward so fast that she was unable to gain enough balance to fight back.

"Miss Estrada," a voice hissed in her ear, "please don't damage my hand. It's the only one I have that works." That voice! She would never forget it. It was the man called Lynch, the first one to contact her weeks ago—or was it months? "About all you needed to attract their attention was a neon light. Are you crazy?"

She relaxed and felt the tears flow as her arms fell to her sides. There was still a possibility, still a chance that she might survive to fight all this madness . . .

"Now I'm going to take my hand away. No noise, all right?"

She nodded and leaned back against the building when she was released.

"What got into you there? Don't you realize those two are looking for you?"

"Who is that man?" she whispered. "The big one, I mean."

"Russian. A Spetznaz. A very dangerous man. Don't you remember? Wasn't he the one . . . at the church . . . ?"

That was it. That was why she was so frightened. "I don't understand."

"Don't bother now. But listen to me, please. We have to get out of this alley, or sooner or later both of us are going to be very dead. Since they really don't know me, the only reason they'd want to see me dead is you—"

"Me?" she interrupted. "Why? Why do the Russians want to kill me?"

"Everybody seems to want a pound of your flesh, Miss Estrada, and they don't seem to care how small the pieces. Your leader, Juan Duran, wanted you back alive at first. Now he doesn't especially care, since his intelligence people explained why they think you blew the whistle on that Pensacola raid. And the Russian colonel, Voronov, is after you because he isn't sure whether you're on our side or Duran's, but he figures he'd be a lot better off if there was no such person as Cara Estrada when he's finished turning Cuba upside down." Lynch grinned and cocked his head. "Make sense to you?"

For the first time since she decided that Juan Duran was the wrong man for Cuba, Cara smiled. She understood why Havana had turned upside down and taken her on a roller-coaster ride. "What are you planning to do?"

"The most important thing is to get you inside the bishop's place, where you'll be safe." It was something that she had no option to argue about. Ryng had discussed the idea of sanctuary during his first meeting with Father Allende and understood exactly why the bishop thought the concept would initially be honored. The military hierarchy might laugh at the idea, but many of them were dead and those who had survived the Spetznaz purge had enough to do without lecturing their underlings about religion. "Bernie Ryng feels you have a great deal more to offer if you remain alive. And I want that car that's sitting in front of the bishop's."

Cara peered toward the front of the alley. "Do you have anyone else to help you?"

"Just you." He smiled again. "You seem to have regained control. With only one arm, I'm not as efficient as I used to be. But before we make up our minds, we've got to see what those two Russians are up to. If they stay, then it may take a little longer," he added as he inched back up to the head of the alley.

"Just as I figured," Lynch explained when he came back to Cara. "The big one wanted to get inside the bishop's place. But it seems they weren't interested in him. He's headed back to their car now, but he left his friend on the steps—waiting for you, I'm sure. I don't know what they'd all do if they saw you coming across the street. Sort of a contest for squatter's rights, I guess."

Cara stared back at him curiously. "I don't follow . . ."

"You don't have to right now. Duran's police think that guy in uniform on the bishop's stairs is one of their own, so they're going to be in for a big surprise when they find out he's one of the bad guys. Here, you remember how to use this, don't you?" he asked, handing her a police .38.

"I know how to handle all of them," she answered.

"I hope you don't need it, but I can't take chances with those guys across the street, since they're on different sides. I want you to work your way down to the next block without being seen. Use that alley. Then come around the corner and walk casually down the street toward them like you don't care what they're doing there. I'm going to be coming from the other direction. There's no chance the Russian is just going to gun you down in the street, but you use that gun if you have to. Just remember, it's going to be one hell of a surprise to all of them when the person they're looking for comes sauntering down the street. While they're all paying attention to you, I'll be coming up behind the car. I want to take care of those two first because they don't care whether you're dead or alive. I'll try to take the Russian, too.''

"What makes you think you can do it all yourself? Are you so good with one arm that you do miracles?'' She was feeling a spiritual renewal surge through her body. Once again she was in a position of power. She had trained in the mountains to lead revolutionaries, and now she saw that her talents were again needed.

Tony Lynch was embarrassed and he looked it. "I just don't want to take the chance of you getting hurt. Now that I've found you, my job is to make sure you stay alive.'' There was no point in explaining exactly what Ryng thought might happen over the next twenty-four hours. His orders were simply to make sure she was protected until the right moment.

"I expect to do exactly that, and I can assure you I'm not afraid of anyone. I also handle a gun as well as you do.'' Saying that renewed her strength. The Cara Estrada she knew and trusted was back in control once again. Her fear of the unknown, the paranoia that had afflicted her early that day, had once again retreated to whatever corner of her soul harbored that strange weakness.

It seemed to work exactly as Lynch anticipated at the beginning. By the time he was in position at the end of the block behind the police car, Cara rounded the corner from the opposite direction.

The Russian posted on the stairs recognized her at about the same time the police did. He glanced nervously from her approaching figure to the police car and back again. Then he turned to face her. His orders were to bring her back to Voronov.

Tony Lynch was a blur as he covered the fifty feet between himself and the police car. The man on the passenger side was about to open the car door when Lynch rose up beside his open window. The only sound was the pop of the silencer as his first bullet drove into the man's ear. As he fell sideways Lynch put two shots into the driver.

Catching Lynch's motion out of the corner of his eye, the Russian whirled. He had his rifle raised to hip level and was able to squeeze off two wild shots. Then Cara's pistol exploded twice, and Tony Lynch saw the man's body jerk awkwardly before tumbling headfirst down the stairs.

Lynch ran around to the other side of the car, his gun pointed at the body sprawled on the sidewalk.

"No need to protect me, Mr. Lynch. If you care to check, you'll find both bullets in the heart."

The same embarrassed look spread over Lynch's face again. Then he winked. "Here, give me a hand," he said as he opened the rear door. "We can't leave bodies lying around in front of the bishop's residence, now, can we?"

Cara nodded and lifted the man's legs as Lynch struggled to move the body into the backseat with his one good arm. "Do you ever apologize for underestimating other people?"

Lynch shook his head. "Nope," he answered with a good-natured grin as Cara went around to the other side to help drag the body into the car.

"See, you can't do everything yourself, Mr. Lynch," she said as she shut the door. "You'd still be trying to stuff him in there yourself with one arm. And I handle a gun quite well."

"Miss Estrada, I owe you one. I'll repay it as soon as I

have a chance to figure out how." He winked again as he climbed into the front seat, sliding the driver's body onto the other corpse. "Now you do have an important job to do. You go in that door and sit tight. There are going to be all sorts of people in this street when these dead guys don't respond. Bernie Ryng, or one of us, will get back to you." He pointed up at the bishop's residence. "That's going to be the safest place in Havana over the next twenty-four hours."

As Cara Estrada moved reluctantly up the stairs of the bishop's residence, Lynch careened down the street in the police car—with three corpses.

Juan Duran was a master builder—*of revolutions*. He was not an executive. He did not care for administering. He did not understand what held governments together other than pure, unadulterated power. *Fear* was what controlled the people. The military was controlled when they understood that their leader allowed them absolute power over the populace. When any of these elements disappeared, there was a hole in the dike.

At first Duran was unable to conceive that the series of events over the previous forty-eight hours could bring his government to the precipice. This was not an indigenous revolution. *The people couldn't possibly be against him.* The problems had come from the outside. But these problems would not disappear. They magnified as each day progressed.

He had distrusted certain elements of his cabinet. Now that a number of them were confirmed to be either dead or missing, he realized he was unable to live without them. The military was designed to function based on the chain of command. Yet, when their leaders were brutally murdered, and their secondary officer corps was decimated, that element of doubt that always exists within a dictatorship reared its ugly head. Which side were they safest supporting? A number of officers hovering just below the command structure knew they were too junior to be executed in a bloodbath. Many of them simply failed to report for duty to a military already under siege. Chaos reigned in the military.

Duran had declared a state of emergency. He placed all military personnel on an emergency status. A curfew took effect immediately. Even as these orders were issued, those close to Juan Duran could almost sense that it was a lesson in futility. He did not understand what held governments together and what ripped them apart. Just as Paul Voronov anticipated, Duran was contributing to his own downfall.

Bernie Ryng was impatient, alternating between pacing about the small room and sitting before the printer as if that would bring it to life. He was awaiting a response from Key West when the beeper on the side table burped twice. That meant Lynch was coming in shortly—the incredible Tony Lynch, Ryng mused as he drummed his fingers irritably. The navy's loss was Alf Hoff's gain. If there was something about Hoff that Ryng recognized the first day they met, he appreciated it even more now. Not only did Hoff have a talent for sensing the right people, the man was the master of understatement. He had yet to make a promise he wouldn't keep. None of that agency bullshit. Whoever he was or whatever he represented, there were no politics in Hoff's makeup. While he got Bernie Ryng because he knew the right people in the navy, he'd also found Tony Lynch well before recruiting Ryng. And he seemed to have a foot in every door. Ryng had yet to request anything that Hoff couldn't deliver.

Just as Ryng was about to head out to the garage, the printer finally came to life, rattling away with another burst transmission. The messages arrived in Havana in exactly the same manner that Ryng's were relayed to Key

West, by satellite. Encoded by machine before they were transmitted, the unintelligible signals were bounced off a satellite to a receiver that decoded them before printing the message for the addressee. It was a complex method, decidedly not as fast or efficient as voice communications, but it was secure. Even before the Soviet's massive intelligence station at Santa Fe was neutralized, there was no way they could trace Ryng to this small complex.

With a state of emergency declared early that evening by Juan Duran, and a dusk-to-dawn curfew, it was time for Ryng's SEALs to pull the noose tight. The Spetznaz had done much of the job for them, creating overwhelming chaos by eliminating much of Duran's military hierarchy in the past twenty-four hours. Not all of those targeted had been hit. Some escaped, many disappearing rather than risk their lives further. Others simply weren't at their headquarters at the time, and there were only a few who gave a good accounting of themselves. Loyalty became a rare virtue. The Spetznaz had suffered some casualties, but the goal had been achieved: Juan Duran was as confused as Fidel Castro must have been when his time came.

Duran's loyal chief of staff, Ricardo Nieves, had surrounded the presidential palace with a cordon of tanks and crack troops before calling the remaining ministers to an emergency conference. Although neither Voronov nor Ryng knew what was said at the meeting, they both could count—seven men were seen entering the grounds to confer with Duran, seven out of the original eighteen who had maintained a tight rein on Juan Duran's new Cuba. All but one were unimportant civil ministers. There were enough present to give advice, to issue whatever directives Duran determined, and to try to make sense out of the increasing chaos. But they were no longer powerful enough to reinstill confidence in the government.

There was no question that some of the provinces had slipped completely from Duran's control—certainly Cienfuegos and Matanzas and Villa Clara, and much of Sancti Spiritus. La Habana province still displayed some vestiges of control, but only because of the number of troops billeted there. Once again Paul Voronov had made his mark, literally controlling thousands of square miles with less than a hundred Spetznaz. His men had turned the peasantry into a rabble clamoring for revenge against Duran's military.

The air force was grounded by both the loss of its senior officers and a realization that those junior pilots who remained available could find themselves either flying for the wrong leader or even against foreign pilots. It would remain in that status unless Duran could perform a miracle of reorganization with those few senior officers who remained. As a result, neither Voronov nor Ryng was concerned with the provinces at the eastern end of the island. And time was against Duran, for Havana had become a city under siege in less than twenty-four hours. Juan Duran had never touched on this problem in the tent at Assdadah.

Ryng stripped the response from Key West off the printer, scanning through the security padding until he found what he wanted. *John Marshall* had acknowledged his orders. In the next few hours the SEALS would be deployed off Santa Fe and Havana. The third group would come ashore near Alamar.

The base of operations established by Tony Lynch, long before Ryng entered the picture, was in the back of a warehouse in the old Vedado section. Lynch was as Cuban as the natives, and he found little problem in hiring part-time artisans to construct a false rear wall in the building. Money remained king, even in socialist Havana, and there were a number of people who assisted with the essential plumbing and wiring that eventually made Lynch's back room into a cozy intelligence center. Bernie Ryng couldn't have expected more when he appeared.

Lynch signaled four times on the beeper. Ryng pushed the button to open the outer doors of the warehouse, then waited until the red light signaled they were again closed. When he peered through the periscope and saw Lynch's grinning face leaning out the driver's window of the police car, he pushed another button for the automatic doors that slid back to reveal a small garage. The police car moved in, leaving the warehouse as normal as any on the block.

"This job gets more confusing each day, Bernie," Lynch remarked with humor as he opened all of the car doors. "How often do you find someone riding around in one of Duran's police cars with three stiffs?"

"You're lucky you didn't get stopped by someone." Ryng waved a hand at him. "You're not even wearing a uniform."

"I considered the idea of borrowing one and dismissed it immediately. It wasn't the holes in their uniforms that bothered me as much as all that blood." Lynch grinned. "Now, that really would have looked silly if I'd been stopped. And I wasn't so sure Miss Estrada would have enjoyed me changing my clothes in the street in front of the bishop's residence."

"I assume she's safely inside now?"

"The last I saw of Miss Estrada in the rearview mirror, she was stepping inside the front door. That's as close as I can come to making a promise stick. I told her she had to stay there until you got in touch with her." Lynch cocked his head to one side. "I wanted to tell her what you're up to, but I didn't think she was quite ready for that."

"Another twelve hours, Tony. Maybe a little more. You're not tired yet, are you?"

"No more than yesterday at this time. It doesn't feel like Hell Week yet, so I must still be having fun. A little exhausted maybe, but I think that's the point they tried to get across years ago in training." Lynch yawned and stretched his good arm. "What's next?"

"The last item, I hope. Whoever Voronov has in mind to take over for Duran . . . probably the one who provided that hit list he used yesterday."

"There's not a hell of a lot of kingpins left, are there?"

They talked another hour, breaking down the list of possible candidates to a half dozen names. Then Tony Lynch changed into a clean uniform that would go with his recently appropriated car. There were only a few hours for him to eliminate five people in order to come up with Paul Voronov's selection. He hoped it wouldn't be the sixth man.

John Marshall deployed a small group of SEALs in their SEAL delivery vehicles (SDVs) off the Cuban coast near Sante Fe soon after midnight. Less than an hour later she again came to all-stop off Havana Harbor. Her sonar operators had been hard-pressed charting a variety of contacts on the surface. Most were fishing boats, either on their way out or returning with their catch. One large freighter had departed before their arrival, and her sounds were fading to the east. But through the rush of sound their computers could find no indication of any military craft in the area.

Carefully, rising toward the surface ever so slowly, *John Marshall* came to periscope depth. There was no electronic radiation from enemy radar, the sky was clear of aircraft, the silhouettes on the horizon remained uninteresting fishing craft, and Havana's lights loomed brightly on their beam.

Even before the first unit departed the submarine off Santa Fe, the second group of SEALs had been ready to deploy. Buddy checks were completed on each other's equipment for the final time. Once they were secure in their SDVs, the captain gave permission to flood the dry deck shelter. With pressure equalized, the hatch opened and one by one the SDVs eased out like newborn fish into their natural environment off the city of Havana.

They were encased in liquid blackness, the water a warm and soft sensation as the open SDVs moved toward the mouth of the harbor. Each vehicle towed a small sled.

Some contained individual weapons, others the explosives intended to neutralize the city. There was total silence as they approached the mouth of the harbor forty feet below the surface. Their electric motors emitted a bare hum. The navigators, huddled in their cram;ed quarters behind the pilot, checked their dead reckoning positions every few minutes, but the lead craft was the one responsible for their location. Her navigator signaled astern at each predetermined mark.

Havana was an old city and the harbor entrance was guarded by two forts, Morro Castle on the northern headland and Punta to the south. An auto tunnel connected Havana East to the main city just below these headlands. The channel passing between the two forts traversed southeast for approximately a mile before opening out into the main harbor with inlets opening to the east, south, and southeast.

When the lead SDV, carrying the unit commander, Lieutenant John Turner, was three hundred yards due west of Morro Castle, the pilot slowed to allow the others to fall into a single line astern. From that point on, the signal lamps were used only by the lead craft, and then only if there was a change from their original plan.

They moved through the channel at a painfully slow five knots, rising and falling with the oddities of the current. Two SDVs eased out of line as the channel opened into the main harbor and headed toward the first major dock complex along San Pedro. The second group broke away as they passed the two largest docks along Desamparado, and the third continued up the Atarés Inlet past the main railroad station to a location where Bernie Ryng would be waiting.

The entire process was completed in the dead of night before the first hint of dawn streaked the eastern sky. SDVs remained on the bottom, their canopies shut tight against the harbor silt. SEALs bobbed to the surface along a vast stretch of waterfront and quietly climbed ashore with their packs. Wet suits and breathing apparatus were discarded and fatigues and weapons broken out. Each man had been through the exercise so many times that no words were needed. They had their assignments and they were confident.

Jorge Anaya had followed instructions. He remained in his villa just off Avenue de los Presidentes in the Vedado section. The street was exclusive, the colonial-style villas dating back to the eighteenth century, and any vehicle venturing into the area certainly belonged there. Even under the current state of emergency Anaya felt totally secure at home.

But security was the only comfort he could enjoy at that point in time. Since he was a man who believed in taking advantage of the odds, his decision to cast his lot with the Russian, Paul Voronov, had also been based on a sense of security. The odds favored him. Juan Duran had antagonized the Americans, who had been willing to live with the power structure in Havana up to that time, and he had also yanked the tail of the Russian bear. The latter decision had been unwise because Moscow considered Cuba an investment, and a wise investor will do everything possible to make sure it pays off. The Kremlin's response had been no different than Anaya expected—they sent a strong arm to recoup their losses.

Jorge Anaya had dedicated his life to the law and to those who used it to advantage. Understanding that ninety-nine percent of the time the winner either had the most money or was the strongest party politically, logic prevailed when he cast his lot with Voronov. Anaya was supremely confident that his brains and judicial background would eventually ensure his control of Voronov before things got out of hand. If Voronov would set the stage, then Jorge Anaya would come forward and take control at the appropriate time.

Anaya's education in reality came in three stages. It was disconcerting the first time he realized that Paul Voronov had written his own script. It was frightening when he saw that a bloodbath was wholly acceptable as a means to an end during the second stage. And he became terrified when it became evident that the Russians not only intended to achieve absolute control in Havana, but that they considered Jorge Anaya as their personal figurehead.

Anaya had been unable to sleep the previous night. While Duran's state of emergency and the curfew contributed to his uneasiness, it was really the bloodthirsty Spetznaz colonel he feared most. It had seemed to him weeks before that Voronov's plans would culminate in Duran's abdication, though he never bothered to determine why it would happen so easily. He was so involved in the fulfillment of his own destiny that he underestimated Duran's tenacity and Voronov's brutality. Now he was haunted by his misjudgment. Visions of disaster chased any hope of sleep from his mind.

His housekeeper had just prepared a full breakfast and set it out on the patio when he heard an automobile pull up outside. Anaya normally paid little attention to the outside world, but now his senses were acute as his nervousness heightened. Pulling back the curtain, he peered out at a police car parked at the curb. A man stepped from the car in the uniform of the secret police. Though he wore a colonel's insignia, Anaya had never seen the man before.

Voronov had explained—no, ordered was more accurate when Anaya considered the manner and tone in which he was told—that Anaya should see no one until Voronov contacted him again. It had been almost twelve hours of what appeared to him to be house arrest.

Anaya, explaining to his butler that he was not at home to anyone, moved out to the patio for his breakfast. His mind was alive with subterfuge. It all depended on how the day might end. His odds could improve slightly if he went along with the Russian for the time being. After this was all over, there was little that could be proved. It would be impossible to establish that he had collaborated with anyone. There were no records to prove anything. There seemed a variety of methods of vindicating himself.

Breakfast was Anaya's favorite meal of the day. There was fresh orange juice, papaya and melon, and bell covers kept scrambled eggs, a special sausage from Pinar del Río, and fresh croissants warm. And there was always a pot of freshly ground Blue Mountain coffee especially shipped in from Jamaica for his personal use. It was expensive, but it was definitely worth the price.

Anaya had finished his juice and was just cutting into the melon when his servant's voice interrupted. "Sir, this gentleman insisted on seeing you immediately."

"If you'll find out what he wants," Anaya answered without turning around, "I'll speak with him after my—"

"You don't seem to understand, Judge, I'll speak with you at my convenience," a voice interrupted. It was deep and impatient.

Anaya spun around to see the policeman from the car carelessly aiming a revolver at the servant. "Why—"

"Your man was trying to do his job," Tony Lynch said. "Don't blame him for interrupting your breakfast. This" —and he waved the gun at Anaya—"is what did the convincing. I thought we should talk about Paul Voronov right now."

"Did he send you?" Jorge Anaya's expression struggled to remain calm. His eyes registered shock.

"He doesn't even know me, but I think he has heard a little bit about me by now." Lynch glanced over the food on the table. "It seems that everyone wants a little bit of your time right now, including Washington, Your Honor. That's where I come from. Don't pay any attention to this uniform. I borrowed it. My name is Lynch and I have a strong interest in what happens in Havana in the next few hours. Paul Voronov isn't going to succeed today. It's that easy." He raised his eyebrows questioningly. "Now, after all that, can we talk?"

Anaya looked down at his hands and the napkin his fingers had twisted into a tiny ball, then back at Lynch. "I haven't much choice, have I?" He was going with the odds again.

"No, not really. But you could offer me breakfast. That spread in front of you looks wonderful, and I haven't eaten since early yesterday." For the first time Anaya saw the infectious Lynch grin. "Been too busy making sure that your boy, Voronov, falls on his face. You see, we really do have something to talk about, and I really am very hungry. How about having your faithful servant here ask the cook to make up the same thing you're having." Seeing the indecision on Anaya's face, he added, "You could survive for a much longer time than you're scheduled to right now."

Those odds again.

Anaya nodded to the frightened servant, who hadn't moved a muscle. "Do what he asks." Then he looked back at Lynch, his eyes dropping to the gun. "I don't think you need that. I have no guns in this house. And if we're going to talk, as you say, we can at least try to do it civilly." From his long years in the courts he understood that one man normally didn't shoot another if there was no threat involved.

Lynch stuck the revolver in his belt and pulled back the chair opposite Anaya. "I'm reasonable when I'm tired, and I'm very tired. But you might reassure your man, or anyone else around, that I'm still very fast with this weapon and that you probably wouldn't survive even if something happened to me. Fair enough?"

"Fair enough," Anaya answered softly. He could see his world crumbling very quickly as Tony Lynch eased into the chair across the table.

Lynch had no idea whether or not he was facing the right man until he'd mentioned Voronov—"Did he send you?'' Anaya had inquired much too quickly. That, and the expression in Anaya's eyes, had been the answer. Of the others on his list, he found out that General Cholas had died at the hands of the Spetznaz, the president of the university was in prison, and the ambassador to the OAS didn't have the vaguest idea of what he was talking about an hour before. No need to visit the other two on his list now. He had his man.

The breakfast was superb and the caffeine injected new energy as Lynch toyed with his victim. When a man was as scared as Jorge Anaya obviously was, the information came easily. Lynch played him like a fish, giving him enough facts to corroborate, guessing at some aspects of what might take place so that Anaya could correct him, and eventually getting a complete admission of the Soviet strategy.

"You know enough to convince me that you are an American." Anaya was making a final attempt at recovering some of his self-respect. "But how do I know that your people are going to be able to accomplish exactly what you claim?"

Tony Lynch looked at his watch. "Have another cup of coffee. It's almost eight o'clock. In a few minutes you are going to hear some loud and very effective explosions. If we go down to the corner of Presidentes, you should be able to see smoke from the direction of the New Plaza. That will be the end of Duran's stage for his kangaroo court. It's symbolic, no doubt about that, but there are going to be a lot of people in Havana who will understand. The other explosions will be coming from the direction of the Prado, right near the presidential palace. Nothing of major proportion—just enough to spread the troops a little thin. And it ought to make Voronov think a little bit, since he'll figure pretty fast his own boys aren't involved." Another Tony Lynch grin lit his face. "Ought to be an interesting day."

•   •   •

Precisely at eight o'clock that morning Juan Duran's New Plaza stage rose skyward in a tumultuous blast. None of John Turner's SEALs were present to admire their talents. They had done their work before sunup and were already at a deserted warehouse near the airport, waiting for Ryng's orders. The sound of more distant detonations reached Anaya's villa shortly after.

Jorge Anaya shuddered. Havana was under a state of siege. The capitol city was at the mercy of a couple hundred foreigners, Americans and Russians, who intended to replace Cuba's government—and soon they, too, would be at each other's throats.

CHAPTER SIXTEEN

General Komarov, who found it difficult to equate Cuba's problems in the past few days with his own, had gone to bed at about midnight and was asleep almost instantly. The actions of Colonel Voronov and his Spetznaz troops were no longer of concern to him. He took his orders from Moscow. Whatever transpired in Havana during the following day had little effect on the huge Soviet installation in Santa Fe because their business was intelligence. It had nothing to do with Juan Duran, and, Komarov hoped, Voronov would return to the motherland shortly and leave him to his job.

The state of emergency declared by Duran did not influence Santa Fe personnel. The Russians assigned there had been separated completely from the Cuban community for security reasons. Dependents rarely left the base, and even the military and civilian specialists required specific reasons to go beyond the barbed wire and mine fields surrounding them. They managed their own stores, which carried Soviet products, much to the regret of many of the Russian civilians who had looked forward to western foods and consumer goods. They even enjoyed their own beaches. The curfew also meant nothing, since the Russians were unaffected within their compound.

Security had been upgraded by Komarov two days before, but that was standard in such a situation. His main concern was the perimeter, and additional patrols were set up around the fences and at the gates to account for potentially radical Cuban nationals offended by the Soviet presence.

Charlie Rand, a tall, skinny, balding SEAL who looked more like a banker, was Ryng's demolition expert. He was the leader of the group from *John Marshall* that departed their SDVs a few hundred yards offshore and swam the remaining distance to the beach at about two that morning.

They encountered no resistance. While wet suits and tanks were buried in the sand near the tree line, Rand's scouts were pleasantly surprised that patrols near the beach and even within the compound remained sparse. Komarov had simply not been concerned with a threat from the sea.

The SEALs mission was to create havoc within the Soviet intelligence system by disrupting communications for at least a twenty-four-hour period. The ensuing confusion would take the advantage away from Voronov. It made no sense to Bernie Ryng to cause any more damage than that because the potential for sustaining SEAL casualties would increase radically. Years of SEAL training were designed to complete the mission without the loss of a single man. Casualties were caused by inadequate planning or mistakes.

The primary targets were the antenna towers that enhanced long-range radio transmission and satellite communications, and the saucer antennae designed to capture U.S. signals. Enlarged eye-in-the-sky photographs had been studied weeks before in Hoff's office. Photo interpretation experts had keyed the targets by their importance to Ryng's mission.

Whether a war is hot, cold, or simply in the avoidance

stage, the most dangerous element remains the human one—the small, highly trained unit. Their personal objectives, other than completing the specific mission, are to arrive undetected, accomplish their tasks in as short a time as possible, and get the hell out. If their mission is carried out perfectly, they suffer no losses. In such cases the enemy's material losses are significant.

At Santa Fe the SEALs were able to set their demolitions without interruption and withdraw to their rendezvous point on the beach. The single personnel loss to the Russians, before the explosives were detonated, was an unfortunate sentry who fell victim to the call of nature. He was unfortunate enough to choose to relieve himself literally on top of the SEAL who was guarding their equipment on the beach. The sentry died without making a sound and was the only evidence the following morning that those who set the explosives came from the sea.

General Komarov awoke to a tremendous blast that blew in the windows of his quarters just as the sun was turning the eastern skies orange. If he had been awake and peering at the sunrise from the windows, as was his usual habit, he would have been torn to shreds by the shattered glass. The dish antenna that had been no more than a hundred yards from the sleeping general lay in a twisted heap. The precious electronic connectors in a nearby structure and the rotating machinery had also been included when the plastic was set.

As Komarov surveyed the wreckage through the shattered window, two more explosions shook the morning air. Turning toward the sea, the general watched as flames surged skyward near the base of two giant towers. The nearest appeared to crumble within itself, its structural steel legs seeming to curl inward like a spider. The second teetered, leaning for a second or two toward the rising sun, before a morning breeze nudged it in the opposite direction. It collapsed full length, crushing the adjacent building housing switching systems.

Other blasts seemed to follow in a pattern echoing the earlier ones. A week later General Komarov would note in his detailed report to Moscow that the selected targets made great sense, considering the events over the following twenty-four hours. In his analysis the general stated that the unit accomplishing the attack intended primarily to incapacitate his station rather than destroy the entire installation. A greater effort would have involved a much larger force and, in all probability, heavy loss of life. It was indicative of a SEAL operation, he claimed, quite possible forty or fifty men.

Although Komarov's troops scoured every inch of the Santa Fe base, there was no trace of the intruders. The body of the unfortunate sentry was overlooked until later that first day.

General Komarov would have been appalled to learn that the raid, which significantly affected Soviet ability to retaliate in any manner and cost them millions of rubles to repair, was conducted by just ten SEALs who were back in their own homes four days later.

The Cuban coastline for about fifteen miles due east of Havana is mostly high and rocky with dense vegetation developing just inland. The resorts do not appear until the village of Alamar. Tom Loomis's SEAL unit, nicknamed the Gray Foxes after their white-haired leader, had been selected to land west of this town near a rocky outcropping.

At about midnight, a couple of hours before *John Marshall* deployed her SEALs off Santa Fe, a Permit class sub surfaced three miles northwest of Alamar. She remained on the surface, her decks awash to minimize radar contact, just long enough to launch two rubber boats carrying five SEALs each. These were not the traditional ''men with green faces'' outfitted in camouflage; instead they appeared to be Cuban peasants. They paddled their small boats to within fifty yards of the shore. Then, using the surf, they piloted the rubber craft in concert with the waves, up and over the rock outcroppings.

As soon as their boats were hidden they moved inland to a drop-off area where Tony Lynch had arranged for two old pick-up trucks that had seen much better days. After loading their weapons and explosives under tarps, Loomis and his SEALs drove to the circumferential highway around Havana. At each major highway and railroad bridge two men were dropped off.

The final target was the major southern highway that merged near the village of Cotorro, the same one used by the Batabanó SEAL unit. Here, Loomis and the remaining SEAL drove their vehicles well off the road. They had practiced this same task back in Virginia, first in the daylight until they could accomplish the job with their eyes shut, then at night until they could anticipate their partner without ever seeing what he was doing.

Once explosives and timers were set, Loomis and the other driver returned to their trucks and retraced their route, picking up each demolition team. The entire process had taken less than three hours from landing until their rubber boats were dragged back into the water.

As the horizon began to lighten to the east, an onshore breeze sprang up, forcing the SEALs to struggle through three-foot waves just to get their boats beyond the beach. Three times the mother submarine's periscope broke the surface in search of the little craft. It was on the final sweep that the two rubber boats were seen, rising and falling like corks in the swells, struggling against the wind. Not a word was said. They'd been through it too often. From the early days of BUDs training, each of them exhausted and shivering, they had been taught that they could handle such a situation—while an instructor was screaming through a bullhorn, ". . .are we having fun yet?"

Tom Loomis's SEALs were already enjoying their breakfast aboard the submarine when the five bridges critical to Havana's exterior transportation system collapsed within seconds of each other. The capital city was physically isolated from the rest of the nation long enough for Bernie Ryng's strategy to be completed. The mission had been accomplished by ten superbly trained professionals who never were recognized and never fired a shot during the entire time they were in Cuba.

Paul Voronov and his men had been able to move through the streets of Havana because they wore Cuban uniforms. Only the military seemed willing to venture forth in Havana with the chaos that marked the day.

Voronov, an AK-74 cradled in his arms, stared through the wisps of smoke drifting across the Prado toward the dust rising near the presidential palace. A loyal unit of Duran's personal troops remained to surround the main building. The demolition had been perfectly executed, even with Cuban troops surrounding the main building, and it had confused his own plans. To an extent he had lost his perspective. At first Voronov complained bitterly to Kurochkin about his men's discipline. There was smoke near the docks by the Desamparado, smoke at the New Plaza—what were these superbly trained Spetznaz doing? It almost seemed they were in the way of each of his carefully planned steps.

The situation became more confusing as each hour passed. With the frantic report from General Komarov arriving soon after the news of the destruction of the highway and railroad bridges leading into the city, it seemed that Juan Duran was suffering from a secondary revolution of sorts—and that was interfering with Voronov's strategy. Yet there were no reports of mutiny in the army. As a matter of fact, loyal elements were vainly struggling to restructure the army after the loss of much of its leadership the previous day.

It became clear only when Kurochkin contacted his colonel half an hour later.

"Say again. I misunderstood you," Voronov said into the transmitter.

"I repeat, Anaya is not in his villa. I can't find out where he is . . ."

"But his servants, they must be there. Surely you can use whatever means are necessary to find out from them—"

"There's no need to do that," Kurochkin broke in. "Anaya's servant said that a man in the uniform of the Direccíon General appeared here early this morning. He used a gun to get in. But the servant is sure the man wasn't in the police. He says that Anaya became extremely upset when he realized that the New Plaza had been blown. Then there were more explosions around the city. Anaya left in the police car with this man."

"Did anyone get a good look at him?" Voronov snapped.

"All that they noticed was that he seemed to have one bad arm, and—" Kurochkin hesitated. He'd never imagined that a single misjudgment on his part could have such a far-reaching effect.

"Go on. Do you know of someone like that?"

"I believe . . ." Kurochkin faltered as the magnanimity of the single favor he'd ever done for an enemy returned to haunt him. "I believe he is an American . . . quite possibly involved with the American SEAL you recognized in the street."

Voronov stared at the radio in his hand. *That face in the crowd!* Of course. That was it. There were days in the past week when Paul Voronov had been so busy that he almost forgot the man—*the one who had beaten him in Panama!* Why? Why, when he recognized Ryng that day in the street, did he ever think that the man would be protecting only American interests? That explained so much. Who else could employ explosives like those in the last few hours?

"Kurochkin, I want you to radio each of your units. Bring them in by the park across from the Academy of Sciences, the one by the intersection of the Prado and Simon Bolivar. We want to see exactly what these Americans will do if we can draw them into a skirmish."

•   •   •

The only SEALs in Havana, in effect in all of Cuba by that hour, were those who had come into Havana Harbor aboard their SDVs. Including Bernie Ryng, there were fifteen SEALs, and Ryng intended to release them as soon as Juan Duran could be accounted for. The Cuban leader was almost certainly done for! His government was in chaos, his military unable to function without suitable leadership. The Russians had seen to that. Voronov's Spetznaz had turned a key section of the populace against Duran. They had also eliminated much of the power structure that kept him in office.

Yet the Russians now found themselves without a secure line to the outside after the destruction at Santa Fe. Sure, they could establish emergency communications, but anything they said in voice transmissions would certainly be intercepted. As a result, they had no way of utilizing the backup forces that Ryng assumed would be available to reinforce a coup against Duran—such an act would be considered an invasion.

The highways and railroads into the capital were destroyed and the air force was unable to support anyone. Five of Ryng's fifteen SEALs had completed the demolition of the control tower at the airport and were already back in the city. And Tony Lynch was waiting with Cara Estrada at the Bishop of Havana's residence. A frightened Jorge Anaya also awaited his fate there.

Juan Duran remained in his chair at the head of the table and stared back at Nieves. His chief of staff had just so much as said that they were losing control of the city. The head of the navy could not be found. The air force was grounded. The army and secret police were in a state of chaos with most of their senior officers either missing or dead. While a loyal element of the police continued to maintain their position around the presidential palace, repeated calls to army barracks close to Havana had gone unanswered. The officer in charge of the secret police, a major, called Nieves each time another explosion occurred nearby, and the chief of staff feared he and his men would soon be gone. The Russian intelligence unit at Santa Fe was unable to function for at least another few hours—and when they were finally able to establish a secure line and report the situation to Moscow, it would still require more time than was available to react.

Not once in the tent at Assdadah had they ever discussed a situation such as this one. Qaddafi had explained any number of times that a ruler who maintains control with an iron hand rarely suffers from a lack of discipline. *Discipline,* thought Juan Duran. *Discipline is not my problem right now. It is total chaos.*

"Who are we fighting, Ricardo?" Duran inquired of his chief of staff. "It seemed that only a few days ago we had few problems," he concluded wistfully. "Now I see what appear to be our own army on the other side of the barricades. Their guns are aimed at our police. Yet my army commander just down the hall, or at least that colonel who we hope is in command, knows nothing about any revolt within their organization. Who? Who?" he asked, spreading his arms in question about the apparently rebel army facing the palace.

"The Spetznaz?" Nieves's eyebrows rose in question, though his expression was one of perplexity. "We haven't been invaded. To my knowledge, there were less than a hundred of them. As of last night, there was no intelligence that the regular army regiment they have stationed here had left their barracks. If not, I don't know who else."

"But . . ." Duran paused to look helplessly at the remaining familiar faces around the table. Not a one returned his gaze. "But who has been responsible for the bombings? Many of the streets are closed. The docks are burning. The airport is no longer in operation." He spread his hands in dismay. "And no one in the army has made a move to step forward. There's no rebellion."

Nieves was the only one willing to look Duran in the face. "There's no other choice. If there's no army to attack this building, we must go out and find who really is behind this." As soon as he offered that solution Nieves also understood who would go. "I will take the responsibility."

Paul Voronov was not accustomed to stalemates. His methods had always had a constancy to them—swift and deadly. With the specter of third-party interference from Ryng a sudden reality, he knew a quick conclusion was a necessity. He was as yet unable to understand exactly the purpose of the SEALs' presence. Obviously they had been on the island for a few weeks—or at least Ryng had been. Yet up until the day before, there had been no indication of their presence, nothing to hint that there was anyone else but Ryng in Havana . . . until one of his Spetznaz teams had been wiped out south of the city. He was certain only the SEALs could have accomplished such a feat. Why the attack had taken place was irrelevent. Voronov remained confident that once his remaining Spetznaz unit was at full strength, and once Kurochkin located Jorge Anaya, he would be able to conclude the assignment. And if there was a shot at Ryng . . .

His thoughts were interrupted by one of his sergeants. "Colonel, I see some people coming out from the center door. Can't identify them yet." He was peering intently in the direction of the presidential palace.

Voronov accepted the binoculars and studied the group moving in his direction. The man in the center, a civilian, appeared familiar. Voronov closed his eyes momentarily to sift mentally through the photographs he'd memorized back in Moscow. Nieves—that was it, Ricardo Nieves—Duran's chief of staff. And his approach would be in all innocence. He would ask with the appropriate shrugs and gestures why Duran felt surrounded, yet there was no visible army. Who was behind this? Why?

Poor Nieves. He was a brave man, brave and loyal to his leader; so loyal that he would even sacrifice himself. Voronov knew that men like Nieves would be naive about the realities of Spetznaz. If he knew that he was the sacrificial lamb, there was no indication. Such brave men, Voronov concluded, shouldn't have to die for a man like Duran.

When Nieves was brought before him, Voronov spoke first. "Would you prefer to live out the day and see your family again?" His voice was sharp and menacing. If Nieves thought he was going to negotiate, he was sadly mistaken.

"I don't know who you are, sir." Though his expression remained firm, fear etched the corners of his eyes. Ricardo Nieves desperately wanted to be brave.

"Perhaps I am the next ruler of Cuba. What would you say to that?"

"I don't understand what you mean," came the frightened reply. "Your accent . . . I don't think you are even a Cuban . . . only the uniform—" He stuttered, indicating the colonel's insignia on Voronov's Cuban uniform.

"If you fail to do exactly as I say, you will never have the opportunity to even know who I am. Please tell whoever is in command of the guard around the palace that they will be spared if they return to their barracks immediately." Voronov was not a large man, but he had stepped forward until he was face-to-face with Nieves. The spare blond hair, the high cheekbones emphasizing the slightly Tatar eyes—all was imposing to a man who had no idea what he faced. "You see, you know neither my name nor why I am here, nor whether you will be alive an hour from now. Only a moment ago I was willing to keep you alive all day, but because you chose to question me, you may only have an hour left. Now, will you order the guard to leave?"

Nieves was unable to maintain his bravado. He was a successful politician but had never been in the army. Men like this one terrified him. "I don't have the authority to order the military. . . ."

"Then you may send one of the men who came out with you back in. Get Duran. He can give the orders," Voronov concluded matter-of-factly. "If he doesn't come out in say"—he looked at his watch and continued—"ten minutes, then you will be shot. Now, who will you send back to talk with Duran?"

Nieves's eyes were as big as saucers. "Why"—he turned to look at the advisors who had come out with him—"I guess . . . I guess he can go." He pointed at a young man in an open-necked shirt.

Voronov grabbed the indicated messenger by the front of his shirt. "You will first tell Duran that his chief of staff will be dead in ten minutes if the guard hasn't been ordered back to their barracks. And the rest of your friends here will die shortly afterward . . . one at a time . . . in full view. Understood?"

The man nodded his head rapidly before fleeing back into the palace grounds.

Bernie Ryng, perched on the roof of a building a block away from the scene, understood Voronov's thinking as soon as he saw Ricardo Nieves die from a bullet in the back of his head. Four others who had come out with Nieves that first time were also killed a few minutes apart in the same manner.

Then Voronov discarded his own weapons and walked with his hands at his sides up to the hastily erected barricade in front of the palace. There was a major who seemed to be in charge who had watched each execution. He had remained fixed at his post, unable to move as each execution took place no more than a hundred yards away. Since there had been no orders from inside the palace, the major had no idea what response would be adequate. These were Cuban troops doing the shooting and their leader was a colonel.

Now that colonel, who was approaching his post, seemed to be unarmed. There was no question that he was dangerous. The major simply had no idea what he was expected to do. He waited uneasily, eventually coming to attention when the man was about ten yards away.

There was no need for Ryng to hear what Voronov was saying to the major. It was probably no different than the offer he'd made to the unfortunate Nieves. The Russian would very calmly review the status of the military situation to the major before explaining that he could march his men back to his barracks right now without danger to any of them. If not, Voronov probably had a plausible story about how they were surrounded by a powerful Spetznaz force. Just the sound of the word—*Spetznaz*—would have the required effect.

There was no fight in the army major. Ryng watched as he collected his men. They hastened off down the Prado behind the two remaining tanks.

"Bring her in," Ryng called into his radio to Tony Lynch. Then he requested acknowledgement from each of his men. Like Ryng, they were perched on the rooftops in the area, two men to a team. Although each carried a high-powered rifle, one of them would employ the binoculars as a spotter as long as possible. The demolition team from the airport had established a command post in the park across from the Palacio de Aldama at the far end of the Prado.

Juan Duran was not a coward. When he pulled back the curtain and saw his guard moving down the Prado, he understood that his time was short. He made a call down the hall to the colonel in command, who reported in a trembling voice that there was no longer an answer at headquarters. He dismissed his remaining advisors, who exuded the smell of fear, and went to his quarters to change into his uniform of choice.

• • •

Paul Voronov watched triumphantly as Juan Duran marched out onto the Prado in his fatigues. It was the first time Duran had ever worn them in public. *If they were good enough for Fidel*, he reasoned, *then let history see me face my enemy in battle dress.*

Duran had no idea whom he would face until Paul Voronov, still a Cuban colonel to all appearances, stepped forward from the group waiting in the middle of the Prado. "You are wise to save the palace," Voronov said. "There was no reason to force us to destroy one of the symbols of your nation."

Duran's arms were folded across his chest. A gun belt with a Soviet-made pistol hung at his hip. He thrust his jaw out as he spoke to this rebel colonel. "I would like to know by whose authority—"

Voronov pulled his own gun from its holster and, before the surprised Duran could react, shot the Cuban three times. Juan Duran had been treated in much the same manner as Fidel Castro.

"Now!" Ryng's order snapped through the radios to each two-man team.

Five shots rang out across the Prado. Five Spetznaz fell.

Only two were hit in the second volley, but Ryng had never expected them to remain sitting ducks, not Spetznaz.

There was a third volley as the Russians scattered for cover, and then selected firing as the spotters identified possible targets. But the intent was to keep the Spetznaz down for as long as possible.

Ryng had imagined what he might do if he were in Voronov's shoes. Considering the situation, the logical move would be down the Prado, away from the shooting. Special forces never attacked blindly. They regrouped, analyzed the problem, and then struck. Bernie Ryng had no intention of allowing the Spetznaz to regroup. There were too many of them.

And Ryng was right. There were no easy targets. One

man at a time picked his way from spot to spot until he was out of sight. They were heading up the Prado. Since the situation was unusual for any Spetznaz, they had no idea they were being herded.

"They're moving your way," Ryng said into the radio. "They should be approaching the corner of Virtudes or Neptuno shortly."

"We're set," came the response.

When Tony Lynch reported he was approaching in his police car about ten blocks away, Ryng ordered his SEALs down to the street from the tops of the buildings. He led five of them up the Prado behind the retreating Spetznaz. The others moved up Zulueta, parallel to the Prado.

"I see them," a voice reported over the radio.

"Go," Ryng ordered. His final words, "We're covering," were lost in the series of blasts ahead of him.

As the rumbling ceased the Spetznaz heard a loudspeaker's mechanical voice echoing through the dust in broken Russian. Bernie Ryng's words gave the impression that a large detachment of SEALs was advancing through the confusion of the Prado. It was enough to make even Paul Voronov uncertain of the size of the enemy force.

Feodor Kurochkin, perhaps out of guilt, volunteered to coordinate delaying tactics so the majority of Spetznaz might drop back. As he strained to catch each word from the bullhorn, he finally understood that he was receiving an offer to throw down his weapons. In the history of his regiment there had never been a Spetznaz who surrendered. The concept shocked him. There was only one response.

Two SEALs died before Sergeant Kurochkin and his small patrol were destroyed.

A surprised Paul Voronov, leading the balance of his men toward the Malecón, barely heard the strange message the first time. Where was it coming from? It seemed to drift upward to his ears. Then he realized the radio speaker on his belt was turned into his body. The faint voice seemed to rise and fall as it bounced against his chest. It couldn't be Kurochkin, he thought. The firing to his rear had been violent, yet it stopped so quickly.

"Colonel Voronov . . . Colonel Voronov . . ." the voice repeated. "I am using your sergeant's radio." *Kurochkin's! He must be dead*! "I suggest you attempt to tune into the government radio station. There will be a message for you. It is intended to save further bloodshed." The Russian accent was fair, but Voronov could tell the speaker was not one of his men. The words were repeated over and over again. The voice and intonation changed as different men repeated the same message. Finally Paul Voronov switched the radio off completely.

There was an old car parked just off the Malecón near Maceo Park. The keys had been carelessly left in the ignition. Voronov reached inside and switched on the radio. As he stared out across the water he heard a woman's voice . . .

EPILOGUE

"This is Cara Estrada speaking from the presidential palace. Juan Duran is dead. I have been asked by Colonel Mercedes, the new chief of staff of the army, by Jorge Anaya, who survives as the senior member of the Supreme Court, and Maria Delgado, the secretary of the Central Committee, to assume the leadership of our nation.

"The killing is over. The injustice has ended. Any foreign troops still on our shores will soon be out of our country. The nation that José Martí envisioned will rise from the horror of our struggle. . . ."

As she continued the voice of Cara Estrada rekindled the vision that the Cuban people had seen when she laid the plans for Juan Duran—the spirit of an Evita.

"We will rebuild our nation under a system that suits the people. It will be neither an American system nor a communist system. Cubans are a unique people. Our races have learned to live together in harmony. Our heritage derives from a basic belief in God. The Bishop of Havana will serve as a member of the committee to design a new constitution. Delegates from each province will come to

Havana and each man will be equally represented. Our goal is to establish a system benefiting each man.

"We have received assistance from the Americans in overcoming both the inequities of Juan Duran's government and a Soviet effort to control Havana. Those people who aided us at the critical moment have left our country. There is nothing more we can ask of a neighbor than their aid in time of need and their willingness to depart so that we can establish a nation suitable to our people.

"I ask the Americans to grant us the necessary aid we will need without the strings that have always been attached in the past. . . ''

Bernie Ryng listened to her first speech while perched on a stool outside the control room of the main government radio station. There was so much about Cara Estrada that had fascinated him, just as she had enchanted many other men. Her beauty controlled any man who saw her for the first time. After that, each one was under her spell as she spoke with that understated authority that had brought even Juan Duran literally to his knees.

When Paul Voronov had disappeared in the direction of Santa Fe, Ryng returned to the presidential palace to see her. Tony Lynch had delivered her there at the same time he had dispatched two of the SEALs to recall Colonel Mercedes, who appeared to be the successor as army chief. There had been no doubt among any men who appeared at the palace that day that the most powerful personality available was Cara Estrada. The colonel was the first to ask her for orders. That was a symbolic gesture which had established her authority. He was demanding a new leader for Cuba. It was a time when his nation required an Evita.

There was one thing about Colonel Paul Voronov that impressed Bernie Ryng as much as his almost successful attempt to control the government through Jorge Anaya—he had an ability, unlike any other man, to escape from an impossible situation. This was the second time. The man had been a prisoner in Panama during the last incident, guarded by troops with M-16s. Yet he had managed to throw himself over the bow of the ship and disappear into the Panamanian jungle.

They had survived *each other* twice now. It seemed almost an impossibility for them both to have escaped unharmed . . . yet, they had. Paul Voronov was the ultimate enemy and that had made victory twice as sweet. But would they ever meet again? Ryng hoped not. The odds . . .

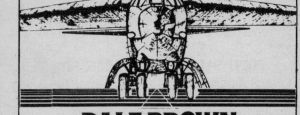